Memories of the Curlew

Helen Spring

Published in 2009 by YouWriteOn.com
Copyright © Helen Spring

First Edition

The author asserts the moral right under the
Copyright, Designs and Patents Act 1988 to be identified
as the author of this work.

British Library C.I.P.
A C.I.P. catalogue record for this title is available
from the British Library.

Notes and Acknowledgments

The idea for this book was originally suggested by my friend Peter Newton, who had written a short history of Gwenllian (Gwenllian, the Welsh Warrior Princess) . Peter believed her story deserved to be better known and would make an interesting novel. I agreed, and Peter has generously allowed me to make use of his research, and has also contributed the poem sung by Meilyr on page 210.

In this fictionalisation I have been true to the few original documents which survive from the period, and where they are non-existent my inventions are what I believe to be most likely.

What comes through the centuries, both from documents and stories handed down by legend, is the undoubted honesty, stoicism and bravery of this remarkable woman, and I have tried to do her justice.

Helen Spring

to

John and Rose

with love

PROLOGUE
(1141)
'THE REUNION'

In the early morning of a rain swept spring dawn, the solitary figure of a bone weary man astride an equally exhausted horse made its way slowly across the plain towards Dinefwr Castle.

To the guards ensconced on the wooden perimeter fence, all superior Welsh archers, the slow moving target offered little in the way of challenge. Bows drawn, they watched as the plodding figure doggedly pursued his way into their killing area through the sleeting rain, which blew horizontally in succeeding grey curtains, obscuring their vision and making it impossible to identify the bedraggled visitor. Eventually he stopped about twenty yards from the gate, a slumped, motionless figure which nevertheless had some defiance in its bearing.

'What is your business here?' A guard leaned over to call out.

'Family business.' The reply was weak above the maelstrom of weather. The guard turned to his companion.

'Did he say family?'

'Yes, I think so.'

The guard leaned down further and shouted, 'Which family?'

The voice came back to them, a little louder now and with a sharpness of authority and frustration, 'I am the second son of Prince Gruffudd ap Rhys! Now, let me in!'

For a moment there was silence, and then as the strangers words were understood and repeated throughout the compound, 'It's Morgan! Open the gate!' bawled the officer of the guard. 'It's Morgan! Wake the family!' He

1

turned to the open mouthed youth beside him. 'Well, hurry, dunderhead!' Still shouting instructions, he ran across the keep yard to the gate, and as he ran he heard his own words re-echoing across the bailey forecourt and up into the castle keep: 'Morgan! It's Morgan! He has returned from the dead!'

Prince Anarawd's much needed sleep was shattered by the pounding on the solid oak door of his bedchamber. Bemused and heavy with sleep, he began to stir as the guard entered the room.

'It's your brother sire, Morgan!' The guard seemed almost overcome.

'We have news?' Anarawd searched the guard's face intently, wanting to know but afraid of what might be revealed. 'Is he alive?'

'Much better sire! He's here!' The guard could hardly curtail his excitement.

'Dear God in Heaven!' Anarawd leapt out of bed and began to pull on a robe over his night-shirt. 'Morgan!' He flung open the door and ran barefoot along the passage and down the steps to the outer door. A hooded figure was being helped towards the keep by two stocky guards. Oblivious to the driving rain, Anarawd ran towards them, stopping a few feet away to regain his composure. Then he stepped forward, and lifted the hood from the visitor's face. The man was wretched and filthy, the features were bony and the beard overgrown and unkempt, but as he raised his head Anarawd instantly recognised his family's trademark, the striking blue eyes of the Aberffraw royals.

Anarawd was almost overcome by a tumult of emotions which threatened to overwhelm him. Gently, he put out his hand and touched the other's cheek, and as he looked deep into the blue eyes he saw them glisten as Morgan said hesitantly, 'Anarawd? Is it you?' before being enveloped in a bear hug. Anarawd took the weight of his brother, and they made their way slowly into the great hall, to where servants were already replenishing the huge peat fire in the centre. Furs were spread across the two large wooden chairs. As the brothers settled, the gentle plaint of a sweet voice which had begun as soon as Morgan entered the hall became louder, and was joined by a soft humming sound as more voices joined in. As Morgan became aware of it he looked across at his brother in anguish and disbelief. Anarawd smiled, and as the humming became a sweet lament of pain and loss, signifying the distress of the time spent apart, he joined in with the great song, remembering times long ago when it had been sung for their father or mother, when they had returned to the family home after long periods of time away. The lament changed to a sweet song of welcome, and then became louder and more insistent, as every throat in the castle joined in, straining to express their joy. As the great sound grew, Morgan too remembered times when he had heard the great Song of Welcome. Those times had been few, as it was only sung to the royal family, and was always a spontaneous reaction of relief and welcome when they saw those they loved return home. Tears ran unashamedly down Morgan's face; never had he imagined the great song would be sung for him. As the song built to its close with a shout of jubilation, he knew at last that he was really home, amongst his own proud Welsh, in the bosom of his blood kin.

As the servants brought ale and bread and meat, Anarawd began his questions. He could see his brother was not well, and needed rest and sleep more than anything else, but he could not help it.

'We had almost given up hope. Where have you been?'

'I have been on display brother.' Morgan took a deep

draught of ale. 'I have been passed from one Norman lord to another, and eventually I found myself at Hereford castle. I have been a kind of novelty for lords who found it amusing to parade a Welsh prince at their banquets. I took their taunts and insults and bided my time. I knew if I could stay alive then one day I should escape. Hereford gave me my chance, and here I am.'

Attentive house servants had brought dry clothing, and before he ate Morgan allowed them to help him from his saturated rags. As he stripped, the sight of the almost mythical chest wound which had been inflicted at the time of his capture was plainly evident to the gathered witnesses.

'So it was true, you were impaled by a Norman sword,' said Anarawd slowly. 'We heard of it, but the Normans claimed they had killed you.'

'They killed many good men that day, as well as our mother and Maelgwn, God rest them both.' Morgan's face was strained, the subject was obviously painful, but he continued: 'I was more use to them alive, it was only my royal blood that saved me. Because of my birth, the Normans liked to show their power by making me suffer any kind of humiliation short of death. Some of my companions taken that day were not so fortunate.' He sighed . 'The men taken alive with me were tormented for the amusement of their captors for days, sometimes weeks. Limbs hacked off, one at a time, this of course after their eyes and tongues had been cut out.' He looked up at Anarawd, and the striking blue eyes held an anguish which struck into his elder brother's soul. 'Ah, my brother,' he cried, almost in tears, 'You have no idea of the cruelty of these Norman swine! I know you grieve for our dear Mother, and for Maelgwn, but if you had seen what I have seen you would not have wished them to be taken alive, and in Norman hands.' He shook his heavy head, and muttered, 'You have no idea brother, there were hangings and crucifixions, and sometimes our followers were burned alive, I cannot speak more of it.'

Anarawd remained silent, he knew Morgan spoke the truth. Even as a child, he had heard tales of the sacking of Worcester and Shrewsbury which had made his blood run cold, long before the Norman invaders had turned their attention to Wales. After a moment, he said, 'At least we have you returned to us, and I thank God for it.'

Morgan managed a thin smile, and then set about the food with a voracious appetite. He was only interrupted when the door opened and an eight year old boy, freshly roused from sleep, his long blonde hair tousled and his eyes bleary, crossed the room and stared intently at him.

Morgan stopped his devotion to the food and stared back, his eyes softening as he took in every aspect of the child. He shook his head. 'It must be Rhys,' he said in wonder. 'I knew he would grow to be the image of our mother.'

'Yes,' said Anarawd. 'Come Rhys; embrace your brother Morgan, who by God's dear grace has been returned to us.'

Rhys was by now awake, but still confused, and he obeyed slowly, walking towards the outstretched arms of this brother he could barely remember, and who he knew only through the stories which had been told to him about the skill and bravery of the great Prince Morgan; the brother who had at last been felled by a Norman sword and had been variously reported as having been either dead or imprisoned.

Morgan had no such doubts. He flung his pitifully thin arms around his youngest brother, and tears ran again as he clasped Rhys tightly to his chest. 'I thought I would never see you again,' he gasped. He gazed with admiration at the boy, who had been so much in his thoughts during the long periods of incarceration, and instantly he was back in the dark cell, making plans for this child, who from birth had been predicted by Meilyr, the wise and revered Druid and soothsayer, to follow in their parent's footsteps, and to become a great leader of the Welsh. During that terrible time, Morgan had sworn that if he ever had the chance to be with the boy again, he would play his full part in the raising and instruction of the lad. At length he released the boy, and Rhys sat down at his brother's feet. His normal high spirits were subdued, as he was torn between knowing and not knowing, wanting to show affection for his brother but feeling awkward, with no real bond to this virtual stranger he had last seen when he was three years old.Anarawd took another draught of ale and called for more. 'If only Dewi was here now, to see this reunion.'

Morgan lifted his head; no day could contain only good news. 'So,' he said, his good humour crushed, 'Dewi is dead then?'

'Dead? Certainly not! He is away for a few days only, to talk with our uncle Owain at Aberffraw.'

Morgan closed his eyes with relief and gratitude. He looked across at Anarawd, the most loyal and devoted of brothers, and at the blonde head of Rhys, now slowly sinking again into sleep upon his knee, and he wished this wonderful day would never end.

It was two days later that the heavy outer gates of the castle were opened again to admit the returning Dewi ap Ifan. Morgan, who had been watching for him since dawn, entreated Anarawd to allow him to stand alone in the centre of the courtyard, knowing his appearance would lift and delight his returning friend, whom they all loved as an older brother.

Dewi was accompanied by two fellow Teulu fighters,

6

royal family house guards, the elite of the warrior class chosen to escort him on his arduous journeys to and from the sacred island of Ynys Mon, or Anglesey, as the Normans and Saxons now called it. As Dewi, now in his fifty sixth year, entered the compound, Morgan noticed his still powerful gait and bearing. Dewi was known by his compatriots as 'The Stag,' for he moved with the power, grace and spirit of that majestic beast, which was celebrated in legend and admired for courage and intelligence. Morgan stood alone in the centre of the courtyard as Dewi approached, now on foot. At a distance of about ten feet Dewi hesitated, staring, and then dropped to his knees, his face transfixed with joy.

'You live!' he cried. 'Curse me for an unbeliever! Meilyr knew! He told it, but I did not have the faith to believe!'

Morgan ran to him and lifted him gently, and the two men embraced as if they were indeed brothers in birth, and Morgan remembered how much his family owed to this wonderful friend. Anarawd joined them, with Rhys bounding at his side, and as they entered the great hall they all rejoiced together, and the long years of suffering and loss began to fade and diminish, in the great joy of their reunion.

That evening in the great hall of Dinefwr, Anarawd, Morgan, Rhys and Dewi held a great court of lament to bear witness to the truth of the events which had ruled their lives so completely over the span of forty years or more. This was the first and last time they came together to tell the great story, and this is how they told it...

ONE
(1097 - 1107)
'A FREE SPIRIT'

Meilyr made his way slowly across the foothills towards Aberffraw. He did not want to come here, for he knew that the harsh times which the settlement had endured were not over, and that there was more to come. He did not want to be part of it, his belly ached with hunger and his thoughts were like scattered leaves in the wind. Oh! to be born a simple tradesman, he thought, a cook or a warrior perhaps, or one who worked with metal or wood. It would be good to know satisfaction in the shaping of something of use or beauty. Why was he born different? Why did his mind always dwell on those things which troubled others rarely? Only when a wandering preacher exhorted them to examine their souls and pray for absolution, did most people stop to consider the many signs and portents which dictated his own life and actions.

Meilyr stopped, and ran his parched tongue over his dry lips. No drink to be had until he came to the stream which bounded the settlement. He pulled a thick stalk of grass and chewed on it for the moisture it brought to his mouth. He was not even sure there would be food for him when he arrived, for the hospitality which had been the byword of the court of King Gruffudd ap Cynan and his Queen Angharad was bound to be frugal in these days of warring factions and never ending incursions by the Norman patrols of the hated William Rufus.

Meilyr strode on, anxious to reach safety before nightfall. 'They will make me welcome,' he thought, trying to reassure himself, 'No matter how hard the times, for though I am but young, am I not already acknowledged as a great bard? Do I not have a Druidic lineage as long and proud as that of King Gruffudd himself? And will they not thrill to hear the wonderful prediction I bring?'

As he walked Meilyr repeated these thoughts to himself to strengthen his resolve. Life was for him a constant effort to accommodate the strictures of the Christian religion and pay due service to it, whilst also making sure that those special arts and abilities of the ancient religion which had been passed down to him were not forgotten. The Archdeacon of Bangor had called those of his profession 'Purveyors of the Black Arts,' but Meilyr knew that his knowledge was part of the old Celtic heritage which must not be lost, for it had served the people well over the centuries.

The strength of his great prediction was still burning within him. There was of course always a new child for King Gruffudd and Queen Angharad, but this one was different. It was rare for the Queen not to be with child, and then only when she had recently been delivered. Angharad the Fair was indeed a stalwart provider for the royal succession, Meilyr considered. Her burgeoning body had already brought forth four older princesses, Mared, Rhiannell, Susanna, and Amnest, who were even now promised advantageous husbands, and there were three princes, Owain, Cadwallon and Cadwaladr.

Now this new child, a child to bless them all, a child to make a difference. Meilyr closed his eyes and tried to conjure the image again, letting his mind sink deep into his dream, when the gentle form of the sweet babe asleep in her crib had dissolved into the scampering child, with thick blonde curling hair and clear blue eyes, who brandished her wooden sword like a boy and climbed recklessly up the mountainside. The image blurred and revealed the woman, still strong and beautiful, as she rode her horse at the head of a great army, who followed her with the resounding cry 'Gwenllian! Gwenllian!'

As Meilyr at last came within sight of Aberffraw, he relaxed a little. The settlement was nothing like the solid stone habitations which had been destroyed by the Earls of Chester and Shrewsbury some two years before, but at least there were some signs that life was returning to the stronghold. There were some modestly constructed timber framed buildings, supplied from the well stocked oak forests of Ynys Mon, with wattle and daub walls and sloping thatched bracken roofs overlaid with turf. They looked as if they would withstand the harshest of weather. Meilyr breathed more easily.

With the destruction of Aberffraw, King Gruffudd and his family had escaped to sanctuary in Ireland, but the canny king had managed to take with him most of his fortune, enough to buy the support of the powerful Viking King Magnus, who had agreed to help Gruffudd in the retaking of his kingdom of Gwynedd. Within a year this was accomplished and King Gruffudd was back at home in Aberffraw, restored to power but penniless and demoralised. The reaction to his return had been a touching surprise to the king. Apparently the Welsh would rather have a weakened leader of their own than submit to the yoke of Norman tyranny. Meilyr had heard of the great call to arms, and knew that in response some ten thousand souls had rallied to the king's side. They were mainly freemen and nobles, but were supported by their bonded auxiliaries, soldiers and servants, mostly physically able but poorly armed and equipped. King Gruffudd had also brought with him from Ireland some one hundred wild Irish mercenaries, who were notoriously fierce. With their double headed axes and infamous thrashing flails they made a bodyguard force to be reckoned with, and their reputation went before them.

Meilyr looked around for any sign of the wild Irish, not realising the king had barracked them in the north of the island, away from the local population, because of their riotous and unruly behaviour.

As he neared the fenced compound, Meilyr saw a small boy, about five years old, brandishing a wooden sword as he was instructed in the rudiments of the warrior arts by his father, who Meilyr recognised as Ifan ap Rhodri, the king's captain of the house guard.

'No Dewi, lift the tip of the blade higher and keep it in front of my face,' he instructed his son, 'In that way you intimidate and distract your attacker before he strikes.'

With a mighty swing he circled his wooden practice sword to the rear and then directed it diagonally to strike the side of Dewi's neck. Sensing the imminent danger, Dewi leapt back, outside his father's cutting arc.

'Well done, lad!' You have all the signs of becoming an accomplished swordsman!' Ifan smiled at his son.

Dewi blushed. His father was regarded as the sword master of Gwynedd and this was praise indeed, although he still did not quite understand why his father drove him to practice sword drill far longer and harder than his peers.

'Meilyr! How good to see you! It has been too long!' Ifan ap Rhodri had already turned his mind to other things and was walking towards the thin stranger, who smiled hesitantly.

'Ifan, it is good to be here again, and to see life returning to normal.'

Ifan shrugged. 'Hardly, but we are doing our best. King Gruffudd will be pleased to see you. He was only saying last week how we miss your stories and your poetry and songs, it will be good to talk of something other than warfare!' He turned to his son, 'Dewi, do you remember Meilyr, our great bard and storyteller? If you are good, you may stay up late tonight and hear him sing and tell us his poems.'

Dewi smiled happily, as his father turned back to Meilyr. 'I have not asked you what brings you back to us,' he said.

Meilyr nodded his head. 'You know me well Ifan,' he said. 'And you are right, I have come for a special purpose, to welcome the new child.'

'Indeed,' Ifan responded, 'And a bonny babe and healthy too. Isn't she Dewi?'

'Yes,' agreed Dewi, who wasn't much interested in babies until at least they could walk. 'I picked her an apple today, a good rosy one, and she took hold if it and wouldn't let it go.'

Meilyr smiled. 'I expect you think it strange that I should come all this way on her account, but I have a portent, she is to be a great leader of the Welsh.'

Ifan stared. 'That small child? And a girl at that? How do you know?'

Meilyr smiled again. 'That, and my prediction for her, is only for the ears of the king and queen. But before I see them Ifan, dear friend, could you please spare some water for washing and a little food?'

That evening, as the court settled around the peat fire in the centre of the large hall, Meilyr noted with satisfaction the circumference of this, the main building, and the way that the few artefacts and war trophies hung around the walls had been displayed to effect. The court was returning to how it should be, even if progress was slow and there was still much to be done. Sword hilts and breast plates glistened in the glow from the rush lights and candles, and the smell of cooking and the peat fire mingled with the sweat of about sixty guests. They had eaten well and consumed a quantity of ale, and were now drowsy and expectant. Dewi settled at his father's feet hardly knowing what to expect, as his senses reeled with the excitement of it all.

Meilyr had been with the king and queen for almost an hour, and they seemed happy and confident. A servant brought in the new princess Gwenllian, asleep in her crib, which was unusual at such a gathering. The king rose to his feet.

'We welcome the bard Meilyr to our gathering,' he said. 'You all know he has the powers to divine and foresee the future, and he has spoken to us of great portents which surround our new child Gwenllian. It is predicted that she will be a great leader of the Welsh, revered in history. Nations as yet unborn will know her name.'

The king waited for his words to be taken in fully by the listeners. Meilyr came forward. 'All is true,' he said. 'All I have foreseen is true, but that is for the future. For now, for tonight, let us celebrate the birth of this sweet child, who comes to us as a sign of hope, in these dreadful times. Let us recall there are things more important than war, let us sing the song of new birth and joy.' He took his harp and played a few notes, and then sang his song to a delicate and unusual melody:

Sleep, Gwenllian, my heart's delight,
Sleep on through shivering spear and brand,
An apple rosy red within thy baby hand;
Thy pillowed cheeks a pair of roses bright,
Thy heart as happy day and night!
Mid all our woe, O! vision rare!
Sweet little princess cradled there,
Thy apple in thy hand all of earthly care.

Thy brethren battle with the foe,

Thy Sire's red strokes around him sweep,
Whilst thou, his bonny babe, art smiling through thy
sleep.
All Gwalia shudders at the Norman blow!
What are the angels whispering low
Of thy father now?
Bright babe, asleep upon my knee,
How many a queen of high degree
Would cast away her crown to sleep like thee!

The plaintive sound had barely died away when Ifan entered without ceremony and made his way to King Gruffudd.

'Another attack on Rhos sire. This time they have pushed us over the Conwy, but so far we have held the west bank.'

'Then we have lost our forts at Deganwy and Bryn Eiryn?' Gruffudd put his head in his hands, as if dreading the reply.

'Yes sire, but at the cost of a dozen of their men to five of our own.' Ifan looked sheepish; he knew this was no answer. The two Welsh held forts were strategically important. He looked carefully at Gruffudd, and saw that the king was having difficulty controlling his temper. Since his return from Ireland the king had done his best to live quietly and refrain from provoking the English king, but Ifan saw that the news he brought had pierced the king's calm exterior. He watched the rush of aggression mount in Gruffudd's face.

'Muster the men! Get my mail and sword! Rhos must be retaken by this time tomorrow, Rufus has pushed me too far this time!'

The gathering broke up in a general scramble to arms, with the entreaties of wives and families ringing around the hall. Queen Angharad laid her hand on her husband's arm and wished him God speed and a quick victory. He grinned briefly and said, 'Guard the little one, if she is to be a great leader we must take good care of her.' He glanced down at the sleeping child, and then at Angharad. 'Do you think it is true? A girl to be a leader? I am not much use with these tales and predictions, whether from priest or bard. Sometimes I think they all speak nonsense just to secure a meal and bed. I cannot think in terms of spirits and such things... and for a girl to be a leader...'

Angharad smiled. 'It is not unknown. Think of the great Boudica, who fought the Romans so many years ago,' she said.

Her husband nodded. 'That is true, but it saddens me. I do not think Boudica had a happy life, and she was beaten in the end.' He winced as the chain mail was strapped to his chest, and took up his great Viking sword, the one which had been given to him in friendship by king Magnus. 'We will talk on these things when I return,' he said to Angharad, and left the hall at the head of his men.

The room, now containing only women and a few servants, fell silent. Meilyr stepped up to the queen, and his words rang out eerily in the fast emptying space: 'Our great King at the head of his men, will scythe the enemies of the free Welsh down like wheat with his great sword of vengeance.'

Angharad thanked him briefly, and then turned to more practical matters. She had heard enough of Meilyr's pronouncements. 'Fetch a wet nurse,' she instructed. 'Gwenllian is awake.'

When Dewi was twelve years old he experienced a moment of clarity which was to inform the rest of his life. He and Gwenllian had been allowed to travel to the King's subsidiary palace at Abergwyngregyn, a few miles from Aberffraw. This was a hall largely used by King

Gruffudd on hunting trips, when he and his followers could make a pleasant stay, sometimes for several days. It was maintained by a small staff, and Dewi and Gwenllian had visited many times, as the lodge was surrounded by mountainous slopes and thickly wooded valleys, ideal for imaginary battles and games. Here among the trees they found lichen-grey outcrops which still showed the remains of ancient settlements, old places of worship and Roman forts. Here they inhabited their imaginary world of kings and queens, soldiers and courtiers, and countless servants, and did brave deeds and fought all invaders, and always the outcome was the same. They would be victorious, and march home together singing a victory song to the rapturous applause of their subjects. In their magical world at Abergwyngregyn there was even a beautiful waterfall, where they would stop and eat the food they had brought with them, and drink the sweet cold water, imagining they were hiding out in the forest, and always plotting campaigns against their enemies.

On this day Dewi had been climbing up a steep mountain path following behind Gwenllian, now seven years old and the essence of naughtiness and enchantment, as she bounded ahead of him. As he reached a flat viewing area he stopped and looked around for her, but she was nowhere to be seen. He called out her name, but the wind brought the echo back to him in silent reproach. He sighed. He was supposed to look after her, to protect her with his life, but she was merciless in the pranks she played on him, and he recognised that this was to be the way of it, as long as she so dictated.

'Gwenllian, I'm not playing this silly game,' he said loudly. He sat down on a rock and pretended to be unconcerned. After a few minutes he got up and strode around a little, but she was still not revealed. She was always doing this, demanding he accompany her into the mountains, never very far, but places she was not allowed to go alone, and then she would torment him by deliberately hiding or running away so they were late home. Always, it was him who was blamed; he had taken several beatings for her sake.

He shouted now: 'Gwenllian, I'm going back now. If you don't come that's up to you. I'm not getting into trouble again.'

He began to walk purposefully back down the path, steeling himself not to look behind him to see if she was following. After about two hundred yards he secreted himself behind a bush and waited. It was a while before she appeared in the distance, laughing and joyous, peeping out from behind a rock. When she did not see him ahead she appeared very surprised, although not worried. She began to run, and called out: 'Dewi, where are you? I'm coming now, we shan't get into trouble, wait for me!'

She ran faster, and as she neared him Dewi stepped out quickly and caught her as she flung herself headlong down the path. She squealed: 'Oh Dewi! That was a good joke! I didn't know where you were!'

Dewi swung her round and round as they both laughed with delight. Then they sat down upon the bracken and picked some bilberries and ate them. Dewi said: 'Gwenllian, I must tell you something. I am almost a man now and cannot continue to play with you all day. You are still a child and don't understand that I must make my mark, and be with the other men, and your brothers.'

Gwenllian laughed. 'Don't be silly, you have always been my playmate, my father allows it. It won't change just because we get older. Anyway, you have to do what my father tells you, it is not up to you.'

Dewi blushed. 'That is true; I will always obey your father. But he will not ever give me a suitable post if I am continually looking after a girl.' He turned to Gwenllian, almost pleading with her. 'My father is captain of the guard,' he said. 'It is a very important post, and I must be a credit to him. I am a good swordsman and fighter, your brother Owain said so only last week, but I will never have a chance...'

'But that is why!' Gwenllian interrupted, her sweet smile showing itself and melting away his crossness. 'That is why you are entrusted to look after me is it not? After all,' she got to her feet and pulled at his hand, 'I'm the most precious thing you could guard aren't I?'

She began to dance her way along the path, her long golden hair bouncing and flying about her. She put on her best wheedling tone. 'If you want to do more soldier things with the boys, we can do them together can't we?'

'But you're a girl,' Dewi protested.

'No I'm not, I'm a princess, and the child of King Gruffudd ap Cynan!' she struck a pose, 'You said I was good with the sword when we practice. And I shall be a great warrior like my father; you have heard the ballads of his great battles.'

'Yes indeed, and you have three brothers who will carry on his great tradition, and I shall fight by their side, and help them,' Dewi explained.

Gwenllian pouted. 'And so shall I,' she said.

Dewi regarded the proud lift of her head, and the stubborn look he knew so well. He smiled with affection. 'Yes Gwenllian, I'm sure you will,' he said.

That evening Gwenllian sat on the skin rugs at her father's feet after supper in the great hall at Aberffraw. She loved this evening time, especially if her father was in good spirits, and she hugged his knee affectionately. She giggled as the big wolf hounds licked her bare feet, and waited for the right moment to speak. Already she understood that she must choose carefully where her father was concerned. At times he was stern and cold, unapproachable to all except for her mother, or one of the other women around him who seemed able to change his mood. At other times, usually later in the evening when he had eaten and drunk well, he would be amiable and even sentimental, and Gwenllian could charm him easily. He was engaged in conversation with her brother Owain, and seemed to be in a good mood. When he turned to take another swig of ale, Gwenllian said, 'Father, may I ask you for advice?'

King Gruffudd smiled down at her. 'And what, my pretty, could you possibly need advice about?'

'It is about my training as a warrior father. I already practice with the sword, and the bow and spear, but I should like to join my brothers when they go hunting, and I'm sure I am big enough now to have my own falcon, am I not?'

Gruffudd laughed. 'I'm sure you are big enough to do anything you wish, sweeting. But when you are twelve perhaps, will be the time to go hunting.'

'Dewi is twelve father. Nearly thirteen.'

Her father looked puzzled. 'What does that have to do with it?'

'Well, if he didn't have to guard me he could go hunting with my brothers couldn't he? So it's only fair he should go now he is twelve. If I went along as well, he could do both at the same time, look after me and hunt as well.'

Gruffudd looked a little taken aback. 'What a little mischief the child is,' he remarked to Owain, who was much taken with his young sister's directness.

'Perhaps it is a little unfair on Dewi,' Owain said now, 'He's very promising, and it's time we allowed him to grow to manhood.'

'You're right,' Gruffudd agreed. 'And what about this little one?' He gazed down at Gwenllian affectionately and then lifted her onto his knee. 'Do you think Owain, you can bring this little mischief to manhood also?'

Owain laughed. 'If you and she wish it father, I've no doubt it will be accomplished. We can humour her anyway, she'll probably change her mind when she finds out it is hard work!'

Gruffudd considered. 'Give her full freedom to develop, and teach her all you can,' he said at last. 'I have not forgotten the prediction at her birth, although it seems unlikely. But Owain, I charge you and your brothers, and Dewi, to guard her well and keep her safe. This little one is our most precious jewel, and I shall have no more children. At least,' he smiled, 'No more children by my Queen, for your mother has stopped her courses, and now it seems her time is spent with more spiritual matters.' He glanced across to where Angharad was deep in conversation with a young prior, and then bent and kissed Gwenllian's golden curls, but the child had already fallen asleep.

'Your young sister has your mother's attributes,' Gruffudd confided to Owain. 'She shows her stately figure, and her strength and willpower, as well as those fair curls. When the time comes, I will be able to make a great match for her, to bring credit to the kingdom. Princesses can play their part Owain, as well as princes. A different part it is true, but sometimes one can obtain lands and fortunes more easily by a good marriage, than by a dozen battles.'

'I agree,' said Owain dryly. 'But in the meantime, until she is of marriageable age, I suppose you and your sons will have to continue to defend what we already hold!'

They laughed, and Owain, planting a kiss on the

child's forehead, picked her up and carried her himself to the nurse.

Next day Dewi was overjoyed to find himself included in the early morning hunting party, which set out with Owain and his brothers Cadwaladr and Cadwallon. The morning was crisp and clear, and Dewi felt the hand of manhood upon him at last as they left the settlement. It would be a hard day but he knew he would be equal to it. He glanced back and saw Gwenllian watching the party depart, and felt a pang of guilt as she waved. He did not return the gesture, but turned away, determined to behave well, and relinquish his position of childminder as soon as possible. Gwenllian had not been allowed to accompany the party, but had been promised lessons in the rudiments of falconry. Her father had agreed she might have her own falcon, as soon as she was able to care for the bird to her tutor's satisfaction.

Gwenllian spent a happy day in this new pursuit, and when the hunting party returned in the gathering dusk, she ran to Dewi with happy anticipation. She wanted to hear the news of his day, but Dewi had become austere and restrained, and seemed embarrassed by her attentions.

'Dewi, what's the matter?' she pleaded, her child's eyes full of concern.

'Nothing' His reply belied his stance, he was too grown up for her now. He was enjoying being with his peers, being part of the grown up brotherhood which did not include women and children.

Gwenllian received the message. 'Just because you go hunting with my brothers does not mean you don't have to look after me!' she said pointedly. 'I want to show you the falcons.'

Dewi sighed. He knew she spoke the truth but he did not like it. 'I will come with you,' he said, following her,

'But I shall not have so much time to spend with you in future.'

'Until we are married,' Gwenllian responded cheerfully. 'Then we shall spend all our time together, because when you are at home, I shall be there, and when you go to war, I shall come as well, and join you in battle. I shall be a fine warrior.'

'Married?' Dewi was horror struck. 'Gwenllian, you and I can never be married!' He came to her side and spoke quietly, urgently.

'Why not?' She tossed her head in the wilful gesture she used when anyone crossed her. She gave her sweet smile and said simply, 'I love you best of anyone Dewi, I always have. Don't you love me?'

One look at her happy face, and he relented. 'Of course I do, but you are a princess, and cannot marry where you will.' He took her hand and led her over to the bird pens. 'Your father will choose a great prince for you, Gwenllian, a much better match than I.'

'But what if I don't like the great prince?'

'That will be no matter. When you are a princess you have to do what is right, and your father will guide you.'

'But some people love their wives and husbands don't they? They marry each other because they like each other a lot? My serving girl Elaine told me she loved her husband very much.'

'Yes, but they are ordinary people, baseborn, like me. They are not of the ruling family, and this love you speak of is not a thing you can understand until you are older.' Dewi wristed a hooded peregrine falcon and stroked it gently. 'I have spoken of these things with my father, and he tells me that even though I am twelve, I am not old enough yet to understand fully.'

'Well....' Gwenllian considered carefully, turning his arm so she could stroke the bird, 'If you can choose because you are baseborn, you can choose me, can't you? When you are old enough?'

'I certainly cannot! Your father will never allow it!'

'He will not gainsay me! I can always charm him! Well...' she considered again. 'Nearly always. Mother says I have the wiles of a witch! I shall not marry before I am sixteen at least. By then I shall understand it all, and be able to beat you in combat!'

Dewi smiled indulgently. She was still a child, and would learn the hard truths of life soon enough. 'Come along my lady,' he said gently, ' We shall be late for supper.'

TWO
(1113)
LOVE AND WAR

Sir Gerald de Windsor regarded his wife gravely. He could not imagine what she was thinking. In the evenings he loved to do nothing other than this, to sit quietly by the fireside with his darling Nest, and just look at her. Looking at Nest was perhaps the greatest joy of his life. He examined her again, more closely this time. Since their marriage fourteen years ago her extraordinary beauty had blossomed from the prettiness of youth into a deep, rich beauty, more mature but infinitely more seductive. Her face now, in elegant repose, bent over her embroidery, showed nothing of the intense pain and tragedy she had suffered in her early life. He considered this, as he had many times. To lose two brothers to the invading Norman forces was enough for anyone, he thought. But to have your father beheaded in front of your eyes, and then to be carted off by the conqueror as a war prize... how had she coped? He thought back to that time, but reflections were hazy and he could hardly recall the journey back to King Henry's court with Nest as a prisoner. I must have been in my cups, he thought ruefully, I did a lot of that in those days. Certainly I remember that she was given the treatment demanded by her high birth. A royal princess of Wales, with a lineage to put even King Henry's to shame, was a prize indeed. Of course he had known what would happen as soon as the king set eyes on her. Sir Gerald's father had been the first castellan of Windsor castle, and his son Gerald had been brought up with the young Prince Henry, and as boyhood playmates they had been close. In manhood Sir

Gerald still understood the King's disposition better than almost anyone. Now he recalled the slight revulsion he had felt as the king appraised the fourteen year old. She had been bathed and robed after the journey, and for all her plump prettiness, she had even then a certain self possession, a look of calm assurance in the dark eyes, which turned men's insides to water. All men seemed to be affected in the same way, and he had been no exception.

King Henry was an old goat, he thought angrily, and sighed. *After all, the king had taken no more than his due, and had treated Nest well on the whole. If he had not taken her himself, she would have been traded to one of the other nobles, and he would never have had a chance.* Sir Gerald was not of high birth himself, but had been born on a farm in Windsor, from whence he had taken his name. When he had successfully defended the Norman built castle at Pembroke against the marauding Welsh in 1094, the then king William Rufus had called him 'our gallant defender', and Gerald had basked in a warmth of recognition far beyond his expectations. When William Rufus had been killed out hunting in what was apparently an appalling accident, it had crossed Sir Gerald's mind that such an accident was providential to the king's younger brother Henry, who had also been present on the ill fated hunt. His private thoughts had only been strengthened when Henry ascended the throne only three days after the accident, and Sir Gilbert was aware that King Henry the First was a man to be feared and obeyed. He had decided, wisely as it turned out, to keep his thoughts to himself and his head well down. His service to King Henry had been exemplary, and he had risen slowly in the king's esteem, although the king had not risen in his. He thought back to that evening when Henry summoned him to attend in the great chamber. To his surprise the king seemed more interested in his personal life than in the defence of his strongholds.

'Why have you never married?' he asked, as soon as Gerald entered.

'I - er - I don't know my lord,' Gerald answered. 'I have never felt the need. Er - I have a concubine,' he added swiftly, in case the king got the wrong idea about him. 'I am fond of her and she keeps me warm enough.' He smiled, wondering what was coming next.

'You can make a very advantageous marriage and do me a service at the same time,' the king announced.

'Then consider it done sire,' Gerald responded cheerfully. 'Who is the lady?'

'The princess Nest,' the king said, noting the look of shock which passed over Gerald's face. 'Surprised? Think she's too good for you? Well you're right, she is.' He bent over and put his face close to Gerald's. 'Of course, you get her because she's spoiled. But only by me!' he added. 'Some would take that as an honour!'

'Indeed it is, sire.' Gerald responded. 'I take it she is with child?'

'Of course.' King Henry was pleased with himself. 'I set my seed as a king should, plentifully!' He leaned over again. 'I did not intend to let her go so soon, but needs must, the queen is becoming anxious, and I cannot have that, as she is with child herself. If Nest's child is a boy, he must be named for me, Henry Fitzhenry it shall be I think. You agree?'

'Of course, and I shall love the child as my own, boy or girl.' Gerald was already thinking of Nest, the beautiful girl who was to be his wife. His mind was racing, making plans.

The king was laughing aloud. 'I knew you would take her, I've seen you looking at her like all the others.' He became serious. 'I wish to be particularly generous on

26

this occasion,' he said. 'In addition to the position of Constable of Pembroke castle I shall give you a large tract of land to the north of the castle as a dowry, where you may build your own domain in time, should you so wish. We must expand our influence right along the Welsh coast. Nest is of the old family, who had their stronghold at Dinefwr, and many of our Welsh subjects still feel that her family should rule in Deheubarth, in spite of our having beaten them roundly. When Nest marries in to our Norman family, the warring factions in that part of Wales may become better reconciled to our rule.'

You devious old lecher, Gerald thought, but aloud he said: 'I'm sure you are right sire, I shall do my best to obtain the outcomes you desire.'

Now, as he considered his wife again as she bent over her embroidery, Gerald wondered if the King had any idea of the tremendous favour he had bestowed on him. If King Henry had known of the happiness and contentment Gerald had enjoyed since his marriage he would surely have found some way to put a stop to it. They had been married now for fourteen years, and Gerald had done all he could to ensure his new wife's comfort and health. It had not been easy at first, and Gerald had wondered if Nest would ever be able to feel any true affection for him. It could hardly be expected, given the way she had been handed over to him like a damaged parcel. She had accepted the marriage as a way of making her precarious position at least respectable, and had thanked him, quietly and soberly, as she said, 'For giving me a settled place, and my child a name.'

The look of meek acceptance on her lovely face had made him feel ashamed, although he had done nothing wrong. After the child, a boy, was born, and was named Henry Fitzhenry on the king's instructions, Gerald found that Nest began to relax a little, and gradually she had come to trust him, and respond not only to his embraces, but to their life together. His main duty was still as the Constable of Pembroke Castle, held in the name of King Henry, and Nest understood that he had to fulfil his duty to the King, although it went against everything she had been born to honour as a Welsh princess. Gerald had never forgotten her joy when they had returned to Wales, and the look on her face when he told her she would be able to live out her life in her beloved Deheubarth, and never have to return to court in England.

'Unless,' he had teased her, laughing, 'King Henry commands it of course.'

He immediately relented when he saw her eyes cloud. 'We shall live so quietly,' he said, 'and I shall carry out my duties so well, that the King will forget all about us!'

By and large, that is what had happened, he reflected. The grant of land north of Pembroke had been the spur to his decision to establish his own great hall at Cenarth Bychan, and he and Nest had planned the building of it together. He was astonished at the pride she took in the new home and its furnishing, and in the welfare of the local people who had now become his tenants. Cenarth Bychan had become their own place, a true home where each of them could escape from the duties expected of them and where they felt no need for show or pretence. During this time Nest had also given birth to two more children of their own, a son named Maurice Fitzgerald, and two years later, a daughter whom they called Angharad. Gerald found almost to his own surprise that he felt a deep sense of love and satisfaction in his young family, something which, as a soldier for so many years, he had neither looked for nor expected.

Gerald was pleased he had worked so hard to ensure they could occasionally escape to Cenarth Bychan for a few uninterrupted days, as they had this month. He knew Nest was happy here, and that made him happy. Now, he leaned over towards his wife and said gently, 'Have you not had enough time at your stitching wife? I fear the candlelight is not good enough and you may strain your eyes.'

She looked up quickly and said, 'I can see well enough, but you are right, it is time for bed. We are making many preserves tomorrow and I have promised to help the cook.'

He watched as she tidied away her work, never tiring of seeing her quick, deft movements. He thrilled at the twinkle in her eye as she turned to him. 'Come, sweeting,' she said, and he followed her to the bedchamber like a lamb.

Later, as they lay together in the big bed which had been made for Nest by an old Dinefwr man who had been a woodworker for her father, Gerald asked, 'Why did you not tell me that your cousin, the Prince Owen ap Cadwgan came to see you a few days ago?'

'Oh husband, I am sorry but I thought it was better not to mention it. After all, he has fought against yourself and other Norman lords for many years. I did not think he would be welcomed by you.'

'You were right about that,' Gerald said shortly. 'The man is a troublesome rebel. As for fighting the Normans, he is his father's son and I do not berate him for that. But he is a cavalier, he fights anyone he pleases, on any whim which takes him. There is no knowing what he will do next; his exploits are the talk of Wales. Cousin or no, you should not have received him.'

'Perhaps not.' Nest turned to Gerald and snuggled into him. 'But he is not my cousin you know, only a second cousin, and he only called to pay his respects to me as his kin, and a princess of the old Deheubarth family.' She sighed. 'Try to understand Gerald, I have so few kin left now. I have two brothers, but Gruff has been in Ireland these sixteen years, and my brother Hywel is still imprisoned. It was good to see a relative, even an unruly one. Owen talked to me of the old times when we were children, when we used to have festivals of music and poetry...'

'Did you?' Gerald interrupted. 'In Wales? Festivals of music and poetry? I thought...'

'You thought! You thought!' For once Nest allowed her irritation to show. 'You did not think at all! You knew nothing about us, but you assumed because we were not Normans we were savages!' She made an effort and her voice became calmer, softer. 'Oh my husband, we had a good system here, our laws had evolved over centuries and were codified by the great king Hywel Dda. We had an established culture of poetry and music, and many monasteries with wise monks who studied plants and animals and who could treat many ailments...' Her voice tailed off, and she sighed. 'When the Normans came, they did not ask any questions, they did not want to know what or who we were. They just killed and took, and killed and took...'

Gerald was quiet for a moment. Then he said, 'And you include me in this ravening pack of wolves?'

Nest met his questioning look. 'You have never shown me anything but respect and love, you are a good man and the father of my children. But I ask you to remember, when you were younger and came here with William Rufus and then Henry's army, do you not recognise what I describe?'

'Perhaps.' A flood of images entered Gerald's mind, images he did not want to dwell on. 'We were at war,' he said eventually, 'And you must understand our Viking blood. It is not for nothing we are called Normans. It is

30

from *Norsemen*, and comes from the time when we were invaded by the great Viking warriors from the North, and their blood is now mixed for ever with ours. We have inherited their great warrior skills but also probably their aggression and need to expand our territory. You do not understand dearest. A soldier must obey orders and seek the outcome his king desires. A battle must be won by whatever means.'

'I understand what you say', Nest replied. 'But we were not at war, we were simply invaded, and when we fought back to protect our own we were told we were rebels. And after a battle was fought and lost, what then? Was it part of the king's desired outcome to pillage, to kill without thinking, to rape the women, old and young, to set fire to the harvest so all would starve?'

Nest stopped. She knew she had gone too far, and recognised that Gerald himself was not to blame for all the terrible things which had happened in her life. She raised herself on one elbow and looked down at her husband, whose jaw was set in a determined line.

'No...Do not answer,' she whispered as she saw him about to speak. She kissed his lips gently. 'I am sorry my dear husband, I should not hold you responsible for everything, and as a soldier, I expect you were better than most. We have had this conversation many times and there is no answer to it.'

'No,' Gerald agreed. 'I am sorry my dear, for the troubles inflicted on your family. But now, we are in control and governance is more peaceful, apart from minor problems with mad half wits like your cousin Owen.' He smiled. 'Don't worry; I'll leave him alone if he behaves himself. If he doesn't, he only has himself to blame.'

Nest snuggled down under the heavy cover of fur, thinking over Gerald's words. She could hardly tell him now that Owen had in fact attempted to make love to her within minutes of being shown into her presence. He had paid many compliments, telling her that he had heard tales of her great beauty, and had wanted to come and see for himself. Now he had, he realised that everything he had heard was as nothing to the actuality before him. Nest was, Owen had declared to the world at large, the embodiment of earthly womanhood in its most perfect form. Indeed, he expanded, there probably was not such beauty among Heaven's own angels. Nest had laughed a little at his romantic pretensions, and had reminded him that she was a married lady. Before leaving Owen had sworn undying fealty to her, telling her that they would meet again in much better times, 'when she was not carrying the heavy yoke of Norman duty,' as he put it.

Nest sighed to herself. She knew she was a beauty, she had been told so often enough, and had heard herself described as 'The Helen of Wales,' but she did not view it as an asset. Her beauty had brought her nothing but trouble. Gerald was right, Owen was a madcap and a troublemaker for sure, and yet there was something likeable about him. She just hoped he would keep well away from Pembroke and Cenarth Bychan in future, so that she would be spared the embarrassment of being obliged to refuse him entry.

It was only a week later that Owen ap Cadwgan proved Gerald de Windsor right. He arrived at Cenarth Bychan secretly under cover of darkness with fourteen of his most trusted followers, who quickly tunnelled underneath the outer defences and despatched the surprised and sleepy guard.

Sir Gerald, already woken by the noise outside, leapt out of bed and grabbed his sword.

'There are too many,' Nest screamed, in a panic. 'Help me.' Together, she and Gerald moved a heavy clothes chest against the door.

'You must get away,' Nest entreated, 'Quickly, they will kill you!' She did not know who was breaking in to their retreat, but only that it could mean nothing but harm for her husband. Gerald was dressing quickly, but as he picked up his mail coat Nest took it from him.

'No,' she said quickly. 'Too bulky.'

There was loud banging on the door. 'How can I get away if I do not fight them?' Gerald asked incredulously.

'Come quickly husband,' Nest took Gerald's arm and led him through to the privy room attached to their bedchamber.

'Down the privy hole,' she commanded. 'Get in and slide down...'

'Down there?' Gerald stared, a look of disgust on his face.

'It's the only way!' Nest was desperate. 'They will kill you! Don't you recall husband, when we planned this place we arranged for the privy fall to come out just on the outside of the walls. No-one will be there, you can get away...'

'But you must come with me...'

'No. They will not hurt me, and I would hold you up...go now...'

The clothes chest began to shake as the door was battered from outside. Raised voices called for help. Gerald climbed into the privy, his nose wrinkled in disgust. Nest leaned over and whispered, 'I have a bag of coins, I'll throw them down after you. Mind who you trust...'

Gerald loosed his grip on the top of the privy and hurtled downwards. Nest threw the coin bag down after him and then ran over and sat on top of the clothes chest. She was still sitting there when Owen ap Cadwgan and his men broke down the door.

At tribute time, in mid October, when the harvests had been accounted and all the calculations made, on a dry clear day King Gruffudd ap Cynan took up his traditional position atop the small hill known as the tithing mound. First the local chieftains, and then the freeholders, followed by the tenantry, mounted the slope one by one to where he stood, arms folded and countenance grave, to receive both their homage and their tithes, which were duly marked off by his clerk. For this ceremony the King was robed in green velvet over his linen shirt and wore the great jewelled torque of state around his neck, and the thin circlet of gold on his head, so that all might know to whom they paid allegiance.

Not all persons who attended were quite sure what was happening. They were Flemish settlers who had been given their land on the instructions of the English king Henry a few years earlier, when his troops had ravaged the land and driven the noble freemen and bondmen, together with their slaves and families, from their homes and livelihood. Following the Norman soldiers were the Flemish peasants, driven from their own lands by the devastation caused by battles in their homeland, battles between Henry and his estranged brother Robert, the Duke of Normandy.

It had been a ten year war since Robert had invaded England in an attempt to wrest power from his brother Henry in 1101. Although Robert had been defeated, Henry had never forgotten his brother's duplicity, and five years later had invaded Normandy at the head of a huge army to put an end to his brother's power base. At the decisive Battle of Tinchebrai near Avranches, Henry had captured his brother and, before his imprisonment, had blinded him. Descriptions of the ferocity and cruelty of Henry's soldiers preceded him, as the army pillaged its way back through Holland and into England, laying waste to farms and villages, putting their own people into any stronghold they did not already own. Eventually, having conquered the south and east of the country, they pushed north and west with an orgy of killing and cruelty, until all England knew who were now the masters. At last they had come to Gwynedd, that unruly area which Henry had intermittently tried to subdue since the failure of his predecessor, William Rufus. The Norman army was followed by a Saxon and Flemish rabble of the hungry and dispossessed, which quickly moved into the hastily vacated farms, settlements and hovels. Those Welsh patriots loyal to King Gruffudd who chose to stay and fight were soon despatched, and after the great wave of invasion had passed and the main army had returned home, King Gruffudd found he had lost many of his loyal chiefs and bondmen, and even more of the local peasants who had formerly claimed him as their King and protector. The trickle of Flemish settlers had become a flood, and no matter how often the king's soldiers removed them and re-instated his own people, others came back to replace them, and eventually after many small battles and skirmishes, they had grudgingly been allowed to stay. The furious King Gruffudd had railed against this, but he had little option, for if he did not allow them to stay, who would farm the land and ensure the next harvest, and the tithes to be paid to keep up his household and army?

Now King Gruffudd stood atop the small hillock, and watched as the scorned Flemish settlers nervously approached him with their tithes of wheat and barley, baskets of apples and the occasional sheep or goose. At least they had come, the king reflected. It was true they had only done so at the point of his men's swords, but nevertheless, they were beginning to conform to the pattern, to make a contribution to the whole. He smiled quietly to himself, at least the grain holds and byres would be full enough to last through the winter. He calculated that if he could just keep a hold on the community, and keep receiving the help he had solicited from his friends in Ireland and Denmark, he could continue to rebuild his stronghold.

It seemed to the king that for years he had thought of nothing but defence, how to preserve his settlement at Aberffraw and his barns and cattle from the passing Norman raiders, but things had quietened a little of late. It had been reported that Henry had decided to let well alone. Apparently his instructions were 'If Gruffudd doesn't attack us, leave him alone in his miserable mountains.'

Now the king winked his eye at a filthy and frightened looking settler, who approached with two hens. The man was taken aback and retreated quickly, but Gruffudd knew he had made a point. Sooner or later these new people in his land would realise that the Welsh king was a better option for them than the Norman invaders, and would be able to give him their allegiance more gladly, and hopefully, in time, this allegiance would include their axes and spears also. Gruffudd was no fool, he knew he did not have the strength to attack the Normans in their new strongholds. But if he could only continue to re-build the kingdom, then perhaps he and his people would have a chance of survival.

King Gruffudd now became aware that the main column of peasants was thinning, and the final miserable tithes were being donated. His presence was no longer strictly necessary. He raised his arm.

'Good people,' he cried, and his commanding voice seemed to fill the air and ring around the valley. 'We have had a good harvest, and I am pleased. Tonight we shall hold a feast to celebrate, and all are welcome. There will be meat for all. Those of you who wish to travel from here and refresh your souls at the church before returning to your homes, are welcome to stay overnight and continue your journey tomorrow.' Then he turned and made his way slowly back to the hall, hoping he had not made a mistake, and that his ever hungry guests would not eat too much.

That evening the king was in benevolent mood as the feasting began. His queen Angharad was at his side, and they were flanked by their four offspring who still remained at home. King Gruffudd watched them with interest. He was immensely proud of Owain, who was proving to be a strong right hand to his father. Even now he was busy, checking in all the guests with the doorward, making sure that those who were seated within the king's hearing were the kind of people who might at least have something worthwhile to say. The king smiled as he looked across to Cadwallon, who was proving to be every bit as good a fighter as his eldest brother, and who, as usual, was anxious for the festivities to start because he was always hungry. King Gruffudd turned to the queen, 'How is it that Cadwallon manages to eat so much?' he asked her. 'I like my food but I'd surely split my belly if I downed the amount he does!'

Angharad laughed, but then her face changed. 'I would that our younger son would down more food like Cadwallon, but I fear all he can swallow is drink.' Her husband followed her gaze to where Cadwaladr, already very drunk, was assaulting a serving maid whilst still draining his ale. Her husband sighed. 'If over indulgence in drink was his only fault I would not complain of him,' he said slowly, 'But I receive reports that worry me.' He bent his head towards Angharad. 'In his cups,' he explained, 'I have heard he criticises me and my actions, and speaks against me. I do not know how I can continue to turn a blind eye. I have always sought to do what is best for the family and our people and he knows this. I fear he has a taste for intrigue as an ox licks salt. It comes naturally to him.'

'He is young and headstrong,' Angharad replied, trying as always to keep her husband equable. 'Remember my lord, you have a daughter who is also young and headstrong, but she loves you dearly and will never resort to devious ways. Take strength and delight in her beauty and accomplishments.'

The king roared out loud with laughter. 'Accomplishments!' he laughed again. 'Gwenllian's accomplishments are not those which are to the credit of a princess. Of her beauty there is no doubt, and it will bring her many suitors, but you said yourself she was the worst of our daughters with regard to sewing and embroidery, or any of the pastimes which are suitable for a young princess.' He looked across to where sixteen year old Gwenllian sat, incredibly beautiful, smiling and happy, and his heart softened. 'She has a little skill with music I understand,' he said grudgingly, 'And her tutor says her languages improve, but even so...'

'Even so,' Angharad said, with a slightly reproving glance, 'You were the one who allowed her to run wild with her brothers, and train as a fighter with Dewi, you can hardly complain if she has turned out to be headstrong and wilful.'

'No, I suppose not.' Gruffudd agreed. He knew his wife was right, as she usually was, although he would not have admitted it. He glanced up as a messenger approached the table. The man spoke to him for several minutes, and when he was gone the king turned to his wife again.

38

'Interesting news,' he said slowly. 'The young prince Gruffudd ap Rhys has returned from exile in Ireland.' He sighed, and turned to a young visiting priest whom Owain had shown to their table. 'He must be a young man now, and I should dearly like to see him. He was named for me you know, this young Prince Gruffudd. His father was my dearest friend...' He broke off; the news of the young prince had clearly affected him.

Angharad understood, and remained silent. The death of Gruffudd's closest friend Rhys ap Tewdwr was never far from her husbands memory. To die in battle was an honourable death, but Rhys had been captured by his Norman enemy, Bernard Neufmarche, and beheaded at Talgarth in front of his daughter Nest and his own followers.

At length the king turned to the table in general: 'Apparently young Gruffudd has gone to his sister Nest at Pembroke Castle.'

'Will he be safe there?' Angharad queried. 'It is but a few months since her husband Sir Gerald recovered her from Owen ap Cadwgan is it not?'

'Yes, and that fool Owen was lucky to escape to Ireland with his life,' her husband said gravely. 'It was a happier fate for him than for many of his followers. Gerald has been merciless over these last years in his search for Nest, it is almost six years since she was kidnapped by Owen.'

'I expect Owen could not stomach the idea of a princess of Deheubarth being married to a Norman lord,' Angharad said.

'Nonsense! He wanted her for himself, that is all! You forget my dear I know this fellow. He makes up his principles by the hour as the whim takes him. He is a great fighter I admit, everyone acknowledges that, and would be happy to give any Norman a bloody nose. But kidnapping Nest was a foolhardy thing to do, it was known Sir Gerald was besotted with her, and would never let him get away with it, no matter how long it took.'

'Let us hope he is still besotted,' said Angharad, 'Or it will be a bad time for Nest. She has two children by Owen you know. I doubt Gerald will make them welcome.'

'If he is a sane man he will know she had little choice in the matter,' said Gruffudd, 'And they are of royal blood so he will be obliged to provide for them. Also, he owes her a great deal. They say she saved his life the night Owen and his men attacked.' He grinned, wanting to share the story with the whole table. 'Pushed him down the privy outfall, so I heard! Imagine how he must have stunk! Nest managed to convince Owen that Gerald had not been there at all that night. But she also did him a greater favour. She persuaded Owen to have Gerald's three children returned under guard to their father at Pembroke. She promised to stay with Owen and be faithful to him if he did that.'

'That must have been hard for her,' Angharad agreed. 'But what about now? She is back with Gerald again but we do not know how he feels about her. After the trouble that Owen caused him, I cannot see him welcoming Nest's brother back to the fold.'

'If Nest is her father's daughter she will not turn him away,' said Gruffudd, 'And Gerald can hardly blame the son for his father's opposition all those years ago. He was only a boy when he escaped to Ireland.'

'Nevertheless,' said Angharad, 'Perhaps it would have been better if he had come to us.' As the King nodded agreement, the young priest interjected: 'He has another brother I believe, who is still imprisoned by the Normans?'

'Yes, Hywel,' King Gruffudd answered. 'He is still in

Montgomery Castle. He did not manage to escape with Prince Gruffudd, he was a small boy and friends hid him for a while, but eventually he was captured. There were two elder brothers too, Gorono and Cynan, but both were killed in that final battle. That was a terrible time, and of course meant the breaking up of the whole principality of Deheubarth. It has been in Norman hands ever since.'

'And now the young Prince Gruffudd returns,' Angharad pondered. 'Imagine husband, how he must feel! His father and two elder brothers dead, his other brother imprisoned and his sister Nest married to a Norman lord! Do you expect him to settle down to a quiet life with all that history behind him? How can he?'

'I can not tell his mind,' Gruffudd answered, 'For I have heard little of him these twenty odd years. I know he was taken under the protection of King Murcart of Dublin, who has treated him well and brought him up with full training in all the warrior arts as well as court etiquette and learning, as befits a true prince. If he nurses revenge in his heart and wishes to recapture his lands he will fail. He has no army and no money, and no real following.'

'But if he arrives here?' Angharad queried. 'We shall make him welcome surely?'

King Gruffudd smiled. 'Nothing would give me greater pleasure,' he said, 'Than to welcome the son of my dearest friend.' He leaned closer to the queen, 'At one time my dear, Rhys and I discussed the possibility of his sons marrying my daughters and my daughters marrying his sons!' He began to laugh. 'This was of course, before most of them were even born! I admit we were both in our cups, but we had the idea that we could amalgamate the principality of Deheubarth with my Northern stronghold and make one great kingdom to leave to our heirs!' He laughed again, 'We were young, then, so young, and thought we could conquer the world. That was before the Normans came.' The king's face changed and his eyes became bleak. 'Now his heirs have nothing at all and I hold on to what I have left by the skin of my teeth.'

THREE
THE PRINCE

The dilemma which King Gruffudd ap Cynan had supposed for Nest was in fact an imaginary one at first. Nest, now happily settled back with Sir Gerald, was ecstatic with joy to see her brother returned. Tears dimmed her eyes as she beheld the handsome young man whom she had not seen since that dreadful day at Talgarth, when they had both lost their father and brothers, and had been wrenched away from all family contact. The young Prince Gruffudd had been whisked away to Ireland by loyal followers before she had a chance to say goodbye, and she had been taken prisoner and escorted to London.

Nest stared at her brother, trying to ascertain his feelings, and regarded with deep pleasure the evidence of his family traits. Yes, he had the look of their father, she thought, appraising the dark hair and eyes, and the tilt of the proud head. The sight of him brought back so many painful memories that she gasped and swallowed, fighting the emotions which welled to the surface. She approached him slowly, recalling the little boy who had played so joyfully, whom she had teased and instructed every day, as an elder sister should, and she wondered if he recalled anything of those days.

'My dearest brother,' she whispered, and traced his face with her finger.

In answer Prince Gruffudd knelt down before her and bowed his head. She raised him up gently and looked deep into his eyes, and then in a moment they had their arms around each other, both tearful and happy, and for the next few hours they hardly stopped talking. Prince Gruffudd was appraised of Nest's history, and was introduced to his nephews and nieces. He did not, however, meet Sir Gerald. Nest explained that although Sir Gerald welcomed Gruff with personal warmth, it would be safer if he was not seen to be openly harbouring the Welsh prince.

'My husband has been good to me brother,' she explained. 'I cannot expect you to approve, but he married me and gave me a settled life in my homeland, and he treats me well. This is how it is brother, and I'm afraid you have to accept it.'

'If he has given you a good life, then how can I complain?' said the prince.

'He lets me have my way in most things,' Nest said. 'I am able to help the local people in small ways. Sir Gerald knows what I do, but he turns a blind eye.'

'And will he turn a blind eye to my being here?'

'Certainly not! He will welcome you here as his wife's brother, but he cannot welcome you as a Welsh prince, if Henry found out he would be very angry. But everyone will find out you are home brother, for I will ask Gerald if I may give you and your followers a banquet of welcome.'

'You shall have your banquet my love,' Gerald agreed, 'But it must be a small one, limited to your trusted friends, and I shall not be able to attend. There must be no trumpeting of his return to the people of Deheubarth. He must not become the centre of attention, or a rallying point for dissention, or an attempt to reinstate the Deheubarth royal family.'

'Of course not,' Nest agreed. 'I have not had a chance to talk to him at length as yet, but I do not expect he has any ambitions in that respect. I believe he will wish to live quietly here. The tragedies of our father's death and the loss of our lands are no doubt still with him, but that was almost twenty five years ago, and he will realise he has to accept things as they are.'

'I sincerely hope so,' said Gerald, not entirely convinced. 'Be aware Nest, that if he chooses the path of opposition I cannot protect him. King Henry would have my head and yours.'

'He will not choose such a path', said Nest confidently, 'For he is not a fool. Now I must attend to arrangements for the banquet.'

It was two days later that Nest finally came to the acceptance that she had been completely wrong in her assumptions. As her brother Prince Gruff settled in to life at Pembroke, and conversation with his newly found sister became easier, he began to reveal to her that it was his long cherished dream to win back his family lands and re-establish the old kingdom of Deheubarth. Nest was horrified, but at the same time incredibly proud of her young brother. He was handsome and accomplished, and expressed thoughts and feelings which she herself had long suppressed for purely practical reasons.

'You know I'm right,' Gruff stated in an almost pleading tone. 'Tell me you agree; you know I have to do this, to honour our father and take back what is rightfully ours.'

They were ambling along on horseback, with only a small escort, on their way to Cenarth Bychan. Nest had promised Sir Gerald she would take Gruff away from the inquisitive gaze of some of the Norman knights in Pembroke. Now she reined in her horse, and waited until her brother was close alongside.

'Gruff, my dearest brother, of course you are right. Do you imagine that I have not dreamed of such things since I was a child?' She leaned over to him, and said fiercely, 'But being right does not ensure success. What you plan is impossible! The Normans have a tight stranglehold on our society here, they have made their mark and the people fear them. You do not know what our people have suffered, you were a child and were not here.'

'That was not my fault,' Gruff responded. 'And I am not a child now. The people may well be afraid, they have had no-one to lead them. All the time I have been in Ireland I have dreamed of this.' His eyes held a dangerous light and his voice filled with passion as he enthused: 'Nest, I have trained hard in Ireland, and King Murcart helped me, his warriors taught me well, I am not without ability or friends. I will first release Hywel from prison, and with him by my side who can stop us? Two royal princes of Deheubarth, together again to rid our country of these invaders once and for all! I seek no favours, but do request...nay... I do *expect* the free Welsh to stand at my side. We will succeed by sheer force of numbers!'

Nest stared at her brother in dismay, as the inevitability of the situation sank into her brain with a clarity which threatened to overwhelm her.

'It is a dream, Gruff, and I see I cannot stop you from pursuing it.' Nest sank down visibly in the saddle. She could see sad endings, and knew that as usual, she was powerless.

'I wish I had been born a man,' she whispered, and walked her horse on slowly.

Three days later Nest returned to Pembroke alone to face Sir Gerald. During the last days she had agonised over whether or not she should tell her husband of her brother's plans. Sir Gerald had been good to her and in spite of everything, Nest knew she had a strong affection and even love, for this Norman knight who had married her, and given her shattered life some dignity and self respect. She did not wish to deceive him, but at the same

46

time had no wish to put him in a difficult position. After some heart searching, and discussion with her brother, she had decided to confide in her husband, but to distance herself where possible from her brother's cause, so that Sir Gilbert could not be held accountable for his brother-in -law's actions.

When Sir Gerald returned to Pembroke that evening, Nest approached him with some trepidation.

'You were right,' she told him. 'Gruff does intend to raise friends and allies, and attempt to re-take our lands. He has left for the mountains.'

'The young fool! I knew it!' Gerald was fuming.

'Please don't follow him Gerald, he poses no real threat at the moment. I do not think he will find it easy, the local men have no stomach for fighting, I do not think he will be able to do what he wishes.'

'Where is he?' Gerald was in no mood to be lenient.

'I...I don't know...'

'You mean you won't tell me!' Gerald gave a great sigh. 'God save me from your vengeful kith and kin! As if Owen ap Cadwgan wasn't enough! Next thing *he'll* be back from Ireland and joining in!' He smote his fist on the table. 'We were just getting back to normal and this has to happen!' A thought struck him, and he turned to Nest swiftly.

'You didn't help him did you? I mean with money...or horses...?'

Her eyes looked away, and he swore roundly. 'I see it's money *and* horses, and ...?' He left the question in the air.

Her eyes were downcast. 'A...a few provisions perhaps...'

'Oh Nest! Nest! How could you? Don't you know what King Henry will do if he finds out that my wife has been helping a rebel?'

'He will never find out. I have sworn Gruff to secrecy. He will never reveal who helped him, and King Henry will not suspect. Gruff understands our situation dearest, and I made him promise...'

'Promise what?'

'Of course it will never happen, but if it did...' Nest was floundering. 'Well... if he ever was successful, I made him promise he would never raise his sword against you personally.'

Gerald was astonished, but he felt a slight glow of warmth, and stifled a smile. 'And did he agree to that?'

'Yes, his agreement was conditional on my offer of help. If we ever do regain Deheubarth, you and I shall still be husband and wife my dearest, and you shall not suffer, I swear it.'

Gerald felt hot tears spring to his eyes, and blinked fiercely. 'The situation will never arise, the young hothead hasn't a chance.' He turned to her, and despite his anger he took her in his arms. 'Nest, if you know where he is...'

'No, my husband. Somewhere in the mountains I suppose, living on mud and fresh air.' She considered. 'He did say one thing though...'

'Yes?'

'About our brother Hywel. He has been in prison so long, I think Gruff might try to free him...'

'No chance of that, Montgomery castle is well guarded.'

'You don't understand. What I meant was that if he did take some action like that, an attack on the castle, it would be exactly what you don't want. He would gain a reputation, whether he succeeded or not.'

'What is your point?'

'Hywel has been in prison such a long time, and he is not a threat. Couldn't you use your influence to get him released at last? If you did it might help. There would be no need for Gruff to attack the castle then.'

Gerald considered. 'It's a thought. It might stop young Gruff from making a fool of himself.' He looked at his wife, and the beautiful blue eyes met his own in the way he remembered. He knew he was being manipulated, but somehow he didn't mind.

'I'll see what I can do,' he said.

The young Prince Gruffudd ap Rhys was in fact well on his way to the mountains of Caeo. It was an isolated and inhospitable district, nestling in the highest reaches of Cantref Mawr's craggy moorland and dense forests. The few followers he had brought with him from Ireland rode with him loyally, for they had known him for many years, and despite the privations of this new existence they trusted him implicitly and believed in the justice of his cause.

After a week of outlaw existence, on a cold wet afternoon in October, Prince Gruff and his band, soaked through and somewhat demoralised, arrived at the substantial holding of a freeman of noble birth in Cantref Mawr.

'We shall try here for food and shelter,' he told his weary friends, 'And we shall be made welcome.'

'How do you know that?' said one of his men doubtfully, trying to wring the rain from his beard.

'Because this is the home of my uncle, my dear father's brother.' Gruff explained. 'His name is Rhydderch ap Tewdwr, and I ask you all to show him the great respect due to the brother of a king.'

Their astonishment turned to joy as the gate was opened to them and they were welcomed by the old man Rhydderch, who embraced Gruff with tears in his eyes. He led them into the best room, and in a very short time the large table was groaning with a variety of meats and fowls, with bread, pastries and pies, cheeses and flagons of ale, brought in quickly by servant girls. It was clear they had been expected.

Gruff gave a great laugh of pleasure. 'I knew you would make us welcome uncle,' he said, 'But I did not expect all this! Some bread and meat would have sufficed.'

'Your sister Nest sent me word by a trusted friend,' Rhydderch explained. 'I was overjoyed to know you were home, and that I should see my dear brother's child again before I die. I will help all I can, but I cannot offer you a home here. It would not be safe. My relationship to your sister is well known, and I am watched. You should understand there are those who will sell you out for a little Norman gold.'

He waited while the famished men seated themselves around the table and then bade them eat. 'Set to, dear friends, for it is all in your honour. My household have been killing fowls and baking this several days in the hope that you would be here soon!' He turned to Gruff and said in his ear, 'Nest tells me you are determined to right your family's wrongs?'

'Yes, or die in the attempt,' said Gruff.

'It would do my old heart good to see it,' his uncle responded. 'But it will not be easy. You need to send out word to rally an army, and I can help with that, for I can advise you who is safe and who are the traitors. You can certainly stay here for this night and rest yourselves, but after that you must set up a camp, well hidden so it can not be found easily, and send for your people to come and find you. I may be able to help on occasion with food and supplies, but I cannot feed an army.'

'Don't worry uncle,' Gruff responded cheerfully. 'Once I have my warband we shall easily find enough

Norman food and supplies for ourselves!'

Rhydderch ap Tewdwr was correct in his assumption that there were traitors who would look for every chance to gather and sell information to the Normans. Even as Gruff and his band were leaving his uncle's settlement at Cantref Mawr, news of their arrival in the area was on its way to King Henry, who had a well established network of spies within the region.

The Norman king immediately sent out instructions to all his representatives in Deheubarth that the irritating young rebel, Gruffudd ap Rhys, was to be captured, dead or alive. Sir Gerald de Windsor received this instruction along with other Norman nobles as a matter of urgency, and became increasingly nervous that his wife's troublesome family would be the downfall of them all. Nest soothed his fears as well as she could, but later that evening, under cover of darkness, Gerald observed her sending a servant away from the castle with a message.

He sighed. *At least the young prince would know the hunt was on for his head,* he surmised. *Someone would find and kill him before long; thank heaven it did not have to be him.*

It was not long before news of the actions of the young Prince Gruffudd ap Rhys began to filter through to Aberffraw. It was hard to distinguish what was mere rumour and what was established fact, but the whole of Gwynedd was aware that the young Welsh prince from Deheubarth was trying to recruit an army. King Gruffudd wished him well, but had major reservations.

'The people will not rally to him,' he told Angharad sadly. 'He was away too long. They know who he is, but not what he is. They do not trust him yet, and of course he has no resources, he cannot pay an army or even feed them.' He grinned at his wife. 'Nevertheless I wish him well, he reminds me of myself when I was young, full of idealism but with no common sense!'

Angharad sighed. 'If one has no ideals when one is young, when can one hope to have them?' she countered. 'The young man has his heart in the right place; let us hope he will survive long enough to come to the maturity you wish for him.'

'Amen to that.' The king was pensive. 'But he is courting disaster. The young friar who arrived from Deheubarth yesterday told me there had been many skirmishes in the area. Gruff's call to arms has not produced many takers, but enough to cause some trouble. It seems young Gruff and his band are hiding in the mountains and coming out to attack any Norman patrol or supply wagon they feel they can take, and they are having some success. They have become a sufficient nuisance for King Henry to send out a demand for his capture, dead or alive.' He sighed. 'I only hope Gruff's actions do not encourage Henry to start another campaign here in the North. We have made some progress these last years, the settlement is growing, and Henry and I have largely kept out of each others way. I do not want all that to change.'

King Gruffudd's words were prophetic, for it was only two days later that an exhausted messenger arrived with the news that King Henry had mustered a large army and was on his way even now with the declared intention of invading north and mid Wales, and exterminating the last threads of Welsh resistance. Within minutes King Gruffudd had given instructions for the whole settlement to make ready to escape to the relative safety of the mountains of Snowdonia. Here, he explained to his sons and Gwenllian, they could dig in and hide, making guerrilla style incursions into the enemy camps and patrols, whereas if they attempted to defend the settlement at Aberffraw they would have little chance against the far superior force of the Norman army.

Even as the frantic preparations were taking place they received unexpected and welcome news from men sent by Owen ap Cadwgan of Powys. The young hothead had already returned from his brief sojourn in Ireland and had heard the same news of Henry's intentions. Knowing that both himself and King Gruffudd would be a priority for King Henry's quick action, he suggested they gather their forces together in Snowdonia to defeat Henry, and King Gruffudd was quick to agree.

As the Welsh king led the procession leaving the settlement, followed by the ever stoic Queen Angharad and her sons and daughter, and all their fighting men at arms, they were joined by every person from the settlement who could either ride or walk, together with their tenants and freemen of the area. Servants and slaves carried all the goods and chattels they could manage, and the beasts were all fully loaded. All understood what was required. The mood was subdued, most had trodden this path before, and were aware of the trials which awaited them. Gwenllian sat astride her favourite horse with the ever faithful Dewi alongside, and was at first inclined to view the whole thing as something of an adventure, but as they travelled further east to gain access to the mountains of Snowdonia, they were joined by many refugees fleeing the approaching Norman army. These people brought reports of terrible atrocities which were being committed by Henry's army as it drove its inexorable way towards them. As Gwenllian listened in horror to the tales of wholesale murder, rape and torture, her heart bled for these poor people driven from their miserable homes, who now surrounded their column hoping for some succour and a degree of safety.

During the next seven days, King Gruffudd and Owen ap Cadwgan acted in concert to attack several advance patrols of Henry's army as it reached the area. There were some light skirmishes and serious fighting on one occasion, when Gwenllian's eldest brother Owain, and the troublesome Owen ap Cadwgan both distinguished themselves by their bravery and prowess. Gwenllian took part in this battle, and for the first time experienced the use of her sword against real flesh and bone. She fought hard and with some success, and afterwards was pleased when Dewi rode up to congratulate her.

'You fought well,' he said, 'As well as any man I've trained of your age.'

'That's right captain,' said a young warrior alongside him. He dismounted, and bowed to Gwenllian, who was still panting from her exertions. 'May I speak my lady?'

'Of course,' she replied.

'Then I will thank you my lady, for I have two men under my command who would be dead now, were it not for your swift blade. One of them is my brother, so I give you added thanks.' He moved to drop to one knee, but Gwenllian caught his arm and bade him stand. 'We all fought together today,' she said, 'And together we shall stand tomorrow. Go and eat now.'

The warrior smiled and turned to join his men, and Dewi said, 'You have made many friends today, for you fought better than expected.'

'But they all know I can fight, they have seen me at practice often enough,' Gwenllian said.

'Yes, but today you proved you can do it in battle,' Dewi said, 'But I urge you, my lady, to take a little care. You were in the thick of it, and could easily have been wounded... or even...'

'Nonsense!' she said happily. 'You were beside me all the time Dewi, so how could I come to harm?'

Dewi's concern was increased next day around noon, when he suddenly realised that Gwenllian and her troop were missing. He had ridden to the front of the straggling army to speak to the king, and upon his return was met by a group of agitated followers.

'We came upon a wounded man sire,' they explained, 'And the Lady Gwenllian spoke to him. He told us that his village and the farm stronghold nearby had been sacked by Norman raiders, and many of his friends had been killed there, he was lucky to escape. He told the Lady that many of the villagers have been imprisoned in the tower house, and that the soldiers intend to set fire to it today and burn them alive, after they have had their fill of the women.'

Dewi was horrified. 'And where is my Lady Gwenllian now?' *My God, do not let her have gone there, she could not be so foolhardy - God protect her...*

'She has taken the troop with her sire, and the wounded man also, to show the way. She said to tell you where she had gone.'

Dewi's throat was constricted. 'Send to the king to tell him what has happened,' he said thickly, 'And tell him also that I have gone after her. I pray to God we shall be in time.'

As Dewi set off, Gwenllian had already reached the sacked village, but found only a few soldiers there, who were quickly despatched. The main force had moved on to the farmhouse, and the sounds of celebration and roistering reached Gwenllian as she approached and drew her troops around her.

'We have the advantage,' she said, 'We shall attack before they realise we are here. Do not allow any firebrands to take hold in the tower, it is full of our people. We must stop this carnage by inflicting our own...'

'Should we not wait for assistance, my Lady?' asked a young captain. 'We do not know how many they are...'

'No. If we wait we may be too late.' *Pray Heaven I am right,* she thought fearfully, *God give me the strength to do my duty* . She raised her voice. 'I have faith in all of you, follow me....' And she led the charge.

It was a swift but bloody battle, and she had been right. The Normans were superior in numbers, but Gwenllian had the element of surprise, and she and her men fought bravely, so that in a short time they had gained supremacy. By the time Dewi arrived, followed closely by King Gruffudd, the battle was over and the villagers had been released from the tower house. They crowded around their liege lord with cries of gratitude and blessings.

'By dear Heaven Dewi,' said the king, moved by the sight, 'I believe our assistance was not needed! Meilyr's prophesy was perhaps right after all, Gwenllian is indeed a leader...'

'Perhaps so sire,' Dewi responded, badly shaken by the event. 'But I shall not let her out of my sight again.'

King Gruffudd included Gwenllian in his list of thanks when he called his family and senior captains to a hastily convened meeting with Owen ap Cadwgan that evening to discuss their strategy for the next day.

'We have lost some good men,' the king told them, 'We are outnumbered but we shall fight on, for although it is hard, we still have a chance to pick them off a few at a time.'

There was a hum of general agreement around the table, which was broken by the entrance, unannounced, of one of the king's trusted Teulu warriors. He rushed in and threw himself to the floor before the King.

'All is lost sire,' he blurted out, in obvious anguish.

56

'All is lost.' He bowed his head and turned it away. The king rose, and, knowing his man well, lifted the warriors head and made him meet his eyes.

'Tell me.'

'It is hopeless sire, we thought to meet Henry's army, but there are two more armies arrived to join him. The Scottish king Malcolm with a great host, and the Earl of Cornwall with almost as many. We shall be overrun in minutes. Even if we manage to get back into the mountains there are so many they can root us out with ease.' The man looked near to tears. 'They await us now sire, and are full of bloodlust, but King Henry stayed them. He says he will retire if you capitulate now, and he will arrange a face to face meeting with yourself and Owen ap Cadwgan within the hour.'

'A meeting to take off our heads as an example!' roared Owen ap Cadwgan, amidst the uproar which ensued.

'We must fight on father!' Gwenllian's voice was added to the tumult. 'We must!'

King Gruffudd's strong tones cut through the noise. 'What we must do is take stock, and think carefully. We have many lives to consider here, not only our own,' he said, directing his gaze squarely on Owen ap Cadwgan. He took him by the arm. 'Let us take a look ourselves, my brave colleague,' he said, 'And see how we measure the chances.'

Owen seemed about to speak, but thought better of it and nodded briefly, and the two men left the campaign quarters together.

The Teulu warrior had spoken the truth. From the rise overlooking the battlefield King Gruffudd could see nothing but a great sea of Norman forces, distinguished by the banners which flew at the head of each section. In the centre King Gruffudd could see the banner of Henry of England, and the figure of the king himself, astride a white charger.

'One of my bowmen could down him from here,' Owen ap Cadwgan murmured in his ear.

'And what would happen then?' King Gruffudd demanded. 'Do you think anything could stop that great number? We have lost, my friend, that much is obvious. All that remains is to decide whether we fight on and die along with all these people,' he gestured behind him to their crowds of supporters, 'Or whether we negotiate and live to fight another day.'

He sighed. 'It is bitter medicine Owen, but I shall surrender and see what terms I can get. I am not in a mood to see my family and my people slaughtered.'

Owen ap Cadwgan gave a short laugh. 'I suppose we should see what he has to offer,' he said, 'At least we shall get near enough for me to slit his throat if I get the chance.'

King Henry's bodyguard saw to it that neither King Gruffudd nor Owen ap Cadwgan had the chance to attack anyone, let alone Henry himself. From the moment that the messengers had delivered Gruffudd's agreement to capitulate, it was clear who was in control. Two separate guard columns were sent to escort King Gruffudd and Owen ap Cadwgan to King Henry's campaign tent. Obviously he intended to deal with them individually.

King Gruffudd was first. As he entered King Henry's campaign headquarters he was astonished to see how well the English king was provided, even on the battlefield. The campaign tent itself was sumptuous and spacious, and Henry was seated on a comfortable couch awash with cushions. He had removed his armour and was dressed in a long red velvet cloak of obvious quality. King Gruffudd stared hard at the long thin face of his enemy, committing to memory the dark eyes and the cruel mouth above the straggling beard. As Gruffudd stood before him, Henry in his turn took his time in surveying his prisoner, who had been allowed no escort of his own. At length Henry called for wine, and when it came he motioned King Gruffudd to a chair and poured the wine himself into two glasses. He handed one to Gruffudd. 'Well, my old adversary, what have we here?' he said. 'Why are you and half your miserable countrymen out on the roadside attacking my poor soldiers? What is this all about?'

The Welsh king smouldered, but kept his head. 'Did you expect that when we heard of your plans to exterminate us, we should simply wait for you to come and kill us all?' he said. He took a swig of wine. It was good, and the glass was finer than any he had ever seen. Damn Henry and his money and his great armies! Gruffudd wanted to grind the glass into the sly old bastard's face.

'Kill you all?' Henry repeated the words as in disbelief. 'I do not want to kill anybody, but you must understand the situation.' His tone became cold and forceful. 'We are in control here, and intend to continue so, I thought that you at least had understood that. That is why you have been left alone these few years past.'

'And what has changed?' Gruffudd could not help but ask. 'Why have you sent a great army to attack us?'

'It is only those who work against us that we shall attack.'

'That is not what I heard from those who were fleeing your army,' Gruffudd burst out, and Henry's mouth tightened.

'Mind your manners when you speak to me! Remember who is the prisoner here! And as for working against us, what about that young rebel of Deheubarth, Gruffudd ap Rhys, he is bent on causing trouble and has killed many of my good men.'

'That is nothing to do with me, or Gwynedd.'

'I sincerely hope so.'

Henry sipped his wine and appeared to be thinking. Suddenly he seemed to make up his mind and leaned forward to Gruffudd. 'Look, I am prepared to be generous to you and your people. You have already surrendered the battle, you had no choice. You are a good ruler I believe Gruffudd ap Cynan, you have put the welfare of your people and your land before your dislike of myself and English rule.'

'Norman rule,' Gruffudd interrupted. 'The poor English are as enslaved as we are.'

Henry laughed, he seemed to find the remark genuinely amusing. 'Well, whatever you call us,' he said, 'I am the King of England and all of Wales, whomsoever may like it or no. The ruling families in your small principalities have had their day, but I shall allow you to keep your crown and all your many privileges, as long as you swear fealty to me. You will continue to rule in my name, and will have much freedom, as long as you collect the taxes which are due to me as your liege lord, and pay them on time.'

He refilled Gruffudd's glass, and raised his own in salute.

'Together we can make it work,' he said. 'Gwynedd will prosper under your rule and I shall receive more dues from her than if I put in yet another Norman overlord who does not understand how your community works.'

This man is not a fool, Gruffudd thought to himself, *he actually wants me to stay because it suits his purposes.* Aloud he said, 'I will swear fealty to you, but on condition it is done in private.'

'You are in no position to make conditions,' Henry said, 'But I understand your reasons. You do not want your officers and people to see your downfall.'

'No, said Gruffudd, 'But it is my family, my sons, that I am really concerned with.'

'I understand,' said Henry. 'As a king I can only commiserate. But your homage can not be in private, I have my reasons too, and my lords and warriors must see you kiss my ring.'

'I will agree to that,' said Gruffudd, as long as my own people do not see it.'

'And your friend from Powys? Will he also agree?'

'Owen ap Cadwgan is his own man. I can not speak for him.' Gruffudd said.

'He is a very good warrior,' said Henry. 'I watched him today in battle. I would rather he was fighting for me than against me. If he will not, I think he must die. He does not have the advantages for me that you do, as a ruler I mean.' He smiled. 'Owen ap Cadwgan could not rule a piss pot.'

King Gruffudd ap Cynan and Owen ap Cadwgan both paid homage to Henry, King of England, that afternoon, before a small assembly of Norman knights, nobles and soldiers. It was a short ceremony, both being required to read out the words which swore fealty to their liege lord, and then to kneel and kiss Henry's ring. This they both did with good grace, for Gruffudd knew that he had saved Aberffraw and his people, and Owen ap Cadwgan had been offered a knighthood, on condition that he proved his allegiance by joining Henry's army in France, where his fighting skills would be put to good use.

'A knighthood? Does that buy your conscience?' Gruffudd hissed at him, as he stood next to Owen, waiting for the ceremony to start.

'It will be a great adventure!' Owen explained,

somewhat hurt. 'I am off to France!'

After the ceremony Gruffudd was released and Owen ap Cadwgan was taken to join his new colleagues in the Norman army, under guard, on Henry's instructions. Henry himself called his close military advisers to him for a small celebration.

'Not bad work today,' he said. 'Two main insurgents dealt with satisfactorily.'

'Are there to be no reprisals in Gwynedd?' the captain of the guard asked.

'No,' said Henry, 'Let Aberffraw stand this time, otherwise it will be years before their harvests provide us with any decent income'. His eyes narrowed. 'That only leaves the young prince Gruffudd ap Rhys in Deheubarth to deal with,' he said slowly. 'We have plenty of informers there. We will put a good price on his head and see what that brings forth.'

FOUR
'LOVE AND FEALTY'

The fact that the kingdom of Gwynedd had been irreversibly weakened by King Gruffudd agreeing to pay homage to King Henry, would not have been guessed at by the casual observer of the scene at Aberffraw, where the court quickly returned to normal. Because of the outcome of the meeting in Snowdonia, the Norman forces had not ventured as far as Ynys Mon on this occasion, and there was little re-building and repair work to be undertaken. Valuable growing and harvest time had been lost however, and the land tillers quickly began work on the soil to prepare it for next years crops of corn and oats. King Gruffudd immediately arranged for provisions to be shipped in from Ireland to help the settlement withstand the winter ahead, and due to the improved relations with the Norman lords to the south, he was even able to receive supplies from Chester, without interference.

Throughout the settlement the people worked with new heart. The threatened disaster had not happened, and the desperation felt only a few weeks ago had given way to relief. The hunters were out early, as the rich forests still could supply good venison for roasting and plenty of small game for the pot, and in the morning air damp wisps of steam escaped from the apex of the corn kiln and rose high into the late autumn sky. House slaves hung out washing on lines suspended between the kitchens and the timber palisades, and babies cried whilst soldiers argued over their duty rosters.

Everyone now discarded the heavy martial leathers they had worn for the flight into Snowdonia, and brought out their lighter and more colourful clothing, and when the bard Meilyr arrived for a prolonged visit, he was surprised and delighted with the general feeling of well-being which permeated the settlement. Sure now of his welcome, Meilyr was a popular and relaxed visitor, and wrote a new poem which celebrated their recent forays into Snowdonia.

On a rare afternoon of freedom, Gwenllian and Dewi rode out to Abergwyngregyn and then walked to their childhood hideout. Gwenllian was sure there would still be blackberries and bilberries to be found on the sides of the valley, and had brought a basket. Dewi grumbled his way along behind her, but softened a little when she stopped and brought out some bread and goat's cheese wrapped in a cloth.

'Here,' Gwenllian commanded, 'Stop your mouth with this, you have done nothing but grouse since we left home. What is there to complain of on such a lovely day?'

Dewi grinned. Gwenllian was right. He sat down amid the bracken which bronzed the hillside and looked about him. It had been worth the climb. The hillside was still aglow with the gold of the furze which covered the lower slopes, and ahead where the land fell away towards the distant sea, the ground was broken by outcrops of grey slate and rock, and scored by sheep and goat tracks. Overhead, the sound of a lark rang sweetly, somewhere so high it could not be seen.

Gwenllian sat down alongside him. 'There,' she said, pointing with her chunk of bread. 'There we shall get bilberries for winter jelly.'

Dewi followed her gaze to the faintly purpled patch a hundred yards away. 'As you please my lady,' he said amiably. 'Although why you have to do it I can't imagine. There are enough servants to gather as many bilberries and brambles as you wish.'

'But I enjoy it,' Gwenllian said.

'And do you enjoy feeding the pigs and chickens, and helping with the horses and making bread and grinding corn?' Dewi asked. 'All of these I have seen you doing since we came home. I have heard remarks around the settlement that you make a better servant than your servants, and I'll swear that last night you missed dinner because you were so tired you could hardly make your bed. What is going on my lady? Have you forgotten your birth?'

Gwenllian was silent for a moment. Then she said softly, 'No Dewi, I do not forget my birth. It is more that, since we went to Snowdonia, I understand my responsibility at last. Being of royal birth doesn't mean you have to do nothing, it means you have to do more.'

'But does it have to be menial tasks?'

'Does it matter? And what royal tasks would I be allowed to do? There is work to be done and I am strong enough to do it.' She turned her full blue gaze upon Dewi and to his surprise he saw tears there. 'Oh Dewi, how the poor people suffered in these last weeks. I have never been so close to them before, I have always thought they were different. But they are not. Whether royal or slave, all bodies bleed and die. I had not seen it so clearly before, that is all.' She sighed, and then looked around her with obvious delight. 'But as for today, this is pure enjoyment. Don't you remember Dewi, how we used to climb up here as children, and the fun we used to have?'

'As I remember my lady, you used to have the fun and I used to take the beatings.' He regretted his remark immediately, as he saw the horrified look on her face.

'Oh Dewi, you are right, I was a little beast sometimes wasn't I? I am surprised you let me get away with it. Do you forgive me?' Her anxious look was so full of contrition that it was all he could do not to laugh aloud.

'I forgave you long ago my lady.'

Gwenllian sighed and bit into her bread and cheese. 'Yes, you did. I know that. You are the most long-suffering and dear man I know. Why are you always so good to me?'

Dewi smiled. 'Because you are my lady and the love of my life,' he said simply. 'I will always serve you.'

Gwenllian, for once, remained silent. They finished their food and began to make their way towards the far patch of bilberry bushes. Then she spoke: 'Dewi, do you remember when...'

'Yes, of course I do,' he interrupted.

'But do you recall I said...'

'Yes.' He would not let her finish. 'You were a child my lady, but you are not a child now. All the same rules still apply. Some things are best forgotten. Come now, let's fill this basket if we must.'

At Aberffraw a training area for warriors had been designated at the far side of the compound which surrounded the settlement, and it was here that Gwenllian was practising with her brothers the following afternoon when a shout went up from the guard that visitors were approaching. Immediately curious, Gwenllian and her brothers watched from the palisade as King Gruffudd's guard, led by Dewi, quickly assembled and rode out to meet them, a group of three riders, approaching from the direction of Aber Menai, the crossing point from the mainland.

After a short conversation, the visitors were escorted by the guard into the settlement, and Dewi dismounted and approached Owain. 'It is Prince Gruffudd ap Rhys my lord, with two of his loyal men from Deheubarth. He craves an audience with the King.'

'But why would he come here?' Owain looked

66

askance at the young visitor, who in spite of his travel weary garb, had an air of authority and a commanding presence. 'Is there not a big price on his head? He takes a chance to brave the road so poorly guarded!'

Dewi dropped his voice. 'I think he has little choice, my lord, I have heard he is hunted high and low by those who seek the reward. I think he hopes to find friends here.'

'Then he has found them.' Owain went over to the young prince and embraced him roughly. 'I am King Gruffudd's son Owain,' he said. 'I have heard much of you, and you are welcome. You will meet the rest of the family later, but for now Dewi will escort you to food and rest. I shall tell my father you are here.'

A huge smile lit up the features of the young prince in response, and he followed Dewi towards the hamlet. Gwenllian was delighted, a visitor was always welcome for news and conversation. *But this one is more interesting than usual,* she thought, *and is incredibly handsome. There will undoubtedly be a big supper to welcome him, and there will be music, and story telling, and poetic verse....* Gwenllian ran inside to find Meilyr, to ask if he had some portent regarding the young prince, but before she could find him she was struck by a much more important thought. *I must bathe and wash my hair, and choose my best gown for the supper tonight.* She called out loudly for her English servant girl Elaine to bring hot water.

That evening at supper the king was in good spirits, and the young prince Gruff of Deheubarth entertained the company with stories of close shaves with some of those who were tracking him in search of Henry's reward.

He seemed to take his precarious position lightly. 'I have one thing for which to thank King Henry,' he said, smiling as he raised his glass. 'When I came home from Ireland I spent months trying to raise an army, but I found it hard to make the people understand my cause, and even who I was, after such a long absence. Word of King Henry's bounty on my head has given me much more standing! The people of Deheubarth have certainly heard of my cause now!'

They all laughed, and the king said, 'Ah Gruff, when you talk thus you remind me of your dear father, we fought together many times you know, and were true friends.'

'I know that sire,' Gruff responded politely. 'When I was a child he would tell us tales of your great victories together, but I do not remember a great deal.'

'I saw you only once, as I remember,' said the king. 'It was when you were but a babe,' he broke off. 'Did you know you were named for me?' he asked.

'I did indeed know of the honour,' said the prince.

'It is amusing,' said the king. 'We have two royal Gruffudd's! I shall call you Gruff,' he decided, 'To avoid misunderstanding.'

Prince Gruff laughed. 'There will be no misunderstanding sire,' he said, with a flash of his beautiful smile. 'I hardly think I shall be mistaken for you!'

Angharad said, 'Oh I don't know, I think I could mistake you quite easily,' and the whole company, including the king, laughed uproariously.

The next day Prince Gruffudd ap Rhys received his formal audience with King Gruffudd. He expressed his heartfelt thanks for the welcome he had received, and stated his joy that he had at last met his father's old ally, and his wonderful family.

'It has warmed my heart to see you,' said the king,

'And to know that your father's memory is still honoured. But it is a long time since those dreadful days at Talgarth, and while you were away the situation has changed. You have lost everything my friend,' he said pointedly, 'And I see that you do not accept it. Perhaps in your shoes I should be the same, but you need to understand the way things are now. Only two months ago, when we were in Snowdonia to escape Henry, hoping to fight him off by the kind of tactics which you advocate, I saw an army ranged against us the like of which you never saw! It was three armies, bonded together, and we should have been wiped out like flies, all of us, had I not negotiated. In your young hot blood you would probably have fought on to death, but I chose to settle, because I needed to save my people, I want my kingdom to endure.' He leaned forward and said quietly, 'There is more than one way to rule, Gruff, and more than one way to fight the Normans.'

'But my situation is not the same,' said Gruff. 'I have no kingdom left to save, only one to win back. If I do not try, I will betray the honour of my birth and my family.' He hesitated. 'I realise you are taking a risk to shelter me, but perhaps Henry will not hear of it, at least for a while. I need your protection sire, but even more I need your help to retake my lands and restore my kingdom.'

King Gruffudd regarded him fondly. 'Have you any idea of what you ask?' he said. 'You ask me to sacrifice Gwynedd in the hope, and I believe it is a vain hope, of taking Deheubarth.' He sighed. 'There is a lot I would do for you, young Gruff, but these matters are more serious and more complicated than you realise. You need to reflect carefully. You have a dream, and it fills your mind until you forget all else. You need to understand that you may have to live with the many deaths which your dream will cause.' He rose abruptly.

'You may stay here under my protection,' he said, 'All other matters are under my consideration.'

'But sire, if you...'

'The audience is at an end,' said the king, and strode from the room.

The days at Aberffraw went by, busy but uneventful, with the whole royal family awaiting the king's pleasure, in the matter of most concern to their honoured guest. Everyone liked the prince, his striking good looks and engaging nature endeared him to all, including the servants. He had a slight accent to his speech, born of his long years in Ireland, which everyone found attractive, and which caused some comment and amusement. Only Cadwaladr occasionally derided the prince's open and natural style, remarking in his usual derogatory manner that 'anyone would think he was one of us!'

It was true. Gruff had been taken in to the Aberffraw community with such enthusiasm that he had become regarded almost as one of the royal family. Owain and Cadwallon were impressed with the martial skills their young guest possessed, and they spent many happy hours together, comparing battle techniques which Gruff had learned in Ireland, with their own highly developed skills. Gwenllian often joined in these training sessions, and after Gruff had got over his astonishment he declared he would wish to have her at his side in any battle, as he had not seen a more accurate blade, or a more deadly strategist. A great deal of laughter and competitive banter accompanied these sessions, and they all became firm friends. Gruff had explained at length the dreams he had for uniting the Deheubarth people under his banner, and both Owain and Cadwallon were hopeful that their father would eventually give their new friend some practical help with arms and provisions, even if it fell short of providing an army. Cadwaladr distanced himself somewhat from these discussions, taking the line that 'Deheubarth business is not our business,' but Gwenllian herself was content to leave the ultimate decision to the king. 'You have heard of my father as a great fighter, and hero of many battles,' she told Gruff shyly. 'But he is also a wise and just man, and he will do what is right, I am sure.'

Gruff smiled back at her, but privately feared that King Gruffudd was no nearer to making a decision than when he had first arrived. The one consolation for his frustration at the lack of action was his daily sight of Gwenllian, who seemed to him to be the very perfection of womanhood. It was not just her beauty, although this was enough to set him back on his heels, but he was deeply conscious that the young princess was both intelligent and caring, and the more he saw of her daily life the more he came to appreciate her qualities. Added to all this she was very strong and fearless, and could use a sword like a man. Gruff had known of women who would follow their menfolk into battle, but it was not often that they played a prominent role, whereas the princess Gwenllian was well qualified to be a captain at least.

The interest she aroused in the young prince was not lost on Gwenllian, who day by day felt herself falling more and more under the influence of this exciting young man. She could hardly fail to notice the effect she seemed to have on him. Time after time she would glance at him, only to meet his eyes, which were already on her with a look of burning interest. When they spoke it was formally and with little real contact, until the day when he found her gathering in some washing which had been drying on the bushes near the palisade.

'Gwenllian,' he said, with some heat, 'I'm sick of this, get rid of that washing and come a walk with me so we can talk. You always seem busy and I have no time with you.'

Gwenllian looked mildly surprised, but she said 'Yes, I would like that. Wait a moment and I'll be with you.'

A moment later she reappeared and they began to climb in the direction she indicated, across the fields and through a small wood at the rear of the settlement. 'Along here,' she said. 'You can see the sea in the distance.'

Gruff suddenly realised someone was walking up behind him. It was Dewi, about ten paces behind.

'What are you thinking of man?' he hissed at Dewi. 'You are not invited. I want to talk to Gwenllian alone.'

'No problem sire,' said Dewi, smiling broadly. 'I'll stay a good way behind so you shall have privacy to talk, never fear. But where my lady goes, I follow.'

Gwenllian laughed as she turned and realised their discourse: 'Don't worry about Dewi,' she said. 'He always comes with me, he's obliged to.'

Gruff bit back the retort on his lips and followed her through the wood.

That walk was to be the first of many over the next weeks, as Gruff and Gwenllian spent much time in each other's company and became close. Within a very short time Gruff was aware that here was the wife he not only desired with all his heart, but needed by his side if he was ever to accomplish his dream of restoring his family's place in Deheubarth. Gwenllian understood his ambitions, and entered into his plans with enthusiasm. She also was full of her own ideas and schemes for helping him to achieve them. Although they tried to be circumspect, it was plain to all around them at Aberffraw that a deep attraction was blossoming between the young pair. The powerful aura which danced between them was almost tangible.

One evening at dinner when Gruff had been explaining to Owain that he thought the Norman strongholds of Llanymddyfri and Narberth could fall fairly easily, he turned to the king and continued, 'And if you feel sire, that you can not help me with men to accomplish this, then I am sure I can gather enough myself, if you will only furnish me with the arms ...'

'God's teeth!' the king roared, rising to his feet. 'Am I to be badgered thus at my own dinner table?' He stormed from the room in temper, and silence fell upon them all like a threat.

Gruff's face was white. 'I apologise...' he said quickly to the queen. 'I spoke without thinking. I did not intend to offend.' He rose to his feet. 'I must go...,' he said.

'Not now,' Angharad said firmly. 'Not now Gruff. The king's temper is quick but it will cool as quickly. 'Let him have some space to become calm, and then I will go to him. No!' she commanded, as Gruff made to protest. 'Leave it for now, but tomorrow you may speak to the king to apologise.'

She smiled around the gathering, and motioned the bard Meilyr to his harp. When dinner had resumed, she said quietly to Gruff, 'My dear boy, he is not angry with you, but with the situation. He is between hard rock and deep water. He would like to help you, but if he does he will draw down the wrath of Henry upon himself and all of us, and I don't think you have an idea of how terrible that can be.'

Gruff met her eyes with a bleak look. 'I do know that my lady, and I will try not to put my case so that it adds to the king's worries. But it is not only that which concerns me. I have, I am...I have become very attached to the princess Gwenllian and I believe she returns my feelings. I had intended to mention this to you first...'

'To sound me out?' Angharad was amused. 'To get me to put in a good word?'

Gruff flushed slightly. 'Something like that I suppose,' he said. 'The problem is, I have nothing to offer Gwenllian but a life of struggle. I am of royal blood but that is of little use without a kingdom. I was hoping that perhaps our mutual feelings might persuade the king to help me, but now I have offended him just when I need his approval most.'

'Don't worry,' said Angharad. 'Let the king settle his temper and I will see what I can do tomorrow.'

Angharad did not have the chance to speak to the king before events overtook them. In the early light of dawn next day, when spirals of mist were still rising from the river below Aberffraw, when none were abroad except for a few women with their pails and kindling for the fires, a column was sighted making its way towards the settlement. The king's guard was quickly mustered, and the warriors, still heavy with sleep, were mounted and rode out with Dewi to meet the column. Owain and Cadwallon were among the first at the palisade.

'They bear King Henry's standard,' said Owain, as soon as it could be discerned. 'It must be the king's messenger.'

'I doubt a hundred men are needed to deliver a message,' said Cadwallon, distinctly nervous.

'Go to the king at once and rouse him,' said Owain. 'I will stay here to receive them.'

By the time the column had arrived at the gate Owain could see they were heavily armed and well equipped. Dewi rode in ahead of the king's messenger, and a small escort of six men.

'It is Henry's messenger,' said Dewi, dismounting. 'He asks for an audience with King Gruffudd.' He approached Owain and said quietly, 'A hundred men or

74

more just to deliver a letter, we need to stay alert.'

Owain nodded in assent and approached the messenger. 'Well, you are early abroad gentlemen, but come in and have breakfast. I am Owain, the king's eldest son. I shall tell my father you are here.'

King Gruffudd had been woken quickly, but insisted on having breakfast and being shaved and properly dressed before receiving what he called 'that bastard's underling.' He wore the gold circlet on his head and the emerald ring of state to receive the messenger in his private chamber, but for all his attempts at outward show, he was deeply worried. 'Be you at my side, my lady,' he told Angharad, 'This is like to be about that young rip Gruff. No doubt Henry has heard he may be here. Where is the prince now?'

'Hiding in Gwenllian's chamber. Don't worry,' the queen said, 'Dewi has joined them there.'

'I should hope so,' said the king, settling into the great chair.

The messenger and his escort entered the room and the king formally welcomed them.

'I have a letter from King Henry, sire.' The messenger went down on one knee and King Gruffudd took the scroll but did not bid him rise. He broke the seal and read the letter slowly.

'What is it?' asked Angharad.

'It is an invitation,' said the king. 'A very cordial invitation to London.'

'London?' Angharad was aghast. 'Shall you go my lord?'

'I think this is an invitation it would be unwise to refuse,' said the king quietly.

'But London! Will you be safe?'

The king motioned to the messenger. 'Get up man. My lady the queen is concerned about my safety on this proposed trip to see King Henry. Can you allay her fears?'

'Certainly sire. King Henry has sent a large force of English nobles and men of the highest calibre, to ensure your safe journey and arrival in London.'

'I see. And if I choose not to go?'

The captain of the escort stepped forward, and his hand tightened on the hilt of his sword.

'Although,' the king continued conversationally, as if he had not noticed. 'I should like to go. A trip to London will provide some interesting company no doubt, and may be worth my while, what do you think captain?'

'I think sire, we shall look after you very well,' the man replied guardedly.

The king's face was like a mask. Then he said, 'Well in that case it is settled.'

The king rose and dismissed the messenger and guard with a motion of his hand. The captain hesitated, and the king said, 'I shall need some time for my servants to prepare for the journey. I also need to give instructions to my son Owain, who will act for me during my absence.'

'As you please sire,' the captain assented. 'But we need to leave in two hours time, to make Chester by nightfall.'

In the privacy of the king's bedchamber Gruffudd ap Cynan gave instructions to his queen and Owain, as preparations were made for the journey.

'We could make a try at these troops of Henry's,' Owain said. 'You do not have to go father, Cadwallon believes we may fight them off.'

'And what use is that?' the king responded, 'Henry would only send out an even larger force and we should pay with many lives, and perhaps lose the stronghold for ever. No Owain, I must go and face him.'

'If Henry is angry, what shall you do my lord?'

Angharad asked nervously.

'The best I can,' replied her husband shortly. He sighed, and added more gently. 'I shall do the best I can for young Gruff too,' he said, 'But I doubt Henry will hear me. He wants that young prince's head, and I shall be lucky not to lose my own.'

In good time all was ready, but as King Gruffudd came into the compound and made to mount his horse, a slight figure leapt forward to speak to him. The captain of the escort was about to intervene, but the king said, 'Don't worry, this is Meilyr, he is a bard, and some say an enchanter, and has the sight.'

'Never fear my lord,' said Meilyr, 'And for your ears only...'

The king bent his head, and Meilyr whispered, 'Never fear my lord, for I have seen your death. It came clear to me, like a memory, in the dancing flames from the fire. It is in a great bed and you are a great age, and with your family around you. I would not have told you of my seeing this vision, but we live in troubled times.'

The king stared at him. 'You swear this is true?'

'It is true my lord. Am I not descended from the great Myrddin, who resided at Bryn Myrrdin and was renowned throughout the land? And did I not foretell that the princess Gwenllian would be a great warrior?'

The king's face grew dark. 'For these words Meilyr, my thanks,' he said, and mounted his horse.

As the heavily armed column moved out from Aberffraw, the whole population seemed gathered at the palisades to watch them go. First were the English nobles and their warriors, riding two by two, with pennants flying, and then King Gruffudd under his own banner, showing the three golden lions against dark blue, surrounded by the few trusted men he had insisted accompany him. They were followed by a further troop of knights and nobles of Henry's guard, and they rode forward to the glint of arms and the clashing sound of chain mail and horses hooves. A thick powdery dust enveloped them as they left, and the people of Aberffraw watched the dust trail become smaller, and a silence fell upon the place as it disappeared into the distance. Their king had gone from them, and all anyone could do now was to await events.

As the days went by at Aberffraw, the young prince Gruffudd and the princess Gwenllian became ever closer. News had come from Gruff's uncle Rhydderch that there seemed to be a surge of support for the Deheubarth cause, and that many men were now awaiting the call to arms. Gruff's frustration was made more extreme by the thought that if he had only received help, at least with arms and equipment from King Gruffudd when he had first asked, perhaps by now some progress could have been made. He had already made sure that when the time was right, Gwenllian would be his. The lovers had made their vows to each other and their love blossomed day by day. The lack of a future home did not seem to dismay the young princess, 'As to that,' she said dismissively, 'I am more anxious for the fight to begin. When we have regained your lands there will be Norman castles to be had aplenty! I shall choose the one I like best.'

When the king had been gone a few weeks, a message arrived for Gruff from his sister Nest at Pembroke.

'I can hardly believe it!' Gwenllian saw that Gruff was almost beside himself with emotion. 'After all this time!' He turned away, and for a moment she thought that it was bad news, as she saw a tear escape and run down his face.

'We must tell Owain and the others,' he cried,

laughing and crying at the same time. 'My brother Hywel is freed from Montgomery Castle and is on his way here! My sister Nest has used her influence and her husband has managed it at last!'

Owain, Cadwallon and Cadwaladr were delighted at the news, and within a few days Gruff's youngest brother arrived, looking pale and thin but full of spirit and wanting to help his brother in any way he could. 'I apologise for imposing myself upon you and your family,' he said to Owain, 'But it was too dangerous for me to go to Nest at Pembroke. Sir Gerald will turn a blind eye when he can, but with a price on my brother's head, Nest felt we would both be safer here.'

'Of course,' said Owain, 'And you are both welcome for your dear father's sake, and your own.'

Prince Gruffudd ap Rhys embraced his brother, unable to believe this was the small child he had last seen being carried away from him by a wet nurse, under Norman guard. 'Oh brother,' he said, struggling to overcome his emotion. 'Do you see now our great good fortune? How can we fail when we have such friends as these, the royal family of Gwynedd, to stand with us?'

As for the royal family themselves, they watched the brothers reunion with much sympathy. 'We were so lucky,' said Gwenllian, 'To have our family close together for so many years. We had hard times when we were small, often hunted and hiding in the mountains, but at least we were all together.'

'Yes,' said Owain. 'Let us leave, and give them time together. I think they have not seen each other since they were small boys, when they were separated at the time of their father's death. They have a lot to talk over now.'

Cadwaladr grimaced. 'Yes, and we have twice the trouble that we had.'

Talking over their tribulations together seemed only to

make the two Deheubarth princes more determined to right the wrongs which had befallen their family. Every day they made plans together, and Gruff seemed inspired by a new sense of vigour for their cause. He confided all his plans to Gwenllian, explaining that he felt the time was perhaps now right for their campaign to make progress.

'Hywel and I together, dearest,' he said. 'We make a good team, and I believe we can go far. Many people in Deheubarth will rally to our call, especially when they know we are together. Two Deheubarth princes of the old ruling family, united to oust these monstrous invaders and rid Wales of the Norman scourge at last.' He smiled, with the infectious enthusiasm which Gwenllian loved. 'I have wasted much time here...' he continued.

'Wasted?' Gwenllian prompted, and he smiled again.

'Well, not exactly wasted,' he said, taking her in his arms, 'But I fear your father will never allow our marriage.'

'We know nothing for sure until he returns,' said Gwenllian. 'He may manage to placate King Henry.'

'Even if he does, my dearest,' said Gruff, 'It will not help me. I am sworn to take arms against Henry and all those of his minions who have invaded my lands and now hold them in Henry's name. He is my sworn enemy and will always be so. It will be a long battle, but with Hywel by my side I am sure we can win.'

'And me? Will I be by your side also?'

'If God wills it, dear heart. I would have you by my side always.'

'Then wait just a while, my lord. Let Hywel rest here so we may feed and care for him until he is fully fit and well again, while we wait for my father's return, when we shall know all.'

And because he loved her, and because she was so

beautiful, Gruff agreed.

FIVE
BETRAYAL

The journey to London proved to be an eye opener for King Gruffudd ap Cynan. King Henry's troop was well equipped and provided, and so a quality of surroundings was ensured which could not fail to impress the Welsh king, who was accustomed to rough travel with his own men, and was unused to luxury, even at Aberffraw. Mainly, they stayed at the best inns to be found, where rooms for the king were already bespoke by messengers who were sent ahead of them, and where King Gruffudd found hot water and good food and wine always awaited him.

By the time they reached London the king was inclined to believe that Henry did not want his head after all. There had been plenty of opportunity to take it on the journey if that was the plan. Nevertheless, as they approached the city and saw the great size of it, and the thousands of warriors practicing their martial skills in the training fields surrounding the castle, King Gruffudd's apprehension increased, never in his life had he seen such a display of power and strength. It was a day of dry cold, when the thick cloud cut across the dark red sun, lying low on the horizon, and King Gruffudd watched the spurts of white breath from men and horses as they toiled at their exertions. As they entered through the great gate, and came upon almost a full mile of outbuildings and servants quarters, with stables, corn mills, carpenters, shoemakers and blacksmiths jostling for spaces along the edge of the well worn path to the castle, the Welsh king thought he had never seen so much business in one place before. There were wagons being unloaded, and others being loaded, drays of hay and fodder, mounted warriors going this way and that, and hundreds of servants and slaves, all about their business among the squawking chickens and barking dogs. It made the king's head spin.

By the time they had entered the castle, and the king had been led along so many corridors he was completely lost, he suddenly found himself in a large chamber, which, the captain of the guard told him, was assigned to him. During the journey King Gruffudd and this man, whose name was Crinan, had become better acquainted, although at a slight distance, as befitted their respective ranks. Nevertheless, Crinan was the only person he knew here, and even spoke a little Welsh, which was almost unknown for an Englishman, so the king asked him if he could find out when he would be received by King Henry.

'I will find out sire, without delay. I understand King Henry is not here, but is expected at any time. No doubt you will prefer some time yourself to recover from your long journey and rest awhile. I will send your bath slave to you right away and have your possessions brought up to you, and see that your men and horses are well housed and fed.'

'Thank you Crinan,' said the king, and waited until the man had left the room before he began to inspect his surroundings fully.

He had never been housed so magnificently. The chamber was large, with a wood fire the size of a funeral pyre burning in the huge stone grate. The enormous bed was supplied with woven hangings and a richly worked cover, and other heavy curtains and hangings graced the walls and door, he supposed to keep out draughts, though this was hardly necessary, because the long windows were glazed with expensive glass, better than any king Gruffudd had seen, even in Chester. The furniture was heavy carved oak, and the large chairs were awash with embroidered cushions.

There was a knock at the door, and two slaves entered, carrying a hip bath which they placed before the fire.

'Will it please you sire, to take a bath?'

'It will indeed,' said the king, and allowed himself to enjoy the luxury.

Only an hour after king Gruffudd ap Cynan was taking his bath, king Henry was doing the same, but in surroundings even more sumptuous. He received Crinan in his bathing robe, and motioned the man to help himself to wine from the table near the large window.

'I understand King Gruffudd is established here?'

'Yes sire, he arrived about an hour before your own column.'

'You have done well Crinan. What is the Welsh king's mood, do you think?'

Crinan was overcome by the enormity of the question, and was fairly sure that whatever he said would be wrong, so he replied: 'May it please you sire, it is not given to the likes of me to understand the moods or reasonings of kings.' Seeing King Henry's brow darken he added, 'But he seems well pleased with the hospitality offered him.'

King Henry nodded, and Crinan noticed the look of cunning which crossed his thin face, a look of guile, Crinan thought, and who could know what devious plan was behind it?

'Good.' King Henry paced a moment and then said, almost as an afterthought, 'You have got to know him a little though? Is he afraid of me?'

Now Crinan knew how to answer, and said immediately, 'Of course sire. I think he has never seen London before, or a palace such as this, I think he is both afraid and overwhelmed.'

'Good,' the king said again, 'Overwhelmed will

suffice for now. I am going to do you a great honour Crinan. I am going to put the Welsh king in your care. I will entertain him at dinner tonight and shall tell him that you are at his disposal.'

'Yes, sire,' said Crinan, wondering what was coming next.

'By the time he leaves here, he must be absolutely sure of two things.' The king came over to Crinan and looked him closely in the eye. When he spoke his tone was so menacing and bitter that Crinan felt himself flinch. 'One, that I am the worst, most deadly and most powerful enemy he could ever have, and that I can and will wipe out him and his people without a second thought.'

'Yes sire,' said Crinan, swallowing.

'And two,' continued King Henry, changing his voice to a light and friendly tone: 'That I am the wisest and most generous of kings to my friends, and that if he becomes my friend he and his people will benefit to an extent he never even dreamed of.'

Crinan swallowed again. 'I understand sire.'

'I hope you do, for you will assist me in this. You will arrange over the next few weeks to show him the awesome power I command. We shall have jousting, wrestling and sword fighting displays and parades of our troops which will make his eyes pop out of his head, so he becomes convinced it is useless to oppose me. What are his weaknesses?'

'Women sir,' Crinan replied immediately. 'At every inn we rested on the journey he would have a young girl, or sometimes more than one, and he was made very angry on one occasion when no girl was available. I had to pay the innkeeper to put up his own daughter, even though he was saving her...'

'Yes, yes,' King Henry interrupted. 'So we have a lecherous old dog have we? That is good. Anything else?'

'He is very fond of his drink sire,' Crinan could hardly believe his own words. He was actually criticizing one king, in the service of another.

'Well, we have plenty of good wine to smooth our way.' Henry seemed pleased. 'Does he hanker for young boys also?'

'I think not sire. I never saw a sign of it.'

'Right,' said the king, 'Then that is settled. You understand what is needed?'

'Yes, I think so sire.'

'Don't think so, tell me!' said Henry impatiently.

'Frighten him to death sire, and give him everything he wants and more.'

The king roared with laughter. 'Well done Crinan. I could not have put it better myself.'

King Gruffudd ap Cynan was like a lamb to the slaughter. The English king's plan worked to perfection, so that at one moment Gruffudd was almost overcome by the power and might which he saw displayed daily, power which convinced him it would be suicide for him and his people to attempt to oppose the great English King.

On the other hand it seemed Henry really liked him. He was treated with great generosity, and the young captain Crinan was told to provide him with entertainment of every kind. This ranged from daily displays of every kind of martial art and archery, to the best wines and food, some of which were exotic items Gruffudd had never tasted, prepared by the cooks brought over from France.

But the best part was the women. Henry seemed to delight in supplying Gruffudd with the most beautiful girls he could find, and the Welsh king descended into a pattern of such licentiousness and degeneracy that King

Henry himself was impressed.

'You are a stalwart old dog!' he roared one evening, when Gruffudd had recounted his exploits of the night before. 'No wonder your people are so sturdy and strong! Their king can set seed like a prize bull! We shall have an explosion of births nine months after you leave here! I can train a new army!'

He and Gruffudd, both well in their cups and almost unable to stand, collapsed with laughter. They laughed so much they had difficulty pouring more wine down their throats. King Gruffudd was almost incomprehensible as he muttered: 'You are a great king sire, I have always known it, but now I know it even better....' He slurped at his wine and raised his glass. 'Even better...' he repeated. 'You have treated me royally and I shall not forget it.'

'You are my friend,' replied Henry, also drunk but a little more in control. 'We great king's should act together.' He leaned over and refilled Gruffudd's glass. 'You swore me fealty you know...'

'I did...I did,' gasped Gruffudd, 'And I shall swear it again... before any man....By God I shall... I know my friends...'

'And I know who are not my friends,' said King Henry, suddenly vicious. His manner changed and he put his face close to the Welsh king, 'That prince from Deheubarth, Gruffudd ap Rhys, he was named for you, was he not? And he is against me!' His voice ended on a roar, and King Gruffudd, stupefied with drink, stared uncomprehending. Gruffudd ap Rhys had never been mentioned before and he had thought King Henry had decided to ignore the matter.

'I am your friend, my lord,' he managed to splutter. 'The prince of Deheubarth is a young rip... it is true...' he tried to gather his fragmented thoughts. He motioned King Henry to lean nearer and said in a stage whisper:

'He is not a problem... he has no army and no influence...'

'Nevertheless he is my sworn enemy and he has raised his hand against me!' King Henry raised his voice, 'And I pledge my unrivalled vengeance on him and his brother...' Here he put his face to Gruffudd's, 'And anyone who gives them quarter...'

Gruffudd stared in sheer terror at the English king's face. He knew he was befuddled with drink and was trying desperately to say the right thing, but no sound came from his throat.

'On the other hand,' said King Henry loudly and with great purpose, 'Anyone who should capture them and deliver them to me, dead or alive, shall have my life-long protection and my gratitude.'

King Gruffudd suddenly found his voice. 'You shall have their heads on a platter within a week of my return,' he roared. 'I swear it, my liege lord!'

Crinan came upon his friend in the tack room, where he was polishing a harness. 'I did not think to find you here so late, I have been looking for you,' he said. 'I have just come from the king, where he entertains the Welsh king Gruffudd and they are both well in their cups.'

The man smiled, 'That is nothing new,' he said.

'No, but I seem to remember... do you not have some kinship with Sir Gerald of Windsor, who is now constable of Pembroke?'

'I do indeed,' said the man, 'My aunt and his mother...'

'Never mind that,' said Crinan curtly. 'I just heard King Gruffudd ap Cynan swear to Henry that he would bring him the young Deheubarth princes heads on a platter within the week!'

The man turned pale. 'No! He would not do that,

surely.'

'My ears did not deceive me I assure you.' Crinan said nervously.

His friend nodded. 'I must send word to Sir Gerald, his wife Nest is their sister, and she has only just been re-united with them...'

'Yes, yes. I remember the princess Nest, when she was at court here,' Crinan said. 'She was so young when she arrived, a gentle soul and a fine person. I served her and knew her quite well. She taught me a little of the Welsh language.' He smiled, remembering. 'She loved to hear a few words of her own tongue. What King Henry did to her was appalling. She was a royal princess, and he treated her...' Crinan stopped, realising he had said too much.

'I am the king's man, ' he continued eventually. 'I serve him and do what I am told, but it does not mean I have to like it. He has the Norman cruelty in him which I have seen so often.' He took hold of his friend's arm. 'You must do what you must,' he whispered fiercely 'But whatever happens, this word never came from me, you understand?'

'Of course, you were never here,' said the man, and as Crinan left the tack room he added softly, 'But God bless you anyway, good sire.'

Queen Angharad was in a happy turmoil. Since the messenger had arrived the previous evening to announce that the Welsh king and his escort was only two days away, she had been busy with arrangements for a warm welcome, and Aberffraw buzzed with life as linen was freshened, bread and sweetmeats were baked and venison roasted, and the hall itself was swept and laid with new rushes. The many arms and war trophies arrayed upon the walls were polished until they glittered in the morning sun.

The family was not spared their share of the preparations, and all were anxious to welcome the king home and to know what had befallen in London. Gwenllian and Gruff were sure that this safe homecoming meant that things had gone well with King Henry, and perhaps that King Gruffudd would relent and allow their marriage and give his blessing. They were discussing this with Owain when yet another messenger arrived, this time for Gruff, from his sister Nest at Pembroke.

The man had ridden hard, and looked all in when he was shown in to the hall.

'God please you sir, but you must...' The man stopped as the queen joined them with Cadwallon, Hywel and Cadwaladr. 'What is it?' Angharad asked, realising something of some import was afoot.

'I don't know...a message from the Lady Nest,' said Gruff. 'Take your breath man, is there a scroll?'

'No sir, just a message entrusted to me, to be given to yourself and Prince Hywel alone.' He looked nervously at the queen and her family, 'I beg your pardon my lady.'

Gruff smiled. 'Nonsense my friend, we have no secrets here, give your message.'

The man looked about him in some distress, and Angharad said, 'Oh, let him give his report privily if he wishes, it may be some embarrassment or other...'

'No!' Gruff was adamant. 'Speak your piece man! Here and now!'

'I am not sure sire...'

'Now!'

'Yes sire.' The messenger looked near to tears, and shuffled uneasily. 'The message is sire...' he took a deep breath, and then in a sudden explosion of words: 'King Gruffudd is on his way here.... and he has promised King Henry to send him your head, and that of your brother prince Hywel, within the week.'

There was silence in the room, a silence of shock so palpable that it seemed to ring and reverberate around them like a bell.

'What?' Prince Gruff was pale. 'How do you have this information? It cannot be true!'

'Indeed it is true sire. The man who brought the news from London is a kinsman of Sir Gerald, and came directly from King Henry's court. King Henry demanded it and King Gruffudd agreed to it clearly and enthusiastically, within the hearing of many.' The man was more at ease now he had got it out at last, and added, 'The princess Nest begs you to leave right away for Pembroke sire. Sir Gerald is of course not happy, but he will not see you both killed if he can help it. The princess Nest will hide you both my lords, and begs you make haste, but secretly.'

'This can not be true!' It was Owain who spoke. 'I know our father is forced to appease King Henry, but surely he would not agree to this!'

'Depends what Henry has paid him surely,' said Cadwaladr, and received angry looks from Owain and Gwenllian.

'Your father would not do this for pay,' said Angharad, 'I can hardly believe it myself, but I do know Henry will manipulate any situation, and it may be the king has become embroiled in something....'

'He would not do this, he could not!' cried Gwenllian. 'He knows Gruff and I are bespoke, and he would never murder my chosen lord!'

Cadwallon, ever practical and cautious, sounded the note of reason. 'We cannot know the truth of this until our father returns. It may be that he is playing some game to confound Henry. In case it is true, for whatever reason, Gruff and Hywel must leave and go to Pembroke to ensure their safety.'

There was a general hum of agreement, and Gwenllian said, 'But they will be safe here surely? Our father will not harm them?'

The silence which followed this remark gave the lie to the belief. Gruff said gently, 'You may be right dearest, but we can not take the risk. We must leave right away.' He turned to the messenger, 'Your duty is well done,' he said, 'and you must have food and rest...'

'Just a little sire, for myself and my companion, then we shall be ready to accompany you back to Pembroke.'

'We thank you,' said Gruff, and turned to Hywel. 'We leave within the hour brother.' They left the room, leaving the others staring at each other in consternation.

Gwenllian knocked and entered quietly into Gruff's chamber, where he was busy with his servant sorting out his requirements for the journey and packing his saddlebags.

He turned, and taking her in his arms said, 'Never fear dearest, somehow we shall overcome these troubled times, and shall be together. Shall you wait?'

'I shall wait.'

'And if your father commands you to take another in marriage? You are of age...'

'I shall refuse.'

'And risk his wrath?'

She smiled. 'And risk his wrath,' she said firmly.

'But dearest, for how long? It seems now that we may not be together until I have re-gained my lands, and that time seems far distant.'

'Whatever the time, I will wait,' Gwenllian said. 'I still cannot believe my father could do this dreadful thing. I am sure that when he returns, even if he is set on it, I can persuade him to relent. He hates King Henry, and your father was his best friend.'

'But he is a king first, and a father second,' said Gruff, 'He cannot risk everything for us. In any case, we cannot risk him finding us here.'

'No' said Gwenllian, 'I agree, but I have been thinking. You and Hywel could go to the church on the coast at Aberdaron, and seek sanctuary there, it is not so far and you will be safe. When my father arrives I am sure we can dissuade him from any promise he may have made to King Henry. Understand that my mother and brothers will all try to help. Then, when he has relented of his promise, and agreed to our marriage also, I can send word to Aberdaron for you to return here. It is a much better idea.'

'It might work,' said Gruff, considering. 'I will do it, but I must have a safe retreat just in case the king cannot be moved. I will send my Pembroke men back to Nest. I will ask her to send a boat to Aberdaron, so we can escape by sea to Pembroke if your father remains obdurate. In any case it may be better than risking the roads.'

'Yes!' Gwenllian was delighted. 'Thank God for your brave sister, perhaps one day I shall be able to meet her, I cannot wait for that day.'

'Yes,' Gruff smiled. 'The Lady Nest is renowned for one thing, her beauty. But there is much more to her than that, as I have discovered since I came home from Ireland. She is brave and resourceful, and you will have to be the same my love, while we are apart.'

'I promise,' Gwenllian assured him. 'And now, make haste dearest, you can be in Aberdaron by nightfall, and I have knowledge of the priest there, he is a sound and saintly man.'

There was no doubt of the mood of King Gruffudd ap

Cynan when he arrived at Aberffraw next day. As he and his troop entered the courtyard Meilyr began the great Song of Welcome, which was only sung for a member of the royal family when they had been away for some time. As the song progressed, everyone joined in, until by the time the king entered the great hall it had mounted to great crescendo of sound. The king waited in the hall, until the last sound died away, and then nodded his head in acknowledgement of the welcome. He did not smile however, and went immediately to his chamber, calling for wine and Queen Angharad at the same time.

Despite all the efforts of the queen and her household, King Gruffudd found fault with everything and everyone, and even roared at Angharad, telling her that King Henry would never stand for the kind of slackness and lack of discipline he found in her house.

'Perhaps that is because King Henry has more money to spend on his household than you have my lord,' she answered him tartly, which stopped him short for a moment. He brushed his hand across his brow as if he had a headache and said, 'Don't cross me my lady!'

'I shall not sire, while you are in this mood,' said the queen, and made to leave.

The king grumbled, 'Stay...stay you a while...' He poured a glass of wine and drank it off. Then: 'Send young Gruff and his brother to me,' he said, and when Angharad began to speak, broke in 'Oh yes, I know, Hywel is here as well, we heard in London he had been released, King Henry was none too pleased, it was done without his knowledge.'

'But they are not here my lord.'

The king started. 'Not here? God's teeth! Where are they?'

'I know not at this precise moment, but we had word... word I could hardly believe...'

The king's face darkened and he spat out: 'What word was that?'

'That you had promised King Henry to send him the Deheubarth princes heads within the week.'

'Who told you?' the king roared, 'Who has been spying on me?'

'No need for spying as I understand,' Angharad said crisply. 'Apparently you shouted it loud enough for the whole nation to hear. When the princes heard the rumours, they left, and who can blame them?'

King Gruffudd cursed under his breath, and the queen quickly crossed to his side. 'Husband', she said, 'Dear heart, what is the matter? Has Henry been at his tricks? I know you would not harm those two fine young men, the sons of your dearest friend. I know you do not mean to do it, but tell me all, and we can perhaps find an answer...'

The king's eyes were downcast, he would not meet her gaze. 'There is nothing to be done,' he said, 'The spear is thrown, and travels on its way, and it will find its target.'

'What do you mean?'

The king shook his head, he had a look of guilt about him Angharad thought, but he said, 'I cannot talk to you now, send Owain to me.'

'As you please. But my lord, please do nothing to hurt the princes, Gwenllian and Gruff are bespoke, and it would break her heart.'

The king's look was bleak. 'If I do not fulfill my promise to Henry there will be a deal more than hearts broken at Aberffraw,' he said, and Angharad felt the cold enter her bones.

When Owain entered the king's chamber he found his father's temper somewhat calmer, but a sombre mood had overtaken the king, and Owain, like his mother before him, felt a sudden disquiet, and had a premonition that any words he could speak would fall on stony ground.

Nevertheless, when they were seated, the king began in a confiding tone: 'My dear son, you are my heir, and although I do not always ask your counsel, and oft do not take it when given, I know your worth and that you will become a good ruler of Gwynnedd. It is for this reason that I wish you to understand what has happened, and why I must find and capture the Deheubarth princes for King Henry.'

'Then it is true,' said Owain slowly. 'You intend to betray them.'

'That is an unkind word for you to use Owain,' the king said, nettled.

'It is one I never thought to use about my father,' said Owain, 'How many times have you told us the stories of yourself and the Deheubarth king, Rhys ap Tewdwr, how you rode and fought together when you were young, and won so many battles and swore undying friendship? Now you expect me to believe you would kill his two remaining sons? You cannot do it father, and I know you will not.'

'Do you think I want this?' the king roared, 'Do you think I would not rather they made great battle against Henry and won? Do you think I do not itch to join them?'

'Then why...?'

'Oh Owain... if you can understand only one thing, understand this. It is impossible. You saw the might of Henry's armies at Snowdonia when we could have been routed and slaughtered, you know it...' He thumped his fist on the table. 'You know it Owain, or you have no eyes to see!'

'Yes, I know it, that is true,' said Owain.

'That day I made a great compromise for this land and my people. I swore fealty to Henry so he would allow me to continue to rule here, and our people's lives would be saved. All of us.' He looked at Owain darkly. 'It stuck in my gullet I can tell you, but I did it, not to save myself but to save my people and the kingdom of Gwynnedd. Now Henry has declared open warfare on the Deheubarth princes I have to carry out my promise, or I risk his vengeance, and that vengeance would be worse than you could imagine. Oh Owain, in London I saw such things...such power of arms...such military might...we have no chance unless we obey. If we do, Henry has promised help and assistance to us. I must do what is right for the kingdom.'

'But how did you come to make such a promise?' said Owain, 'Did you not negotiate? Say you would rather not be drawn into the dispute, or some other device...'

'I was...I was in my cups...and Henry tricked me... one moment he was friendly...and the next minute threatening to kill us all...' King Gruffudd flushed as he looked at Owain's stony face. 'It is easy to be wise now!' the king shouted. 'You were not there!'

'He outwitted you, because you could not resist his wines,' Owain said dismissively, 'I expect there were other favours and hospitality you enjoyed also. You forget father, I know your tastes better than most. And for this, the two Deheubarth princes are to die?'

'Do not dare to teach me my duty!' the king yelled, 'You are not king yet! And if we do not appease Henry you never will be!'

Owain rose and walked over to the window. 'And where father, is the honour in ruling a kingdom bought by betrayal?'

'Honour?' The king spat out the word. 'Honour is for the young and naive, those who have not learned that it is not easy to rule, that in the search for the greatest good sometimes one has to compromise...I have to put the kingdom first...'

'And the princes? Gruff and Hywel?

'I will not kill them,' the king said more quietly. 'But they must at least be taken and delivered to Henry. He knows I can find them more quickly than his own troops. He expects it of me.'

'So he will kill them himself.' said Owain. 'I will not tell you where they are father.'

The king gave a bitter laugh. 'I already know,' he said, 'Even the servants knew where they had gone. I have already sent a troop out after them, to Aberdaron.'

The priest at Aberdaron was enjoying his first mission. The bishop at Bangor had told him he had been selected for it because it 'was a quiet spot, with few souls to minister, and plenty of time for the contemplative life.' It was clear the bishop thought that this particular young priest was the contemplative type. Father John knew himself that this was not strictly true. Although he enjoyed reading the scriptures and particularly the writings of Saint Augustine, he admitted to a fondness for music, and in his wilder moments, even dancing. He surmised that the reason people thought of him as something of a hermit, including the bishop, was because of his speech. He knew what he wanted to say, but sometimes his jaw would go into a kind of spasm, which meant the words would only come out with a stammer, and sometimes not at all.

Now Father John stood outside the church door, facing the captain of the king's troop, and his speech had completely deserted him. His jaw dropped open and his mouth worked, but no sound came.

'Come now father,' the captain said kindly. 'We know they're here. We've already searched the village and there's not been a boat since last week, so we know they're in the church. You go now and fetch them out to us.' He smiled at the priest and nodded. The priest still had not uttered a word, he was clearly petrified.

The captain tried again. 'You have to fetch them,' he said. 'It is the king's orders. He wants to talk to them.'

'Are you sure he doesn't want to k...k...kill them?' The priest had found his voice at last.

'What he wants with them is no business of mine, nor yours neither!' The captain said briskly. 'If you don't fetch them out this instant, we shall go in and get 'em.'

'No you shall not!' Father John said loudly. To his surprise his voice came out clear and firm. It must be a miracle, he decided. A strong presence of God filled him, and he spread his arms wide, as if defending the church door, and cried, 'This church is a holy and sanctified place, and men bearing arms may not enter, and all who seek sanctuary shall find it.'

The captain looked astonished, and his men began to mutter amongst themselves.

'Your king will not thank you,' continued the priest, 'For desecrating a holy shrine in his name.'

'Well, we won't do that,' said the captain, attempting reconciliation. 'You just go and fetch them out, they'll surely do as you ask, and we'll be on our way.'

Father John drew himself up to his full height, and felt the power run through his body and along his outstretched arms.

'Do you not fear for your very souls?' His voice rang out again, clear and distinct. 'There is a warning here, a warning of the great fires of hell, and eternal damnation, to any who dare to break the sanctity of the Church.'

The troop of soldiers backed away, discussing the matter, some crossing themselves. One or two would have entered the church with daggers drawn, but most were in fear for their immortal souls, and would have none of it. Eventually the captain decided to send a messenger to the king at Aberffraw and ask for further instructions.

'We shall not enter without the king's express order,' he told the priest. 'But I shall remain here at the door to make sure they can not leave.'

Father John nodded, and went into the church, closing the door firmly behind him. Then he collapsed on the floor in a quivering heap, and the princes Gruff and Hywel came out of hiding from the room behind the altar, and hastened to lift him up, and to give him a little wine to revive him.

Even while the young priest at Aberdaron was making his first and only impassioned defence of the sanctity of his church, the boat sent by the Lady Nest was rounding the headland and making for the small harbour. Because of the location of the church, chosen for its sheltered position in a small valley, it was not visible to the captain and two men of his troop who stood guard at the church door. The captain had no concerns that his quarry could escape, he had ensured that there was no rear door to the church, and was content to settle down on a bank in the watery sunshine and await instructions from the king.

Inside the church Father John had recovered his wits and smiled enthusiastically when Hywel told him the boat would arrive any minute. 'You found the way my lord?' he asked, 'The tunnel is still useable down to the valley bottom?'

'All the way,' said Hywel, 'Although I'll not say it does not stink in places from lack of air, and the spider's webs are thick as spinning yarns. My torch almost failed several times, but we can use this tunnel, certainly. Our servant and Nest's messenger are already at the far end, watching for the boat. From the end of the tunnel it is a short way to the harbour.'

'We shall not forget your help this day Father John,' said Gruff, gripping the priest's hand fiercely.

'It was f...f...fortunate I knew of the t...t...tunnel,' the priest responded. His stammer had reappeared. 'I have never used it m...m...myself, but my p...p...predecessor had it dug so that the b...b...barrels could be raised more easily from the v...v... village.' Seeing the question in their faces, he explained: 'The p...p...previous f...f...father had some dealings I u...u...understand...er...er...in the w...w...wine trade.'

'I see.' Prince Gruff was relaxed enough to laugh. 'Then God bless him.'

'He's d...d...dead, my lord. He d...d...drank himself to d...d...death.'

'Then God bless his immortal soul,' said Gruff, 'And yours too father.'

He took the burning torch from Hywel and led the way down into the dank tunnel.

Two hours later, as the captain still dozed in the warmth of the mid-afternoon sun, the boat carrying the two escaping princes had already left Aberdaron point and was on its way. Now the immediate danger was over, Prince Gruffudd ap Rhys was overwhelmed by a feeling of deep depression. Hywel attempted to cheer him, and reminded him that they had escaped with their lives, and had cause for celebration.

'But this means I can never marry the princess Gwenllian now,' said Gruff. 'Her father is so set against me he will never agree.'

'We have great plans to accomplish brother, and all you can do is cry over a woman! Have some sense, and gather your courage for our great enterprise.'

'That is just the point Hywel. It is a great enterprise, and I had thought she would be there with me, my support and strength. You do not know her so well yet, but she is not just a woman, she is the princess Gwenllian, and her prowess in battle and her keen mind and stout heart would have meant all to me.' Gruff's handsome head drooped. 'I do not know, Hywel, if I can do it without her.'

'Come now, it's not so bad,' said Hywel, 'If she is all you say, perhaps she will defy her father and come to you.'

'I doubt it,' said Gruff, determined to be miserable. 'King Gruffudd will have her watched; she will be almost a prisoner herself. As for us, we shall have to rely on the generous spirit of yet another Norman lord, Gerald de Windsor.'

'But you said he was a reasonable man, and devoted to our sister?'

'That is true; I think he will do what he can. But he is answerable to King Henry, and where that viper slides all shades of poison follow. King Gruffudd would never have raised his hand against us but for that cunning bastard! Now we have lost the friendship of a king, and I have lost a glorious wife.' Gruff raised his head into the face of the wind, as the small boat made its way steadily southwards. 'I tell you Hywel, Henry thinks he has us beaten but I've hardly started yet! Just give me the chance to take on that devious cur and I'll cut out his heart and feed it to the dogs, I swear it!'

'That's more like it!' replied Hywel, smiling into the wind.

SIX
ESCAPE

Back in Aberffraw Gwenllian was elated. News had just arrived that the troop which had been sent to Aberdaron to arrest the Deheubarth princes had returned without them. When news of Father John's refusal to allow the men at arms inside the church had been brought back to the king, he had been white-lipped with temper. When it had been explained to him that the captain was reluctant to incur the fires of hell for either himself or the king, he had ranted at length on the extent of the captain's stupidity.

'What need was there to break the sanctity of the church? You fool; you should explain to the priest that you need to enter only to worship there, for the good of your souls! Leave all your weapons outside, except perhaps a concealed dagger to quietly persuade the princes, and once you are inside you can take them with little trouble, eight against two, even you should be able to manage that!'

'I see sire.' The messenger was in awe of the king and could hardly think straight. 'So I am to tell the captain...?'

The king sighed and then explained, as if to a child: 'You are to tell the captain and the priest that it is my order that you all lay down your arms and go gently in to the church, to give thanks and to pray. When you find those inside who should not be there, you will assist them out, and so they can be brought back here, where they belong.'

'Yes, sire. It shall be done, never fear.'

King Gruffudd had put his head in his hands, and

called for wine.

Now the whole troop was back again, and the princes were not with them. Gwenllian was not privy to the stormy interview between the captain and her father, but learned later that the princes had not been in the church when eventually the soldiers had entered, and must somehow have made their escape earlier.

King Gruffudd was not available to anyone for three days. When he reappeared he was cold and distant to the family, even Owain and Angharad. Gwenllian's attempts to distract or amuse her father were met with complete rejection, and the once happy relationship between father and daughter was strained and aloof. Still, knowing Gruff and Hywel were safe, she attempted to repair the damage. One evening at dinner, she tried to remind him of one of their stories. 'My lord,' she said, in a break in the hum of noise, 'Do you remember when I was a child, we used to...'

'You are not a child now Gwenllian,' the king interrupted harshly. 'Do not behave like one.'

Angharad tried. 'She is only trying to lighten our dinner conversation my lord. We have all been under a great deal of strain and worry over these matters, and...'

'Strain and worry?' the king interjected. 'What do any of you know of strain and worry? Which of you will deal with Henry when he hears of the prince's escape? You will feel strain and worry enough when he sends his army against us!'

'Do you think it will come to that?' asked Owain.

'How can I tell? You never know which way Henry will shift.'

'I am sorry to have displeased you father,' Gwenllian said in a small voice. 'I did not intend to, but I love prince Gruff, and I cannot pretend I do not.'

'Remember my lord,' said Angharad, before he

could reply. 'Remember when you wanted to wed me? You defied your parents, who would have had you marry higher in rank. You knew your heart and mind, and followed them.'

'That is true, but I was a man and knew what I was about.' For a second a brief smile flickered across the stony face and he said kindly. 'I made the right choice and do not regret it, except that you have brought up my children to cross me.'

'Never sire!'

'Nonetheless, I am king,' Gruffudd continued, as if she had not spoken. 'I am king and my rule shall have sway, whether or not I have the loyalty of my family.'

He looked around the table as if to dare anyone to speak. No one did.

The princes Gruffudd and Hywel arrived at Pembroke castle within two days. They were received with great affection by their sister Nest, particularly Hywel, for she had not seen her youngest brother for many years. She kissed his dear face, almost a mirror image of Gruff, and then hurried them to private quarters she had prepared, without the chance to meet Sir Gerald or any of the main members of the household.

'You know the difficulties here for us all,' she said, 'Sir Gerald knows all I do, but he does not know it officially, and does not want to. If King Henry should ever investigate here, Sir Gerald can deny any knowledge of my actions, and I can take full blame.'

'And would he allow you to do that?' Hywel asked, slightly shocked.

'I do not know the answer to that,' said Nest, as if it had not occurred to her before. 'I know he is a good husband and father, and allows me much freedom. He will not willingly do anything to harm you. You will be safe here for a while at least, until we know what the future holds.'

'I think that is already decided,' said Gruff. 'The future holds a great deal of hard battle and anguish for us both, and for you too Nest, if you help us. We had almost two days on the boat to decide on our plans. We cannot stay here kicking our heels while the Normans, Saxons and Flemish invade our country at will and take our lands and our livelihoods so that the native born Welsh have no place in their own country.' He took the glass of wine which Nest offered him and raised it. 'We intend to fight! We intend to give Henry and his minions a bloody nose, and that includes all those traitorous Welsh who toady to him for pay and betray their own neighbours and their country.'

'Amen to that,' said Hywel, raising his glass also. 'And we pray you can help us dear sister.'

Nest held aloft her own glass and said, 'Whatever I can do to help, you know I will do it without reservation.'

They raised their glasses together and drank, and Nest wondered if it was just her imagination or a trick of the light, or did a shadow briefly cloud the open window and chill the chamber as it entered and passed through? She sipped her wine and reflected on her family's history, and knew in her bones that their father, Rhys ap Tewdwr, had joined in the toast with them.

In less than a week the Princes Gruff and Hywel had established the base for their activities. On the advice of their uncle Rhydderch, they had chosen a site far in the upper reaches of the river Twyi, which was an area of dense tangled forest at Caeo, in Cantref Mawr. The heavy woodland provided almost impenetrable safety, in contrast to its surrounding area of barren heath and moorland, where any approaching threat could be easily seen. Nest had provided money and provisions, and as

Rhydderch spread the word, men began to arrive to join the two princes in their fight for justice.

The incursions into Norman held holdings and land began right away, first with a small force of followers, some of whom were filled with patriotic fervour, and some who were lured by the promise of acquired wealth through sack and plunder. Gruff led from the front in all these first excursions, and was ferocious in attack and merciless in victory. His style was reckless in the manner of the Irish who had taught him, and was a process of attack and withdraw, and attack and withdraw again, which suited the territory and the targets which he had identified. Soon, word of the brothers exploits spread like wildfire through the mountains and valleys of central Wales, and this led to enhanced numbers coming to train with them in Caeo, and increasing plunder for the victors.

The princes Gruff and Hywel were not the only ferocious fighters, some of the warriors who had joined them had suffered immeasurable cruelty from the Norman seizure of their lands and the murder and pillage which accompanied it, and they were set on revenge. There were many individualistic fighters for freedom who would vie with each other for the most number of kills, and their actions spread terror and panic throughout the area.

Growing day by day in numbers and in confidence, Gruff and Hywel now planned for more lucrative victories. They began a series of raids on Norman strongholds, beginning with the fortresses at Llanymddyfri, Narberth and Abertawe near Cardiff. Under the old Deheubarth banner, and calling themselves the 'sons of the dragon,' they attacked the wooden palisades and outer defences with impunity. They swept down like an avalanche on the fortresses, and climbed, tunnelled or torched their way through, in a hail of thrashing swords, arrows, spears and axes, and those who had been brave enough, or foolish enough to remain to defend the strongholds were quickly dispatched. The fortresses were torched so that no remnant of Norman occupation would remain. Then came victory over the fortress at Aberteifi and then the garrison at Aberystwyth, and all the time, as the great Welsh army grew, so did the fame of the great warrior Prince Gruffudd ap Rhys and his valiant brother Hywel.

Gwenllian pursed her lips and turned her back on her mother. She could no longer bear the quiet and insistent stream of common sense which came from the queen's mouth. She knew her mother was right about many of the points she made, but none of them reached her heart, or quelled the deep ache which had been there since Prince Gruffudd had left.

Now Angharad, sensing her daughter's loneliness, came over to where she stood by the window and embraced her.

'Do you think I do not understand your feelings, dear heart?' she said gently. 'Of course I do, and I understand that you love Prince Gruff deeply and cannot imagine life without him. But what you propose is not only dangerous, it may well condemn you to an early death and the loss of any real chance of a happy marriage and all that can bring. Think of any children you may have...'

'That is exactly what I think of!' Gwenllian burst out. 'If I stay here I either have to marry where my father decides, against my heart's dearest wish, or I can wait, and wait, hoping that some day Prince Gruff will prevail, and may send for me. Years will go by and we shall have spent our youth apart!'

'But he has nowhere to live! And if what we hear of his actions is correct, he will not live much longer anyway! King Henry will not allow...'

'But he is doing well, mother.' Gwenllian interrupted. 'He has made great inroads already into Norman positions and destroyed their strongholds, and his influence is growing. Men flock to his banner daily. I can help him!' Gwenllian's voice became impassioned, 'I am not like you mother, you know I can wield a sword as well as any man, and hold my own with spear and dagger! I can fight with Prince Gruff, I believe in his cause and feel impelled to assist him.'

'And what of your reputation as a virgin princess? If Gruff does not marry you...'

'We shall be married,' said Gwenllian firmly, 'And as for other choices in marriage mother, I need none. I shall have none but Prince Gruff.'

'And your father?' Angharad said gently.

'He will never agree, I know that now,' said Gwenllian bitterly. 'But he knows that if Aberffraw was ever under attack from King Henry, then I would be the first to fight with my brothers at his side. I am not disloyal mother, I am not!' Hot tears sprang to the beautiful blue eyes and then her head came up with a look of such despair and anguish that Angharad knew that this must be resolved. She took her daughter's face in her hands and gently wiped away the tears which ran unheeded.

'I know you are not like me, dearest,' she said gently, 'And I have not forgotten the predictions made for you at your birth by Meilyr, of which we have told you many times. I always hoped....hoped that perhaps they would not be true, that I could keep you near, to see your marriage and watch your babes grow, but I see now God has other plans for you.'

'Do you mother?' A look of hope lighted the tear dimmed eyes. 'Then will you help me?'

'No,' said the queen softly, 'I cannot help you, the

king would never forgive me. But Owain will help you, I shall talk to him.' Now it was the queen's turn to shed a tear. 'Heaven knows how I shall miss you, my dear child, but you have my blessing, and we know how to ensure help when you go to meet Prince Gruff. You must write to his sister Nest at Pembroke.'

A week later King Gruffudd, still harsh and steely eyed, rode out from Aberffraw to attend a meeting of local chieftains at his subsidiary hall at Abergwyngregyn. Gwenllian, heavy hearted but firm in her purpose, dressed in her travelling clothes of plain mantle and leather tunic and breeches to ensure she would attract little attention. Then she made her tearful goodbyes to the family and her childhood friends, and mounted her horse.

Angharad was too distressed to attend the palisade to see Gwenllian depart, but Owain and Cadwallon were there, and even Cadwaladr turned up at the last moment and wished her well. Dewi was in charge of the small escort which Owain had insisted should attend her on the first part of her journey to Aberdaron, and his face was like stone as the escort made ready to leave.

Owain took the bridle of Gwenllian's horse. 'You have everything you need, all your weapons and the suggestions I made?'

'Yes Owain, I have all to make me reasonably comfortable in the mountains.'

'You will not be comfortable sister, be assured of it.'

'No, but I shall be safe with Gruff,' she looked at her brother's much loved face, and bent to kiss him. 'You are like a wet nurse, brother,' she said. 'But I would not have it otherwise.'

Owain sighed. 'Remember Gwenllian, if times are too harsh, you always have a home here.'

'I'm not sure father would agree with you.'

Owain's reply was vehement. 'Gwenllian! Tell me you

know it! You can always come home. I will deal with father if need be.'

Gwenllian nodded. 'I know it brother, and do not worry. I shall be safe.'

She gathered up the reins and her horse pranced and whinnied as if aware of the sad atmosphere of leave-taking which all present were feeling. Then Dewi gave the order and they were away, through the great gate and out over the bridge and into the landscape of a new life for the princess of Gwynnedd.

As the journey progressed, the princess herself experienced a distinct feeling of loss at leaving her childhood home. She glanced at Dewi, plodding stolidly ahead, and wondered about his thoughts. *Was she still the 'love of his life,' as he expressed it on that day up on the hillside at Abergwyngregyn?* His loyalty and concern for her welfare was without question, and when she thought of Dewi she knew she loved him too, in a way so deep it hardly needed expression, but which was quite different to the overwhelming passion she felt for Prince Gruff. *Did Dewi approve of what she was doing? Would her father's anger when he returned be taken out on poor Dewi, as it had been when she misbehaved as a child?* She shuddered as she realised that if King Gruffudd was angry enough, he might even raise arms against the Deheubarth princes and try to kill them in the name of King Henry, and return herself to Aberffraw. Gwenllian reflected on these things as they made their way along the Llyn peninsula, and her mood was heavy with misgivings. Nevertheless, as they made progress, this mood gradually gave way to excitement as they rode further towards Aberdaron. Safe in the breast pocket of her tunic was the reply from Nest, which had made the journey possible and urgent.

It read: '*A boat will collect you at Aberdaron point*

on the early morning tide in two days time. Be there!'

At Aberdaron Gwenllian was able to visit Father John at the church, and from him she learned of the tunnel, and how Gruff and Hywel had made their escape. She and Dewi stayed with the priest for the night, and sat until the early hours talking of old times, and of times yet to come. Dewi was supportive of Gwenllian's plans, but expressed fears for her safety.

'I shall be well, my dear friend,' Gwenllian assured him. 'You know Prince Gruff will keep me safe.'

'But my lady...'

'I know Dewi, I understand. You have always been my friend and protector, but it is different now. I am full grown and can take care of myself, and the thanks for that are due to you.'

Dewi smiled briefly, but did not speak again, for he thought the words would choke him.

Gwenllian, selfish in the pursuit of her own wishes, and looking forward to being with Gruff again, had no inkling of the frustration and grief which tormented her old friend.

Early next morning Gwenllian, accompanied only by her maid Olwen, boarded the boat for Pembroke. Dewi watched as the small vessel pulled away, and prayed that one day he would see her again. Then he gathered his troop together, and started back for Aberffraw.

Gwenllian had heard tales of the beauty of the Princess Nest, but nothing she had heard prepared her for the classical grace and elegance of Gruff's sister, who greeted her with warm affection when she arrived at Pembroke two days later. As she had done when her brothers arrived, Nest quickly took Gwenllian to her prepared room, and was at length to explain her precautions, when Gwenllian said quickly:

'No explanations are needed, I know the risks you take

to receive me here, but you were my only means to contact the prince. I hope I cause no trouble.'

Nest laughed out loud. 'Trouble has been my lot since I was born my lady, I do not know how I should ever live without it.' She regarded Gwenllian with affection.

'My brother has made a good choice,' she said. 'He told me of your beauty and also of your skill in swordsmanship and the warrior arts, which was hardly believable.' She took in the open and honest young face which Gwenllian turned towards her, the long golden braids and the travel stained leathers, and smiled. 'And yet now I see you at last, I think I do begin to believe it'. She laughed again, and motioned to the servant to pour wine. 'You must be tired after your long journey,' she said, 'It was a brave thing you did to come here.'

'Oh no,' said Gwenllian. "I had an escort to the boat, and once aboard the journey held little danger.'

Nest met her eyes and held them. 'That is not what I meant,' she said, dismissing the servant.

Gwenllian sipped her wine. 'Does Prince Gruff know I am coming?' she asked.

'No,' said Nest. 'I thought it best to wait until you were here. I was not sure, not really sure, that you would come. I thought perhaps your family would persuade you against it.'

'Nothing and no-one could have done that,' Gwenllian replied, 'But all my family support me in this, save my father. When can I join Princes Gruff and Hywel?'

'After at least two full days rest,' said Nest firmly. 'We must send you to him looking your best, and it will take me a little while to organise your journey without rousing suspicion.'

It was four days later that Gwenllian rode into the clearing in the dense forest at Caeo where Gruff and Hywel had their headquarters. It had been a hard journey, using little known roads, some of which were hardly more than wild animal tracks. They had eventually arrived at the home of Gruff's uncle Rhydderch, where they had been provided with a trusted guide to take them to the mountain retreat. As they entered the clearing, Prince Gruff, hardly able to believe his eyes, ran across and almost dragged Gwenllian from her horse.

After their tearful greeting, he took her across to the fire, where venison was roasting on a spit. 'I cannot believe you are here,' he said, and took her into his arms as the firelight flickered and danced, and the warriors crowded around, to get a look at the young princess of whom they had heard so much. 'I will never, never, forget the sacrifice you have made to join me this day,' he whispered. 'Now you are here, I shall be twice the man I was.'

SEVEN
NEW BEGINNINGS

After the sweet exultation of their reunion, and several days during which the only thought on Prince Gruff's mind seemed to be constant lovemaking, Gwenllian and her prince eventually settled down to more serious matters. Gwenllian, although accustomed to occasional rough and ready life in the mountains since childhood, was horrified at the conditions which prevailed in the Prince's camp.

'This place is not fit for animals, never mind human beings,' she complained to Gruff, 'How can you live like this?'

'It was chosen for its security and inaccessibility, not its living conditions,' Gruff growled in response. 'I have hardly had time to sleep and eat, you seem to forget I have been fighting the Normans.'

'And that is what you must continue to do,' Gwenllian said sweetly. 'I will see what can be arranged. My dearest, when your warriors have been fighting so hard, they need a good place to sleep and recover, somewhere dry and warm. Think what this place will be like when winter comes.'

Gruff could only agree, as he and Hywel rode out on yet another raid with their fighting warriors, relying on information they had of a Norman patrol which should be appearing within a few hours far below in the valley, and where rich pickings might be expected. They left behind them a ragged band of men and women who had come to join them in the forest, some from the settlements in the valleys below, but many of whom had been forced by first Saxon and then Norman incursions, to flee higher and higher up the mountainsides to the high scree which could hardly support life, apart from the few sheep or goats they could rear, and the odd capture of a hare or pigeon. They were still not quite sure of their place in this new army, but they knew the names of the old family of the Deheubarth princes, and were sturdy and savage fighters. Now Gwenllian persuaded these men and their women followers to clear some of the woodland area, and construct a small bower for herself and Gruff. It was made in the old way, from bent wattle and hazel boughs driven deep into the ground and bent over and intertwined with twiggy shrub branches and rushes when these could be found. Gwenllian had seen this work carried out in Gwynedd all her life, and showed the rather surprised helpers how to mix the straw and horse dung to make mud to fill in the larger holes, to ensure it would keep out the worst of the winter cold. Then she and two of the women gathered bracken for the bedding.

'We must gather plenty of bracken while it is dry,' said Gwenllian. 'After the autumn rains come there will not be another chance. A comfortable winter depends on what we do now.'

Having been sceptical and somewhat dilatory at first, when her helpers saw the finished result they discussed it between themselves, and were eager to repeat the work and fashion dwellings for themselves. They came in a group to Gwenllian, small mountain people, with dark hair and skins so weather-beaten by hard living, that they seemed almost part of the forest itself.

'May it please my lady,' said their leader, in an accent of the old Welsh, which made it almost incomprehensible to Gwenllian, 'Is it fitting that we should build such huts for ourselves, in the like of that we built for the prince?'

'Yes, it is fitting,' said Gwenllian, 'We must all be able to withstand the winter. Decide on your own spaces and clear the land and gather your boughs. Cooking stones inside will be useful too. Although we shall cook and share our meat together, it makes sense for each to have a place to warm the air, and to brew the ale with honey to keep out the chills. I will help you, and we shall all help each other.'

They stared at her, and then went away muttering to themselves, but after a few minutes they began to clear the woodland, hacking away at the trees with their sharp and sturdy axes, used for anything from slicing a man's skull in battle to jointing a deer or felling trees, as now.

Next they set to work with mattocks to remove the tree stumps and level the ground. Their energy was prodigious, and Gwenllian was impressed at the speed with which the small huts mushroomed amidst the woodland, each with its own space but with mature trees left to provide shade and cover, so that anyone approaching from the valley would not have been aware of the camp now being created in the density of the forest. It seemed laziness itself not to help them, and so Gwenllian joined the women collecting bracken, and then supervised the mixing of the mud, which they had not quite mastered as to consistency. She also helped with preparation of the evening meal, made usually from game and whatever roots were available, and occasionally a good mutton stew from a carcass sent up from Gruff's uncle Rhydderch, who provided both supplies and news whenever he could.

After about a week the place was transformed, and Gwenllian expected the mountain people to rest from their labours. To her surprise they again approached her, with their leader, whose name was Pwul, as spokesman. He seemed very aware of his status as the speaker for them all, and straightened his hair and pulled his ragged sheepskin into line as he asked: 'Is it fitting to ask my lady about the Prince Gruffudd ap Rhys?'

'Of course it is.'

'Then my lady, you can tell us true. Is this prince truly the son of the great prince Rhys ap Tewdwr, who was killed by the monster Bernard Neufmarche at Talgarth, as is told in our story?'

'You are right. It is he, and his brother Prince Hywel is with him also.'

The group of men conversed together, but their speech was so fast and their language so strange that Gwenllian could hardly understand a word. Then Pwul turned to face her again.

'This was our understanding my lady, but we were not sure. Now we are sure.' He fidgeted, and then said, 'And will this prince, when he has recovered the lands of Deheubarth, be a prince for all of us? Will we be a part of his kingdom? Since his father's death we have had no prince, and no-one to turn to for redress when we have suffered wrong or grievance.'

'Of course,' said Gwenllian again. 'The prince Gruffudd ap Rhys will be a prince for all the people of Deheubarth.'

Pwul turned to his followers and discussed this with them. Then he said: 'We shall fight for this prince, for he is of our own people, and we had thought he was gone forever.' Pwul hung his head. 'We should have been with him, fighting for him, not building huts.'

He seemed ashamed. Gwenllian said: 'Building the huts is important work, for my lord and his men will need shelter and rest when they return. And my lord will fight many battles to regain Deheubarth. He will need you to fight for him on another day. When he returns here you can tell him these things yourself.'

Pwul's eyebrows shot up in alarm. 'Oh no, my lady, I could not speak to the great prince himself. But if you will, when he returns you may tell him of our loyalty, and that we shall send our runners into the forests and the mountains, for there are many still there who will join him.'

'I will tell him, Pwul, and he will be grateful.'

Pwul nodded, and for a second Gwenllian saw the flash of blackened teeth. 'Then we are satisfied,' he said, 'And we shall build more huts now for prince Hywel and the warriors, who will also need a warm place this winter.'

When the troop of exhausted and hungry warriors returned four days later, there was great amazement at the re-organised camp which now awaited them. Gruff was more than pleased, and when Gwenllian told him of her conversation with Pwul and the mountain people, and how they had worked to build the camp, he listened carefully and then went over to where Pwul sat outside his hut, skinning a hare.

Before the man could get to his feet, Gwenllian saw Gruff put out his hand to stop him, and stoop down at his side and spend several minutes talking to him quietly before returning to his own hut to shed the trappings of war.

Pwul, for his part, gathered his followers to him with tears in his eyes. Their prince, he told them gravely, had addressed him as 'brother.'

Some of the warriors who had rallied to Prince Gruff's side had been less than enthusiastic about Gwenllian's arrival in their midst, believing that their prince could well be distracted from his purpose by such a lovely interloper. The new huts and improved conditions at the camp helped to soften their attitude somewhat, and they agreed between themselves that perhaps the arrival of the princess had some advantages after all. However, a week later, when Gwenllian announced her intention to accompany them on a raid against a Flemish settlement, the arguments broke out again.

'There is no place for a woman in battle,' one of the men complained bitterly, as they prepared to leave.

'Aye,' agreed another, 'It will take three men to keep her safe.'

'I think not!' Prince Gruff had joined them unannounced. He strode across to where they were grouped around the fire. The men were apprehensive, but Prince Gruff did not appear to be angry. He smiled at them. 'You do not have my advantage,' he said, 'So I understand how you feel. I would not have believed it myself if I hadn't seen it with my own eyes. I watched the princess Gwenllian train and fight with her brothers at Aberffraw, she is a skilled swordswoman.'

The men were silent. Then one of them said, 'Perhaps that is so, my lord. But training and practice is not the same as the real thing, and we would fear for your lady's life.'

Prince Gruff smiled again. 'This will not be the first time she has been in battle. I have been told she acquitted herself well against King Henry's troops in Snowdonia. But let us see for ourselves. Today's efforts should be little more than a skirmish, but there will no doubt be much blood shed, Norman blood of course!' The men laughed their approval, and the prince added, 'Let the princess come alongside me, and then the responsibility is mine alone. Let her prove her worth as a fighter, if she can.'

The men nodded, but doubtfully, and there was some muttering as they mounted their horses and made to depart. Gwenllian joined Prince Gruffudd at the front of the column, and as they rode out there was a good deal of boisterous banter and camaraderie. One of the warriors towards the rear shouted, 'Well, if he's mad enough to risk a woman as beautiful as that, he may be just mad enough to re-gain his lands! Myself, I love to follow a madman!' There was a ripple of laughter through the ranks, and the column moved slowly on towards its target.

When the column returned late that evening the mood was very different. The attack on the Flemish settlement had been entirely successful, and the men were jubilant as they had only two wounded to counter the severe loss of life they had inflicted, and the raids had produced much plunder. But the jocular comments were all about the princess Gwenllian, who had fought, as one warrior described it, 'like a man'.

'No,' said another, 'Better than a man I say! Better than most men anyway!'

'She is lithe and slender and can leap about with that sword of hers,' said an older man. He had obviously seen much fighting, as evidenced by the scar tissue on his face and arms.

'She can certainly move better than you, old man!' said a young captain, laughing.

The old man was not annoyed. 'I could move well enough in my time, which is why I am still here,' he said pointedly. He cleared his throat and spat into the fire. 'Our princess is another *Buddug!* The English had a warrior queen all those years ago to fight the Romans! Now we Welsh have our own!'

'She has a zeal for the fight,' agreed the captain, 'And I shall follow her, and her beloved prince, until we are victorious!'

Such was the talk over the evening food, washed down with copious draughts of ale, and as the evening went on the exploits of Gwenllian on this first skirmish became ever more brave and successful during the telling.

Prince Gruff and Gwenllian stood together in the opening of their hut and listened to the raucous shouts coming from around the camp fire.

'I saw you kill two men,' said Gruff thoughtfully. He smiled. 'It seems to have risen to fourteen! On this day, perhaps, a legend has been born!'

Gwenllian laughed. 'It was two,' she said. 'It was hardly a real battle. I will make up the other twelve soon enough!'

Gruff smiled. 'I know you will. But what happened today was important. They now accept you as their own. There is only one thing which will improve matters even further in their eyes, and in mine.'

'And what is that?' Gwenllian queried anxiously.

Prince Gruff's voice was soft. 'Marry me,' he said, and delighted in the joy of her smile.

On the day of the wedding of the Prince Gruffudd ap Rhys and the Princess Gwenllian, the sun decided to shine, almost as if in celebration itself, and in atonement for the many dark days which had preceded it. It was early spring, and the space cleared in the settlement was surrounded by the sparkling white of the 'February fair maids' which bloomed profusely under the rays of sunshine piercing the heavy hanging oaks, now in green bud but still to attain their full leaf.

Long tables were set up, and food and drink plundered from the Norman and Flemish settlements was spread out on long wooden boards. There was a plentiful supply of meat and bread, supplemented by pastries and sweetmeats sent for the celebration by Nest and Gruff's uncle Rhydderch. Nest had been instrumental in all the arrangements, and had arranged for a local priest, who was sympathetic to Gruff's cause, to attend and perform the ceremony of marriage.

As they awaited the priest's arrival on the morning of the wedding, Gruff was nervous.

'Heaven knows I had not imagined I should be married under the trees,' he said. 'I had thought it would be done properly in a sanctified place, as is only right for my family. And for you dearest,' he turned to Gwenllian, 'This is not what was planned for your wedding day.'

'No indeed,' she rejoined, but without rancour. 'But we must cut our coat according to the cloth we have. And the marriage will be sacred, and lawful. We must once again thank your sister Nest for the priest.'

'Let us hope he arrives,' Prince Gruff said. 'For we cannot marry without a priest, and late as it may be, I would have our union blessed before our babe makes its presence known.'

'He is here,' Gwenllian cried, pointing down the valley, 'I see a cart approaching, and two horsemen with it.'

'Two?' Gruff queried. 'Perhaps he brings his assistant. But why a cart?'

'We shall find out in good time, my love,' said Gwenllian, 'I must go and braid my hair with ribbon and put on my best gown, for this is my wedding day!'

She ran off towards their hut and Gruff smiled, her pregnancy, which they had only just realised, did not seem to inconvenience her in any way. Half an hour later, as the cart and the two horsemen made their way slowly into the clearing, Gwenllian re-appeared, beautiful and shining with happiness. She approached the riders, who were heavily cloaked. 'You are welcome sir,' she said to the priest, as he slid from his horse.

The second visitor dismounted and shook off the enveloping cloak, and Gwenllian and Gruff were transfixed with joy.

It was the princess Nest.

The formal part of the wedding took only half an hour,

and was held in the open air in the forest clearing, as it was such a pleasant day. The air was dry and the warmth of the sun could be felt by the several hundred people who had made their way up to the camp from the valley below. Word had spread rapidly through the small villages and towns of Deheubarth, that their newly returned prince was to be married to the beautiful princess Gwenllian, daughter of King Gruffudd ap Cynan of Gwynedd, and everyone was anxious to attend such a prestigious event, even though it was held in such circumstances. Since Prince Gruff's return the people had heard of his exploits against the Normans with something like disbelief; they had been waiting for such a moment for many years and could now hardly credit that it was happening at last. All the morning the track to the camp was filled with farmers and villagers, freeman and bondmen alike, with their wives and sometimes their entire families, all intent on the good day of celebration which they had been promised.

After Gruff and Gwenllian had made their vows before God, and had also been handfasted in the old tradition by the binding of their hands together with ribbon, the feast began. Prince Gruff and Gwenllian sat together at a table at the end of the clearing, raised a little higher than the rest, with the Princess Nest on one side and Prince Hywel on the other. All those attending the feast filed past them in order of precedence, and were announced by Gruff's uncle Rhydderch, who acted as doorward for the day. It was a good choice, since Rhydderch had a good knowledge of all those who attended. After they were presented, the people took their seats on the long benches, and it took over an hour for all to be seated.

There were several bards at the feast, and all took turn to sing and play in strict order of precedence as was the custom, each attempting to outdo the others by their sweetness of voice and their eloquence. Long after the sun had dimmed and the rush lights were lit, everyone sat entranced, as they listened to the traditional stories, songs and poems, and to end the celebration the bard Idwal sang a gentle song of love and honour which he had composed especially for the young couple.

Then Gruff and Gwenllian retired to their hut, and all the guests and their families began their long journeys home in the failing light. It had been a perfect day.

The following morning the princess Nest had to leave them, with promises that she would do all she could to help their campaign. She set off on horseback, accompanied by uncle Rhydderch, (whom she was supposed to be visiting) and escorted by Hywel and the now well armed and trained bodyguard.

Gruff and Gwenllian gave orders for the restoration of the camp, and then took a moment to relax together and contemplate their new life.

'The campaign will be hard, dearest,' Gruff said, 'But we grow stronger by the day. We have many more followers as a result of the wedding, and several local chieftains have said they will raise groups of men and train them to be ready to follow when I give the order. During the spring and summer we shall recruit followers and train them while continuing our plan of local raids. It will take several months, but by Autumn we should have enough seasoned men to attempt our first real battle, a blow against King Henry which will not only make him smart, but will strike at his very heart.'

'Do you know what this target will be?' asked Gwenllian.

'Yes. If I am right, and we work hard throughout the spring and summer, by autumn we should be ready to attack Carmarthen castle.'

During the ensuing months prince Gruff's plans were accomplished more or less as he had hoped. It was a good summer, and with so many new and willing helpers, their camp in Cantref Mawr took on a more settled and permanent structure. Gwenllian's face and arms became nut brown from her many hours of exposure in the summer sun, and despite her pregnancy she took an active part in many of the raids which were still routine whenever they had good information. Often Gwenllian organised and led these excursions herself, as the information on likely targets arrived when prince Gruff was already engaged elsewhere. On these occasions the warriors followed her banner enthusiastically; aware now that she was a wise strategist as well as a fierce and determined fighter, and it would have been a brave man indeed who would have tried to use the argument of her pregnancy to dissuade her.

Nevertheless, she inevitably grew heavier and more sluggish in her movements as the summer progressed, and although it was a bitter disappointment to her, when at last the time drew near for the long planned attack on Carmarthen castle, she recognised that she would be unable to take part. Despite continuing her battle training all summer alongside Gruff and Hywel, during which many more men flocked to their cause; by early autumn Gwenllian found herself tired and ungainly in movement, the child was making itself felt. Gruff was secretly relieved at Gwenllian's decision that although she would accompany the army, she would remain in the safety of their last camp, and not be exposed to any further risk by taking part in the actual raid. Although his wife had acquitted herself well during the skirmishes and raids of the last months, Gruff knew it was inevitable that at some time she must surely be exposed to injury. He consoled her with assurances that she would remain his eyes and ears, as he now had a network of spies throughout the countryside, many of them the local clergy, who could be relied on to relay information about Norman movements.

'Hold you here, my darling,' he said to Gwenllian, as they talked together in their makeshift camp only two miles from Carmarthen. It was mid afternoon, and the sun washed the camp with drowsy warmth, as if to dissuade them from the very idea of undertaking killing and carnage on such a beautiful day. Prince Gruff was keyed up in anticipation of the coming battle, and needed to clear his mind. 'I need you to be in charge of this place, and shall send you word here,' he said now to Gwenllian. 'If we should fail and I am captured or killed, go to your brother Owain for help.'

'But Gruff....'

Gruff smiled. 'I know, I know. But dearest, I have to say this to you and you must hear me. In such a case your duty would be to safeguard our child which you carry.' He smiled. 'I am not expecting defeat my darling. On the contrary, I believe we shall succeed, for we are well prepared and shall take them by surprise. I plan to attack at dusk, when they least expect it.'

Gwenllian nodded. 'Our plans are well made my lord, and I believe too that we shall prevail. But I beg you sire...' Her beautiful eyes clouded, and a frown flitted across her brow. 'There are many traitors here, born Welshmen who have traded their duty to their country and now sympathise with the Norman cause for gold. They are the ones I fear, there are many in Carmarthen who have sworn to fight off any attack, and our men may hesitate to draw the blood of their own kin.'

'You are wrong,' Gruff said. 'Our men will not hesitate to kill these traitors. They may speak little about them, but it is not because they are not aware of the threat. Rather, they are ashamed to even acknowledge them as Welshmen. They are worse, far worse, than any Norman invader who seeks conquest for his own ends, or for loyalty to Henry.' Gruff's voice became bitter. 'I seek no favours, but do expect the free Welsh to stand at my side. Those who will not do so may cower in their hiding holes and stew in their own remorse. But those who take arms against me, those who join my enemies, may expect every torment and revenge which I can inflict upon them, and this is well known.'

'I know my lord, I know.' Gwenllian said quietly. 'But I caution you my love, because these traitors will not always show their true colours. I beseech you, watch for the knife behind your back.'

'I will be careful,' Gruff responded. 'And you, dearest, take rest when you can, and care for our child, for he will be the heir to all I fight for.'

Advance surveys by Prince Gruff's spies had determined the best means of access to Carmarthen castle, and it was plain that stealth and secrecy were paramount. Under the long shadows cast from a sun slowly sinking over the horizon, Gruff's men scaled the high palisades in complete silence, until they were all assembled on the ramparts in the growing darkness. Suddenly, an ear splitting yell rang out, and the attack began. The bewildered defenders were hardly shaken into action before Gruff's men were upon them, and as hand to hand combat followed within the castle, Gruff's prophecy about the vengeful Welsh was carried out, as the invaders hacked to death both Normans and their Welsh lapdogs. Revenge for the betrayal of their country was sweet to the warriors, as they took the castle without mercy. Then, bloody from their exertions, they plundered every item of value and set about stripping the castle down to the bare earth, to remove every last vestige of Norman occupation.

As the drama inside the castle was unfolding, Hywel and the troops under his command rode in and ransacked the unsuspecting nearby town. They put to the sword all those Norman vassals who might have been tempted to go to the assistance of the beleaguered castle, as well as anyone who attempted to oppose them. Homes and trading places were systematically burned, and the whole town put to flight, so that when Gruffudd ap Rhys eventually left the smoking ruins of the castle and joined Hywel in the town, there was little left to do. The battle had been bloody and merciless, and Gruff and Hywel and their warriors had matched their Norman counterparts in vengeance and fury.

The brothers embraced each other, and called their followers together. Gruff sprang up onto a table, hastily brought out from an inn, and addressed them.

'This night has seen a great victory', he told them, 'And as the dawn will approach, so will the dawn of light and freedom for our beleaguered country. This battle is only the first, but it shows the way we shall prevail against the invaders. We have lost a few of our brothers, and we mourn them, but King Henry has lost many more, and a great castle, and the obedience of his lapdogs who thought he could protect them.'

A great roar went up from his army, they were still full of bloodlust and the arrogance which had accompanied their victory. Prince Gruffudd went on:

'For years our people have feared the name of Henry, the Norman invader. Now it is the turn of the Normans, and Henry himself, to fear our name. Yes! My name, Gruffudd ap Rhys, descended from the true house of Deheubarth, and that of my valiant brother Hywel!'

The roar went up again, and the roistering went on until mid-day.

EIGHT
WINNING AND LOSING

Gwenllian soon heard the news of the victory at Carmarthen Castle, at the camp near the town. Almost immediately, now that the battle was over, she decided to return to their retreat in the mountains at Cantref Mawr, there to await the birth of her child. If male, the child would be the heir to the Deheubarth kingdom, and his safety was paramount. Although Gwenllian had played a major part in planning the strategy of Gruff's campaign, she accepted that she could not risk her own or the child's life, and now needed to be circumspect. There was however, another reason which made her decide to seek the safety and peace of the mountains. Lurid tales had reached her of the lecherous roistering and feasting which had followed the victory at Carmarthen, and her husband's name had been at the forefront of these stories. She was well aware this was partly intentional. Gruff was keen to have the local populace fear as well as respect him, in order to keep his followers loyal. They regarded the spoils of war as their right, and indulged in rape, looting and even murder as part of their reward. Gruff in particular, was reported as having done more than his share in the capture of several young women who were kept with his entourage for his personal pleasure. Gwenllian was not surprised by these events, being accustomed to her father's and her brother's activities at Aberffraw, but she could not help but feel a slight hurt when Gruff did not even bother to enquire as to her welfare. When she sent a message to him that she was about to leave however, he responded by riding out to the camp and visiting her tent.

'So you are for home, dearest,' he said, as soon as he

entered. 'It is probably for the best.'

'I think so,' she responded, a little tartly. 'You seem to have plenty to keep you here, and I must take care for the child.'

Gruff laughed. 'You are angry that I have taken my fill of so many women,' he said. 'That is good, I like you to be a little possessive of me, it pleases me to know of it, but you cannot deny a prince the spoils of victory.'

'And what of my spoils?' Gwenllian said, smiling. 'Did I not contribute to the victory also? So may I take my pleasure with any young man I fancy?'

Gruff's face darkened. 'Do not even jest about such a thing, Gwenllian,' he said. 'It is not seemly.' He sat down next to her and took her hand. 'You know I do not wish to take you when you are with child,' he said, stroking her belly. 'Our child is most precious to me, and to you also, I know that.' He stroked her cheek. 'Rest assured dear one, if it pleases you to hear it, there is no other I can enjoy as much as my own dear wife. But as much as I shall miss you, I will be happier when you are back safe in Cantref Mawr.'

'And so shall I,' Gwenllian responded. 'At least your amours will not be under my nose.'

Gruff laughed again. 'Then we shall both be happy. But I did not come to see you to speak of such unimportant matters. You are not only my dear wife, but my companion in arms, and I would discuss strategy with you, for you are my right hand in all I do. I have a mind to make Cydweli Castle my next target. It is well defended but we are strong now, men rally to us by the hundreds each day, as they hear of our success. I think we must take the moment.'

'I agree,' said Gwenllian. 'I only wish I could be with you. But Cydweli will be a great prize, and I too believe we can take it now. I just hope....' She faltered.

'Hope for what?'

Gwenllian was reticent a moment. 'I would wish... I would wish my lord, that the bloodshed and devastation would not be so great as at Carmarthen.'

He thought a moment. 'You are right,' he said. 'It is time for the Welsh to experience what it will mean to be free again under their own rulers. But there is another reason to let Cydweli Castle stand, to keep it habitable and comfortably provided.' He turned and looked into Gwenllian's eyes, and in that moment she felt she could forgive him anything.

'When we have Cydweli,' he said, 'You will come back and live there. It is well situated and will be the perfect place for the birth of our son.'

When Gwenllian returned to the mountain camp in Cantref Mawr after a tiresome and uncomfortable journey, she received a warm welcome from those who had remained to secure the settlement. Chief amongst these was the wife of Pwul, the mountain leader. She was a coarse looking and heavily boned woman named Rhiannell, who was known as a reticent and quiet person. It seemed she had gained confidence during the absence of her husband, and now, against all appearance, showed a tender and caring nature. Rhiannell was quick to notice that the princess Gwenllian was exhausted by her long journey, and each day brought some small treat she had made, or a potion distilled from the herbs she found in the woodlands. Not wanting to disappoint her, Gwenllian drank each bitter mixture as instructed, and to her surprise found that within a short time she was feeling much better.

'Rhiannell seems to know much of the herbs and medicines to be found hereabout,' she mentioned to Olwen, her maidservant.

'Indeed, my lady. I understand she is much skilled in the old arts, and has a potion to cure almost anything. She has on occasion been summoned by the local landholders, especially when there is a difficult birth, or a broken bone.'

'Has she indeed?' Gwenllian pondered a moment. 'Send her to me,' she said.

When Rhiannell arrived Gwenllian came straight to the point. 'Your potions have done me much good Rhiannell, and I thank you,' she said.

Rhiannell's heavy face flushed with pleasure. 'I wish only to serve you, my lady,' she said.

'Thank you,' Gwenllian responded. 'Please sit so I may talk to you.' She waited while Rhiannell made herself comfortable and then said: 'When I lived in my father's home at Aberffraw, we had there a wise man named Meilyr. He was a poet and a bard, but he also knew the healing arts, for it is said he was descended from the great Myrddin, who served King Arthur long ago.' She hesitated. 'I miss Meilyr,' she confessed. 'I miss his advice and his knowledge, especially when our warriors are wounded and we can do little but watch them die.' She smiled at Rhiannell. 'I hope I may count on you, especially as I come near my time.'

Rhiannell nodded her head with averted eyes. Then she burst out, amazed by her own temerity, 'Your time will not be long, my lady.'

'That is right,' said Gwenllian, smiling. 'That is why I wished to see you. I understand you are skilled at birthing and the healing arts.'

The woman's ugly features flushed with pleasure. 'I have always done these things,' she said. 'They were told to me by my mother and my grandmother.'

'Then I hope, Rhiannell, to depend on you when my time comes,' Gwenllian said eagerly, 'For I tell you truly

I know not what to expect.' *And how can I tell you how terrified I am,* she thought. *I could face any battle more easily than this awful birthing, this womanly thing I have heard of but of which I know nothing, other than it is very painful.*

'It will be a great honour to serve my lady,' Rhiannell said. 'Do you know when the birth will be?'

'I surmise it will be in Autumn,' said Gwenllian, 'Perhaps just after harvest time.'

'If you will permit me to look at your belly and feel the size,' said Rhiannell, 'I may be able to tell you the time within a week or so, and as the time comes near, to within a day or two.'

Gwenllian smiled her acquiescence, and lay down on her cot. Rhiannell made an exploration, pushing down hard on Gwenllian's firm flesh, as if she could truly feel the life under her hands.

'Yes, in the Autumn,' she said eventually. 'But perhaps a little earlier than you think.' She restored Gwenllian's clothing, and said gently, 'At the time of the harvest, as the corn ripens, the child ripens also.' Her voice took on a sing-song quality, and she swayed, trance like, her hands moving in a soothing pattern just above Gwenllian's body. *'In the golden time,'* she intoned, *'The stalks are gold and full, the sea runs smooth and the trees are mottled brown. The wind is but a sigh and the ox is in the yoke...all will await our golden prince.'*

Gwenllian felt a sense of peace envelop her as Rhiannell's voice softened to a mere whisper. When she awoke she felt peaceful and relaxed, more settled than she had felt for many weeks.

Prince Gruffydd ap Rhys made good his promise to Gwenllian. As the Welsh patriots surged towards Cydweli Castle in their hundreds, every man knew that the only damage to be inflicted was to be on the Norman troops within, and any who raised a hand against them. The castle was to be saved and kept in good order, so that the Princess Gwenllian could be kept safe there in some comfort, to await the birth of her child. This knowledge gave even the roughest soldier amongst them a sense of right and purpose, and an affinity with the house of Deheubarth which they were sworn to defend and obey.

Using the same tactics of surprise and stealth which had served them so well at Carmarthen, the Welsh army, now swollen to almost twice its size, swarmed upon Cydweli like locusts. With their new found confidence soaring they fought like fiends, and although the stronghold put up its best defence, the overwhelming power of the oncoming Welsh could not be denied. The Castle was taken with the loss of only a few of Gruff's men, and within hours the Prince had it secured and defended, and immediately sent a patrol to inform Gwenllian of their success, and to escort her back to their first ever true home.

'I am happy this day,' he remarked to Hywel, as they watched the patrol depart. 'And for you brother, my grateful thanks. You acquitted yourself well.'

'Gwenllian will be safe here,' Hywel responded, 'And I believe brother, you have another reason to rejoice. With your wife living here, and this place becoming our central stronghold, King Henry will receive the clearest message. He will know now that his hold on south Wales is not secure.'

In Cantref Mawr news of the great victory at Cydweli reached Gwenllian even before Gruff's patrol arrived. The news had spread far and wide and the countryside was aflame with patriotic fervour. In Cydweli the prince was surprised and overjoyed to receive messages of support and goodwill not only from farmers and small landholders, but also from the priests and monks of the local churches, who sent gifts of food and medicines. When Hywel attended his brother in the great hall at Cydweli, he found that their fame had spread even further.

'Come hither Hywel,' Gruff called to him. 'See how we are now sought for our help.' He indicated a weary looking band of men who were gathered around his seat.

'These are men from Ceridigion,' Gruff said. 'They have brought me a written deposition from the local leaders there. The people are being driven from their homes and lands by Flemish and Saxon raiders.'

'It is true sire,' said one of the men, flinging himself to the ground in front of Hywel in an attitude of supplication. 'I know you are not of Ceridigion, but it is said that you fight to free all Wales of these hordes who follow upon the tails of our Norman conquerors. We are weakened so much we can fight no longer. If you cannot help us, all Ceridigion will be overcome, and the only place for the free Welsh will be in the mountains, where these Flemish and Saxon dogs fear to go.'

'Get up sir,' said Hywel, taking the man's arm. 'You are right that we fight for the freedom of all Wales, and we have no need to see a good man on his knees before us.'

Prince Gruff rose to his feet. 'Hear me my brothers,' he said, raising his voice so that all could hear and report his words truly. 'We have heard the cries of the people of Ceridigion, and have read the deposition sent by its leaders. We shall not turn deaf ears to the plight of our countrymen.' He seemed to grow in height, as his gaze travelled right and left, ensuring all could see and hear him. He raised his sword arm. 'I vow....' he stated in a clear voice, 'I vow before you all, that I shall drive out these settlers who have taken your lands and homes by force, and shall clear your beloved country of these invaders. More than that, I shall drive out the Norman lords and their vassals who have occupied your lands for so long.'

A great wave of cheering and blessings erupted throughout the hall, which Prince Gruffudd calmed by holding up his hand. 'In this great enterprise I shall have beside me my beloved brother.' Here he caught Hywel's arm and raised it high. 'You already know of his great fighting skill, which has brought us this far. Together...' Here the brothers strode forward with arms raised in entreaty: 'Together,' repeated Prince Gruff, 'We shall rid our lands of this Norman pestilence for ever. Tell the people! Now is the time! Join us!'

The room erupted in a swell of cheering and noise. The delegation from Ceridigion swore to raise more men for the cause, and left hastily to take the news to their beleaguered compatriots that help from the Deheubarth princes was on the way.

Prince Gruffudd turned to Hywel, his eyes shining. 'The time is come at last brother!' he cried. 'All Wales will join us!' And Hywel embraced his brother, and his prince, with tears in his eyes.

Only a week later, as the princess Gwenllian arrived back at Cydweli and settled herself into the comfort of life there, she was brought the news that hundreds more men had rallied to the standard of Prince Gruffudd ap Rhys as he crossed the border into Ceridigion. She turned to Rhiannell, who had become a constant companion, and who had travelled with her to Cydweli. 'Rhiannell,' she cried, 'Do you hear the great news? Our cause is on fire, the princes make great progress!' Her voice dropped, and she added sadly, 'I only wish that I could be with them.'

Rhiannell only nodded in her quiet way, but after a

moment she said, 'I understand your feelings my lady, for you are a true warrior, everyone says so. But we have our duty to do in other ways.' She coloured slightly, and then said diffidently, 'I too, my lady, am proud on this day. For my husband Pwul is with them, and his heart will be joyful at these events.'

Life at Cydweli was more settled and comfortable than Gwenllian could recall since the days at Aberffraw. She had brought her maid Olwen, as well as the ugly but infinitely kind and capable Rhiannell, to be with her as she awaited the birth of her son. News reached her from time to time of the progress of her husband as his army journeyed further into Ceridigion, and she and her ladies discussed the reported tales of battles and skirmishes late into the night. The arrival of any patrol was eagerly anticipated, and when Olwen ran to the princess with news that a troop would be in the courtyard within the minute, Gwenllian ran quickly down to the great hall to greet them, in spite of her increasing girth.

The lead rider was already coming through the heavy oak door as she went to meet him. For a moment she did not recognise him, but when he pulled off his chain hood a gasp of astonishment and pleasure broke free from her lips, and her heart leaped for joy.

'Dewi! Oh my dearest friend! Dewi! Can it really be you?' She looked deep into the kindly blue eyes which returned her affectionate greeting with a look of hungry appraisal which lingered over every part of her, as if to assure himself she was really there. He opened his arms wide and she flung herself into them.

'Dewi! I can't believe it!' She was almost smothering him, and he became aware of the astonished gaze of the ladies and bondmen gathered around them.

'My lady!' He gently disentangled her, and murmured, 'My lady, remember you are married now. I appreciate the welcome but this is hardly seemly...' He motioned to the assembled courtiers, and Gwenllian recovered herself, and turned to face them.

'Please join me in welcoming my oldest friend and protector from Aberffraw. He is the captain of the guard there and most trusted by my father King Gruffudd. We were children together and he is like a brother to me.'

The group visibly relaxed, and a few smiles appeared. 'Let us have wine and food to welcome our guests,' Gwenllian ordered, 'And see that the men are housed and fed.' She turned to Dewi: 'This is a surprise indeed.' Her face changed suddenly. 'There is not...It is not bad news?'

'No, my lady, far from it. All are well at Aberffraw, and life continues as usual. King Henry seems to have forgotten your father for the moment...'

'Yes.' Gwenllian agreed. Then, with a mischievous smile: 'King Henry has other things on his mind.'

Dewi smiled dryly. 'So I hear.'

Gwenllian led him to the large comfortable chairs arranged in the hall, and waited whilst food and wine was brought and her guest was made comfortable. Then she turned to Dewi uncertainly: 'My father.... he allowed you to come here?'

'Yes.' Dewi responded quietly. 'In fact, I am here on his orders, although it has taken me some time to find you. The king learned what happened at Carmarthen, and was concerned for your safety, especially as we heard you were with child.'

Gwenllian blushed slightly, and Dewi thought he had never seen her look more beautiful. 'It suits you,' he said gently.

'Yes, I am happy about it, in the Autumn, about harvest time.' She gathered her thoughts. 'As you see, I am perfectly well and comfortable, and protected also.'

'Yes, but your mother the Queen worries, and the King has heard of your exploits against the Normans. He is proud of you...'

'That's why he wanted to kill my husband and Hywel I suppose...'

'He would not have killed them...'

'He would have handed them over to Henry, and that's the same thing.' She regained her composure. 'So you were sent to confirm I was well?'

'More than that. I have been sent as your permanent guardian and escort, until after the birth.' He smiled lightly. 'It seems it is what I was born to do. I did it all the years you were growing, and now your father thinks you have need of me again.'

'How dare he? After all his opposition to us, does he think we shall allow him to decide what I need or don't need?'

Dewi sighed, and made no answer for a while. Then he took Gwenllian's hand and raised it gently to his lips. 'It is so very good for my old heart to see you, my lady.'

She relented immediately. 'Your heart is not so old Dewi,' she said. 'Not much older than my own. And it is very good to see you too. I was only... I am still a little angry with my father...'

'He loves you, my lady. And still worries about you.' He hesitated, and then; 'Do not think he does not admire what Prince Gruff and his brother are doing. He does, and is with you in spirit if not in arms. He just needs to be sure...'

She stared at him. 'Be sure? Sure of what?'

'That you are protected if it all goes wrong...'

'Goes wrong? How could it go wrong? All Wales rises with us, we are defeating Henry at every turn....'

'Of course. But just in case...I am to tell you there is always a home for you at Aberffraw...'

140

Prince Gruffudd and Prince Hywel stood together and watched the burning torch that had once been the fortress of the Earl of Striguil at Blaenporth. The siege and taking of the stronghold had lasted for a few hours only, despite strong resistance from its defenders. It had been a bloody battle, with severe loss of life inflicted on the brave occupants of the fortress, but in the end, sheer force of numbers ensured that the Welsh army would prevail. Men had continued to rally to the Deheubarth standard from the moment the princes crossed the border into Ceridigion, and the influx of new volunteers continued day by day, and their losses appeared to be slight.

'Another good day brother,' Prince Gruff remarked. 'And I vow it is good to see you. When I looked for you in the fray there was no sign of you, and I was not sure how you fared. I was then told you were already in the keep.'

Hywel laughed. 'That is true,' he said. 'That is a good captain you assigned to me brother, the one called Geraint. There was no holding him once we had entry. It was a bloody business, and I'm sure we have killed a few score of these Norman lackeys.'

As if in answer to his remark, Geraint himself appeared, still bloody and dishevelled.

'We have the tally, my lords,' he said. 'Heaven be praised, we have lost but one man today, to over one hundred of the enemy.' He fell to his knees. 'God has been with us this day'.

Prince Gruff raised Geraint to his feet. 'That may be,' he said, 'And I pray that it is so, but we have been served well by your own strong arm Geraint, and we give thanks to you for this day's service.' He turned to Hywel. 'How can we fail now brother, when we have such numbers with us? These are good, loyal people who have given us their support, and we must let them know the tyrant has been overthrown.'

Geraint grinned, he anticipated what was coming. 'The inner keep is well stocked sire,' he said, 'Apparently the people were taxed to the bone, and the surplus is stored here.'

'Then see to it Geraint,' Prince Gruff ordered. 'Just as we did in Deheubarth, all surplus which has been wrung from the poor here must be given back to them. Fair tithes are due as always, but to bleed the people so they can barely survive has been the everyday work for these Norman vassals, and we shall have none of it. I charge you, Geraint, as I trust your fair judgement, to distribute the surplus fairly.'

'It shall be done, my lord,' he said, and as he departed he turned with a smile.

'They are already calling you their liberator, my lord,' he said. 'With this new gesture you will become their friend.'

When he had gone Prince Hywel asked, 'Shall you give a dinner tonight, to celebrate?'

'No,' said his brother. 'Tomorrow there is another battle, another skirmish, another farm or settlement to be reclaimed. A light supper and an early bed for me brother.' He took off his chain hood and ran his hands through the black curly hair. 'A light has shone for us today, and we must follow that light while it glows. The times are with us and we must fight on now, before Henry has chance to regroup and send reinforcements.'

'Indeed,' Hywel agreed. 'Let us prepare for tomorrow.'

'Tomorrow,' echoed Prince Gruff. 'Tomorrow we start the march to Penweddig.'

Penwedigg proved not to be the great battle Prince

Gruff had expected. For years he had heard tales of the infamous Norman settlement, and the fear and penury they had visited on the people of the region, and he was prepared for a hard fight to take the settlement. However, word had reached Penwedigg two days earlier that Prince Gruffudd of Deheubarth, with his great horde of Welsh followers, was on his way to them. The terrified inhabitants fled to the coast to take shelter behind the substantial walls of Cardigan Castle in Aberteifi, and the settlement fell without difficulty.

Encouraged and emboldened by the ease of his progress, Prince Gruff and his brother, with their army and bands of followers, pressed on to northern Ceridigion, to the Norman fortress known as Ystrad Peithyll. This stronghold was owned by the steward of the Earl of Striguil, and had received orders to stand fast.

The fortress was a pitiful sight within minutes. The defenders of the settlement were simply overwhelmed and torn to pieces by the avenging Welsh army, who saw a chance to vent their spleen on their tormentors, and who tore through the garrison in a wave of killing and fury.

Prince Gruff did not waver in his objectives. He gathered his lieutenants about him, and together with Hywel, still with reddened sword in his hand, outlined his plans.

'You are jubilant, my brothers,' he told them. 'And you are right to be so, for you have done brave work this day and our success feeds on itself. But now we must push on to a greater prize, the castle of Aberystwyth!'

The room fell silent, as the gathered throng reflected on the power of the great castle, and its formidable garrison, which since its earlier sacking had now been rebuilt. This would be a hard battle indeed, and they were unsure of the outcome.

Sensing their mood, Prince Gruff raised his voice.

'Yes, it will be a great test, and will not be easy. But think, my friends, only think what we have done so far, and what the capture of Aberystwyth will do to Henry and his plans! He can never survive such a blow! It will be the turning point to our cause! If we take Aberystwyth he will know he can never subjugate the Welsh!'

Some growls and murmurs of assent followed his words, and he continued: 'I know you are weary, as indeed am I, so let us now rest and eat, and take a refreshing sleep, for we are the victors. But tomorrow, my friends, we leave this miserable place of Ystrad Peithyll. It has been for us merely a killing field, not a battle, and are we not warriors, who need the fire of opposition? Tomorrow we march for Aberystwyth, where we shall meet our destiny, and engage our enemies in true battle.'

Two days later, as the great Welsh army came within sight of the castle at Aberystwyth, many were so weary they could hardly put one foot in front of the other. Prince Gruffudd gave orders that they should stop at Plas Crug, which was within shouting distance of the castle, so that everyone could rest and build up their strength before the battle next day. Within an hour the whole thousand strong army had made camp and was engaged in cooking food and easing their aching muscles.

'My lords, is this wise?' The princes were in their makeshift headquarters tent, and it was Geraint who spoke. Prince Gruffudd turned from washing at the communal bowl to listen to him. 'Is what wise?'

'Sire, we are in full view of the castle, they can see the extent of our forces and where they are located...'

'Exactly!' Prince Gruff responded, smiling. 'Even now they will be quaking in their boots at the numbers we have assembled here. Seeing how many we are will make our task the easier.' He smiled, and took a drink from the wine flask. 'Geraint, dear friend, they can not match our numbers.'

Geraint was still troubled. 'Not here sire, we outnumber them certainly. But we do not know if they have already sent for reinforcements...'

'You mean from the castle at Ystrad Meurig? I sincerely hope not, as I understand they have many horse there.' He turned to Hywel, 'How think you brother?'

Hywel was subdued. He was bone weary and needed sleep. 'I doubt they will have had time to send for help,' he said. 'And if they have, it will not be here before tomorrow.' He smiled, 'And by then we shall have taught them a lesson.'

'If we attacked now,' said Geraint, we should be sure to teach the lesson without any interference.'

'You think so?' Prince Gruff said quietly. 'Go and look, Geraint, look closely at our men. They have marched hard and long. They are in no condition to fight and have no stomach for it now. By tomorrow morning, after food and a night of rest, they will acquit themselves as we know they can, and we shall have our victory. This will be a hard fight, and every man must give his utmost.' He put his hand on Geraint's shoulder. 'Arrange what guard you can,' he said, 'But make sure every man gets some sleep. Then rest yourself, my dear friend. We shall have need of your skill tomorrow.'

But Geraint did not enjoy his nights rest, and neither did any of the Welsh army. Less than two hours later, as the guards spied a large body of horsemen approaching from the direction of Ystrad Meurig, a hail of arrows assaulted the resting Welsh army from a nearby wood. In sudden panic, the foot soldiers could do little as men fell around them under the sustained attack.

'My lords, we are attacked!' The princes Gruff and

Hywel, having only just succumbed to sleep, struggled up and fumbled for their chain mail. Emerging from the tent, they saw to their horror that the advancing horsemen had already reached the outer parts of the camp, and that the castle gates were open and a huge army of horsemen were streaming out towards them, followed by foot soldiers, while arrows continued to hail down on the centre of the camp from the nearby wood.

'They had archers concealed there,' gasped Hywel, 'They must have been there even before we arrived.'

Prince Gruff did not reply, he already had his sword in his hand and was leaping into the fray. The trap had been sprung, the sleeping Welsh army had been surrounded and was fighting for its life, and the sounds of many men in a death grip, one with another, filled the darkening sky.

Gwenllian lay only half awake in her big bed at Cydweli castle. On Rhiannell's advice, she did not now rise early in the morning, as had always been her habit, but stayed abed a little longer, so that the child would receive extra rest. Rhiannell was also adamant in her instructions that although Gwenllian should take gentle exercise during the day, she should go to bed early, and lately Gwenllian had begun to feel that her life had become one long period of lying around, just waiting... waiting for something to happen. Sensing her boredom, Dewi had sent to Aberffraw for some hunting birds, as even in pregnancy this could be a daily diversion for the princess, who was still not inclined to embroidery. During the hours she was abed, Rhiannell had developed the habit of coming to sit with her mistress and tell some of the old stories of the mountain folk, to keep the princess amused. Now Rhiannell intoned her long tale, half song and half poetry, as Gwenllian drifted in and out of sleep, telling her of the great golden bell in the church at

Llandaff, which had been made by Bishop Oudoceus with his own hands from butter, and was transformed to metal overnight because of the bishop's godly virtues. Now, she sang, the bell sat in pride of place on the altar for all to see. Gwenllian smiled, secure and content, dreaming of the great bell of butter and her confident future.

Olwen suddenly interrupted her reverie. 'A messenger my lady, he comes from the Prince Gruffudd.'

'I am coming.' In seconds Gwenllian was out of bed and on her way to the great hall. 'Go to find Dewi, and ask him to join me right away,' she instructed Olwen, who hastened to obey.

The exhausted horseman was being brought into the hall as they arrived. As soon as Gwenllian saw his haggard face and the ragged state of his appearance, she feared the worst. Stumbling forward, he flung himself at her feet.

'You are from Aberystwyth?' It was Dewi who spoke, leaning forward, his face intent.

The man was still gasping for breath, but nodded, and then, raising his head, gave a cry, almost a wail, of deepest anguish.

'Tell us,' Dewi said, motioning a steward to fetch a stool for the poor wretch. 'What is your name, and what did you see?'

The man hung his head, but once seated he sighed and made an effort to gather his wits. 'All is lost, we were routed,' he said. 'My name is Geraint, I am a senior captain with the princes of Deheubarth. We had many great victories, but by the time we got to Aberystwyth we were all exhausted, and Prince Gruff decided we should rest overnight, and face the battle next day.'

'What happened?' Gwenllian spoke for the first time, and her voice was soft.

'Oh my lady, we did not know it, but reinforcements

had already been sent for, and we had hardly made camp and settled to rest and they were upon us from all sides. As soon as the horsemen from Ystrad Meurig appeared, the gates of the castle were opened and they attacked us. There were archers in a nearby wood unknown to us, and they did great damage…'

'And my husband?' Gwenllian hardly dared speak.

'He told me to ride here to warn you,' Geraint said.

'Then he is alive? Thank God!'

'In truth my lady, I know not. There was a small group around the princes, but we were under attack, and Prince Gruff bade me break out and bring you the news.' His words faltered. 'It was plain…it was plain all was lost. He instructed you are to leave here immediately, as with the Welsh army broken the Normans will waste no time in trying to recapture Cydweli. You are in great danger my lady…'Gwenllian turned to Dewi. 'What think you captain? Can we defend…?

'No we can not.' Dewi responded firmly. 'Prince Gruff is right, we must leave right away.'

'But Dewi…'

'No!' His voice was harsh, but he bent down and took Gwenllian's hand gently.

'Do you not understand my lady? Prince Gruff would have you protect his child…'

Her eyes met his, and misted over. 'Of course.' She turned to Geraint. 'My husband was still alive when you left?'

'Yes. He and prince Hywel were in the centre of a group who were trying to break out and get away, but there seemed to be only twenty or so left…'

'Twenty or so?' Gwenllian's face showed her horror. 'But I heard there were nigh on one thousand that followed him.'

'Yes.'

They all stared at each other, and Geraint's face was bleak as tears began to streak down his mud stained face.

It was Dewi who broke the silence. 'Come now,' he took Geraint's arm. 'You shall have some food whilst we prepare to leave, then you must come with us.'

'To Cantref Mawr,' said Geraint faintly. 'The prince said you were to hide in Cantref Mawr...'

'Make haste my lady,' Dewi instructed. 'We leave within the hour.'

The journey to Cantref Mawr was difficult and fraught with danger. They took with them all the loyal staff and followers from Cydweli, knowing there was no hope of successfully defending the castle should the Norman troops arrive. Gwenllian was grateful to have Dewi's strong support and advice on the journey, but her thoughts were chaotic. *Did my father know this would happen? Is that why he sent Dewi to me? Oh, dear God, please protect my beloved husband and send him safely home. Can this be the end of his dream? The end of all his hopes?*

Once in Cantref Mawr, having successfully evaded the numerous Norman columns which were patrolling the lower area, they set camp again and began to reinforce the settlement, with Dewi and Geraint, now recovered but still very sombre, giving the instructions. There had been few people left at the settlement, but they hastened to help, white faced and anxious at the news the party had brought with them.

They had been there less than a day when Prince Gruffudd and his escort, a small band of only a dozen men, still bloody and bedraggled, rode in. Gwenllian's momentary relief at the sight of him was immediately overshadowed as she saw the pain and grief which was indelibly etched in his face.

'Oh my lady,' he gasped, as soon as he alighted from his horse, 'Deheubarth is lost, all is lost, and Hywel...' he could hardly say the words... 'Hywel is slain...'

In the subdued scramble of tired horses and men, scurrying women and smoking fires, Rhiannell stood apart, her heavy features sombre. Then, as she went to fetch water, a quiet plaintive cry escaped her, repeated as she bent to her task. Her husband Pwul was not among the small band who had returned.

NINE
'BIRTH, DEATH AND REVENGE"

Gwenllian raised her face to the watery sunlight and drew in some deep breaths of fresh air. She had walked to the far corner of the cornfield and now turned and began to make her way back. It had been one of those misty autumnal mornings with a hint of coldness at dawn, but now the sun was attempting to make its presence felt, and Gwenllian was enjoying her daily release from the fetid atmosphere of the farmhouse. She glanced behind her to where Dewi and Rhiannell followed, deep in conversation, making their way through the remaining corn. Most of it was already gathered in, and only a few labourers were scything their way slowly across towards the farmhouse, with the women gleaners following in their wake.

Gwenllian waited for Dewi and Rhiannell to catch her up.

'Come on,' she admonished them. 'Why are you so slow?'

'We are enjoying the morning, my lady,' Dewi replied. 'And you are too quick. There is no need to rush anywhere.'

'Indeed there is not.' Gwenllian murmured. *I am still waiting, and it seems I have been here for ever.* She ran her hands over her enormous belly with impatience, she was grateful for the safe place her husband had arranged for her, in the isolated farmhouse of one of his most trusted supporters, but she felt as if she was in prison.

Rhiannell moved to her side. 'It will not be long now, my lady,' she said.

The words were hardly out of her mouth when Gwenllian was gripped by a terrible pain. She doubled over and clutched Rhiannell.

'Is…is this it?' she gasped.

Rhiannell smiled. 'It seems likely my lady.'

'Well do something!' Gwenllian cried. 'I cannot give birth in the middle of a field!'

'No chance of that my lady,' Rhiannell soothed. 'Just wait a few moments and then you will be able to walk.' She took Gwenllian's arm. 'We shall take a gentle stroll back to the farmhouse together. It will not be for a long time yet.'

Turning to Dewi, who stood rooted to the spot, she said: 'Go ahead Dewi ap Ifan, and let them know my lady is on her way.' Seeing Dewi's face she added. 'There is not a problem. All is prepared.'

Dewi began to run towards the farmhouse, and Rhiannell called after him, 'And then you must send word to the prince.'

Dewi would have liked to go to the Prince himself, for he was a man of action and had felt very confined by his guard duties. The Prince however, had made it clear that he was to stay at Gwenllian's side at all times as her personal bodyguard, and so Dewi sent a trusted man with word to Cantref Mawr that the Princess Gwenllian was about to give birth. Dewi could not imagine how it could be that the Prince could bear to be away from his wife's side at this time, but the Prince had explained that he must remain to rebuild his shattered army and continue the fight, even though he now had little support. He also felt that the risk to both himself and Gwenllian was so great that different locations would ensure better safety, and with this Dewi could not argue. Even the princess Nest could not help them now, as the Deheubarth prince still had a price on his head and refuge at Pembroke was out of the question. She had, however, contrived to send some money to a local priest, which had been passed on to her brother covertly.

By the time Gwenllian had returned to her small room in the farmhouse, the pain had returned again. She made several slow circuits of the room, supported by Dewi, stopping when the contractions started, and continuing when they eased. Rhiannell meanwhile, had found an old night-gown, stripped the bed and then covered it with an aged quilt. Now she turned to Dewi with a smile. 'Time to go sire,' she said quietly, taking his arm.

Dewi's brow knitted anxiously. 'But I....' he stammered. 'I'll be nearby. If my lady needs ....'

'I shall fetch you, never fear,' Rhiannell soothed. She pushed Dewi gently out of the door. He stood there, staring at her, his face unreadable. Rhiannell smiled again. 'You cannot birth the babe for her, Dewi ap Ifan. Go now.' She closed the door in his face.

By the time Prince Gruffudd ap Rhys arrived at the farmhouse Gwenllian had been in labour for almost twelve hours. Dewi rose to welcome him with relief, but tried to dissuade him from entering the small room where Gwenllian lay. 'Rhiannell is with her,' he told Gruff, 'And I think it must be bad for it has been such a long time. Rhiannell will not let anyone enter, she says it is women's work....'

'Women's work be hanged,' said Gruff, his voice becoming angry. 'This is my son and heir coming into the world, I must know what is going on...'

Without another word he burst into the room, and stopped short at the sight of his wife, her hair soaked with perspiration and her face bright red with the effort of a contraction. She clamped her lips together and gave a groan. Rhiannell turned, and seeing the prince, dropped a deep curtsey.

'What is happening?' Gruff said anxiously. 'Is all well?'

'Yes, sire. It will not be long now, perhaps an hour or so.'

'But is all well? Do you need another helper? What is that blood...?' He peered at the ooze of dark red as Gwenllian eased herself slightly.

'Nothing to worry you sire,' Rhiannell said. 'It is only a small amount, often happens.' Seeing the prince did not look reassured, she added, 'It is only when there is bright red blood, and a lot of it, that there is a problem.'

Prince Gruff nodded slightly, then leaned over to his wife. 'You are doing well, my dearest, our son will be here soon and it will all be worth it.'

The look she gave him was one of pure contempt, but she only said. 'I know now why women call this labour. It is very hard work.' She shook her head in a determined negation and then clenched her teeth as the next pain took her body.

'Go...' she gasped. 'Please go...'

The prince nodded and left the room with Dewi, who had been standing in the doorway. They went into the farmhouse kitchen, where the goodwife had prepared stew and ale for her distinguished guests. Prince Gruffudd drained his drinking vessel and called immediately for another. 'Drink up Dewi,' he said. 'This will be a great day. Today my son will be born! We must celebrate!'

Dewi did not even smile. He looked coldly at the Prince and then said, 'It might be a girl. What will you do if it is a girl?'

Gruff took another swig of ale, 'Then in that case, she will be brought up to be strong, like her mother. And Gwenllian will produce another child, a son, as quickly as possible.' He began to eat hungrily, and as Dewi watched and waited for the next hours to pass he felt a great sadness sweep through his bones, as if it would drain him of all energy, and leave him helpless. In the darkness of

154

the night he saw the child, the girl child, running and skipping through the meadows and clambering up the mountainside, and he followed her, guarding her, guiding her, like that other small girl, long ago in Aberffraw.

Dewi ap Ifan need not have worried about the child. It was a son, a very healthy and beautiful child, who, after all the struggling and pushing from his mother, and the gentle pummelling and massaging by Rhiannell, had suddenly shot into the world just before dawn.

Rhiannell gently washed the child and wrapped him in a piece of good cloth the farmer's wife had provided. She leant down and gave the child to Gwenllian, who gazed on him in pure delight.

'A lovely son, my lady,' Rhiannell breathed. 'He is perfect in every way, and is a sign of hope sent to us in these sad times.'

'He is more than that,' said Gwenllian, touching the tiny fingers. 'He is a child of freedom, born free in a free place, and is surrounded by loyal friends. He will fight for freedom for his people as his father does.'

Rhiannell grunted. She did not care for talk of fighting when the sweet child was hardly yet in the world. She began to prepare the fresh water for Gwenllian to wash, but her mistress said: 'Leave that to Olwen, she can care for my needs now. You must take the prince to his father, for you have helped to bring this child and the honour shall be yours.'

Rhiannell's face flushed dark with pleasure, but she took the child and carried him carefully to the farmhouse kitchen. Both Dewi ap Ifan and Prince Gruffudd were dozing, but quickly came alert as Rhiannell entered. She handed the child to Prince Gruffudd.

'Your son, my lord.'

'The Prince Anarawd,' breathed Gruff, examining the tiny form carefully. He turned to Rhiannell; 'He is healthy?'

'Very healthy my lord, all seems well.'

'All is well, indeed, all is well.' He turned to Dewi. 'Come look at my son Dewi! The heir to the Deheubarth crown! Is he not a fine boy?'

Dewi smiled. 'A fine son indeed, you are a lucky man sire.' He turned to Rhiannell. 'How is my lady?'

'She is well sire. Very tired but that will pass in a few days. Have no fear, she will be well.' She turned again to prince Gruff: 'My lady is being prepared sire, and will be ready to see you in only a few minutes.'

'Good.' The prince handed the baby back to Rhiannell, and as she left the room he said, 'The princess Gwenllian is my wife, Dewi.'

'I know that sire,' Dewi looked puzzled.

'Do you? I just wondered. You asked after her as if she were your own.'

Dewi's eyes fell. 'I am sorry if I presume sire. It is only that I have known the princess for many years, and her father...'

'I know, I know. Her father has appointed you her guard and protector.'

'That is my honour sire.'

There was a moment of silence, and then Prince Gruffudd said quietly. 'You do not have to protect her from me, Dewi ap Ifan.'

'Of course not sire.' Dewi lifted his head and their eyes met and held. 'But I may have to protect her from the places you may lead her.'

Their eyes still held, and neither would look away until a few moments later the goodwife entered with more ale to celebrate the good news.

King Henry seemed to be in what was for him, a benevolent mood. The arrival of the messenger from

Aberystwyth had changed the king's countenance from one of sullen forbearance and erratic flares of temper, to one of almost jovial camaraderie. Crinan watched as the messenger was dismissed with thanks and a gold coin, and as he observed the laughter and congratulation which followed, he recognised something else which lingered in the king's expression, something he had seen before, and which always made his flesh crawl. It was an edge of granite, of cunning and calculation which Crinan had learned to treat with due caution.

'We have them now!' The King observed with a smile. 'It seems the so called Prince of Deheubarth escaped, but not for long. His younger brother at least was slain, do we know if Prince Gruffudd was wounded?'

'I think not my lord.' A young squire came forward. 'I was not at Aberystwyth but was near Cydweli at the time. I was told that the Prince's wife, the Lady Gwenllian, who was residing in Cydweli with her entourage, had quitted the castle in haste to meet him at their mountain stronghold.'

'She was not at Aberystwyth?' the king asked. 'I understood she was some sort of she-dragon, who could ride and fight like a man ...'

'That is true my lord,' said the squire. 'But she was heavy with child and so was resting at Cydweli when Aberystwyth was attacked.'

'God spare me from warrior women!' said the King, to much laughter. 'I admire this Prince; he must have a great sense of duty to get him an heir on a warrior woman with a face like a horse!'

'Oh no, sire,' the young squire responded innocently. 'I am told the Princess Gwenllian has great beauty...at all events...long fair hair which she wears in a woven shank when she goes into battle...'

The King stared at him. Then his face broke into a

157

smile. 'At your age young sir, we all thought every woman was beautiful.' The group around him laughed and joined in the banter, until the Bishop Osbert, hovering nearby, suggested they should all give thanks to God for the great victory at Aberystwyth.

King Henry looked faintly irritated for a moment and then said, 'Of course, Bishop. Of course you are right. But not here and now, we must give our prayers full attention, especially on these important matters. Go you and make it the subject of tomorrow's worship, you will need time to prepare.'

The Bishop was quick to obey, and the King caught Crinan's eye. 'Is that other Welsh prince here?' he asked. 'Owen ap Cadwgan? I believe he is back from France is he not?'

'Indeed sire,' Crinan responded quickly. 'He has been awaiting an audience this last week...'

'Send him to me.' Crinan noticed that cunning look again, and as he moved along the corridor to find his quarry, he wondered idly what fate was in store for the young prince. Crinan did not really care, for he had heard that Owen ap Cadwgan was an arrogant fool, and was aware of his past history and of the abduction of the princess Nest, whom he remembered with such affection.

He came upon the prince in an ante-room, dozing in a chair.

'The King will see you now, sire,' he said.

Sir Gerald de Windsor was tired and irritated by the time he reached the inn just outside Winchester. He was wet and cold, the winter seemed to drag, and overall it had been an unlucky twelvemonth for weather, the grapes were poor abroad and the ale sour at home, and the price of wheat a scandal.

He reflected dryly that this was what his life had

become, he who had always been a soldier, now reduced to worrying about crops and weather. To be constable of Pembroke castle meant more responsibility than simply guarding Henry's interests. He was supposed to win the hearts of the Welsh people, and that was not easy. To be a soldier was a much more simple life, he decided, but then.... But then he had the Princess Nest for his wife, and so nothing else mattered.

He pulled up in the muddy courtyard of the inn, and looked around him cautiously. He had been here before; it was a place Henry often used as a meeting place when he was on the road. Sir Gerald knew immediately that the King was not here today however, and that he was not expected. There would have been much more activity if that had been the case. The message had seemed urgent however, so Sir Gerald gave quick instructions to his manservant, and entered the building.

Through the dark smoky atmosphere he could see that the place was not crowded, a few local farmers and tradesmen were drinking ale and the landlord approached quickly and bowed low. 'You are welcome my lord,' he lowered his voice. 'The King's messenger awaits you sire, through here, if you please.' He led the way through the low room and into a separate chamber. It held only a table and some rough seating, but there was a good fire, and heavy curtains to contain the draught. A man stood up. He was of average height and bearing, with long brown hair and direct blue eyes.

'Landlord, bring us your best wine and food for our guest.'

When the landlord had left he turned to Sir Gerald. 'You do not remember me sire, but I have seen you before, at King Henry's court. My name is Crinan, and I have orders for you direct from the King.'

Sir Gerald nodded. He removed his ring-mail shirt and

sat down wearily at the table. 'It is so long since I had specific orders I thought the King had forgotten me.'

Crinan smiled. 'The King forgets nothing, sire.'

'I am aware of that.'

The wine arrived, and Crinan poured it into tankards and they both drank deeply before any further conversation, content to relax and warm themselves. Crinan said, 'How goes Pembroke? We hear you do well there and all is fairly quiet?'

'I do my duty.' Sir Gerald replied. He decided he quite liked this young man. He smiled and said, 'The bard wrote a new song only last week for us, it says: *There is a woman in Pembroke who surpasses all the women of Wales, she has dark flowing hair, she is beautiful beyond all dreams and is skilled in many crafts... and all men who see her, sigh with longing...*'

Crinan laughed. 'Ah! The princess Nest, life at Pembroke must be fine indeed! I was privileged to serve the lady, and she taught me what Welsh I have.' He leaned towards Sir Gerald, 'You will be particularly pleased with your orders my lord. For the King has only two days ago given orders to your old rival, Prince Owen ap Cadwgan.'

Sir Gerald bridled at the name. 'That man was never my rival; he is simply a wild dog! I am ashamed that King Henry should have him in his employ! The man has no honour, he not only turned traitor to his own people, but...'

'I know sire, I know,' Crinan interrupted. 'I am well aware of your history, and that of the rebellious cur. The King tends to agree with you.'

'Then why does he employ him?'

'He is a good fighter, he did well in France, and his allegiance to King Henry kept Powys quiet for a time. But he has no loyalty to anyone except himself, and the

King is well aware of it. Nevertheless, he can be useful at this time.'

The door opened and a dish of steaming meat arrived with some coarse bread. Sir Gerald began to eat hungrily and then said, 'Tell me the plan.'

'You have no doubt heard of the defeat of the Welsh army at Aberystwyth?'

'Of course, my wife has been much upset. Her younger brother Hywel was killed.' Sir Gerald suddenly stopped eating, and then said slowly: 'You do not have orders for me to seek out the other brother, Prince Gruffudd, and kill him?'

'No indeed. Rest assured. The King understands your predicament, although of course he expects your loyalty...'

'He has it.' Sir Gerald was slightly relieved.

'Owen ap Cadwgan has that mission my lord. He is despatched already, and his orders are to seek out and destroy the remnants of the Deheubarth insurgence.' Crinan looked at Sir Gerald with a wry smile. 'The King easily persuaded him to do this duty with the offer of sufficient gold,' he said. 'It will not be a difficult task for Owen ap Cadwgan, he knows the terrain of those infernal mountains and has his own spies, he will soon find them out.'

'I do not doubt it,' said Sir Gerald. 'He will probably do it well and quickly, but I do not understand what the King requires of me?'

'When Owen ap Cadwgan has done his work, you and your men will arrive to strike from the south, ostensibly to assist him,' said Crinan. 'You will be a little late, and you need not be involved in killing Prince Gruffudd or his men, but in the confusion it would not be surprising if our enterprising young Owen lost his life also, would it?'

Sir Gerald started: 'You mean King Henry gives me

permission…?'

'He demands it of you. You may kill the vicious dog that you have such reason to hate. The King reminds you that this Owen ap Cadwgan is a thorn in his side as well as yours.'

Sir Gerald smiled, reflecting that it was not such a bad day after all, and Crinan refilled the wine tankards.

Crinan had been right about the intelligence available to Owen ap Cadwgan. Within a week he had ascertained that the remnants of Prince Gruffudd's army were at Cantref Mawr, and a day later at dusk he and his loyal Powys troops were surrounding the settlement. This was not an easy task, as most of the camp was within the woods, and as Owen was determined to mount a surprise attack, he gave orders that the whole area was to be encircled to make sure that this time the Prince of Deheubarth would not escape. The preparations were almost complete before anyone inside the camp was aware of the enemy's presence. Guards were necessarily thin now, and by the time one alert man had sounded the alarm, it was too late.

'We are surrounded sire,' cried Geraint, as he arrived at Prince Gruffudd's hut to find him pulling on his mail hauberk.

'Then we must fight!' Prince Gruff stormed his way out.

'It is too late, my lord! We have no chance; they have a ring around us.'

'Then here we must fight and die. Let us muster together in the centre to make a stand.'

'We are already doing that sire, but you must try to break out.' Geraint caught hold of Prince Gruff's horse which had been brought up quickly.

'No! I will not leave my men, few as we are...'

'Please sire! You are our Prince, if you are killed then all is lost for ever! You must survive! Also you can save many. If you are gone we can surrender and sue for our lives.'

At this Prince Gruff mounted, albeit reluctantly, and Geraint quickly marshalled a few trusted men as escort.

'Over there sire, on the western side of their ring! The undergrowth is thick and there are fewer Powys men there. It is a chance for you. I will mount the defence here.'

For a moment the dark eyes of Prince Gruffudd met the vivid blue of his trusted captain's gaze. He knew it was good advice.

'God bless you dear friend,' he said. Then, spinning his horse, he and his escort dashed towards the western edges of the ring of attackers, screaming their defiance in a tumult of whirling swords and axes, the outriders pushing the Powys men away just long enough for Prince Gruffudd and a few men to break through the ring and away. Then they turned, determined that none should follow, and fought like the patriots they were, and spears and axes clashed and rang out their deadly purpose, until the last man was down and their cries and their blood mingled with the oncoming darkness now creeping over Cantref Mawr. Among them lay Geraint, still handsome in death, his blue eyes open, regarding with an unswerving gaze the dark scudding clouds above.

When Owen ap Cadwgan learned that Prince Gruffudd ap Rhys was not among the dead he gave immediate vent to his fury. He did not intend to return to King Henry with his mission incomplete. He barked orders for the whole area to be put to the torch and for all dwellings to be destroyed, and a troop was summoned to follow the escaping Prince.

When the Norman contingent under Sir Gerald de Windsor arrived only minutes later, they were met by a confusion of burning and destruction which was still under way. Sir Gerald had told his men they were to deal with some 'Welsh insurgents,' and so on his order they set about their task with enthusiasm, as the Powys men reeled with surprise and dismay. As soon as Owen ap Cadwgan appeared from his hastily made tent, he was pierced by several arrows, three of which found their way into his neck, arm and his right leg.

Sir Gerald made his way quickly to the front of the melee, shouting to his men to desist. 'Stop fighting,' he shouted, 'There is some confusion here...'

'Indeed there is!' A Powys captain pushed his way forward. 'We did not know you were coming sire,' he said to Sir Gerald. 'The Deheubarth men are routed, and all are slain. We have already won the day and needed no help from you!'

'All are slain you say?' Sir Gerald picked his way towards him.

'All except the Prince Gruffudd sire. He escaped with a few men, not half a dozen. I was about to mount a troop to follow him...'

'Then do so man!' Sir Gerald said imperiously. 'Do not delay! I will clear the field here and then return to Pembroke. Quickly captain!'

'But sire, my lord is wounded and perhaps...'

'I will see to him.' Sir Gerald walked over to where Owen ap Cadwgan lay, bleeding but still alive. He turned to the captain. 'Hurry! I am senior officer here now! Do your duty! And take a good contingent with you.'

The captain hastened to obey, and after they rode out Sir Gerald bent down over Owen ap Cadwgan. 'At last, you dog...' he murmured. 'No hero's death for you.'

His axe came down efficiently, and it was the work of

a moment to castrate his prostrate victim. Owen was alive just long enough to choke on his own genitals as they were stuffed into his gasping mouth.

TEN
'HOMECOMING'
(1117 - 1127)

It was three months before Dewi could persuade Gwenllian to leave the farmhouse where she and her son Anarawd were still in hiding with her small band of helpers. News had come to them of the events at Cantref Mawr, and although Gwenllian knew that her husband had once more escaped with his life, she realised he was now in gravest danger, as he moved from one safe house to another to evade the Norman patrols which still hunted him.

During the intervening time, the Princess had sent messages to her mother at Aberffraw, begging her to intercede with her father and ask, for the sake of the child, that she be allowed to return home. Eventually permission arrived, and King Gruffudd even went so far as to send his daughter a personal message, in which he assured her, *'I will take no action against that headstrong prince, your husband, if he wishes to visit us here in Gwynedd, which is known for its hospitality.'*

'Come home Gwenllian,' Queen Angharad entreated in her own message, *'Come home and bring your beloved child to safety.'*

On the day Gwenllian left the remote farmhouse where Anarawd had been born, many tears were shed. The farmer's wife in particular, always so reserved and subservient, clung to the Princess like a leech, begging her to stay.

'I cannot, my dear friend,' said the princess, 'But I shall always remember your kindness to me, and I ask of you one last duty.'

'Anything, my lady.' The woman was tearful.

'I ask that you pray for me, and for my dear husband and family. You can do that in the quiet of your days when none shall see, and you cannot be blamed for it. I must put you and yours in danger no more.'

Then she rode out, dressed in the same battle clothing she saved from Cydweli, with Dewi at her side and her son, swaddled well to keep out the cold, carried close by Rhiannell, and followed by Olwen with Dewi's manservant.

They took little used back roads which were hardly more than cart tracks, and as they rode quietly through the glades of mighty oak and ash, with holly and thorn beneath, and saw the wild roe stare at them, knee deep in the long grass, and heard the pheasant call, it was as if the present time receded, and Dewi and Gwenllian remembered the days of long ago, when the world had been the woods and hills of Abergwyngregyn, where they had played and sung, before they had understood the ways of men. And in this pleasant lull Gwenllian thought of Meilyr the bard, and the songs he had sung in the great hall at home, and she felt a magical aura surround her, so that when Dewi stopped in a small clearing and said they would make camp for the night, she hardly knew where she was.

'Shall we be safe here, do you think?' she asked, as she dismounted.

Dewi smiled. 'Safer than if we tried to find shelter in some cottage or settlement,' he said. 'Who knows who may be loyal to us in this wild place? We are well armed, and will be a match for any who may have a grudge against us, I believe.'

'I am sure so, Dewi,' she said, and turned to take the child.

Two hours later they sat together near the fire, and Gwenllian reminded Dewi of the songs of Meilyr which had run through her mind that day. They sang but a few lays together, because the words eluded them, but became mellow in the attempt, and Gwenllian remarked upon it.

'I have not seen you smile much, Dewi ap Ifan, not since we left Cydweli.'

'That is true,' he admitted. 'Except for the day Anarawd was born. But the smell of Rhiannell's good soup has lightened my spirits.'

Gwenllian smiled. 'There is a spit of pheasant and partridge, and larks and buntings too, I'm sure I could forswear all French cooks if Rhiannell would only cook for us forever.' She became pensive. 'It has been a tragic time for us all,' she said, 'Apart from the birth of my son. And I am aware you would rather have been with my husband at Aberystwyth than playing nursemaid to me.'

'You are wrong,' Dewi said. 'I do not hunger for battles which are not my business.' He saw her dark look at this and added, 'Your husband is a brave man and I have always wished him well. I would he had been successful, and regained his lands and driven the invaders from Deheubarth, but it was always impossible. He tried valiantly and he failed, as your father always predicted.'

'But he raised a great army! All Wales was ready to support him...'

'Yes, and where are all those loyal souls now?'

They both fell silent; it was carnage too great to think upon. Eventually Dewi said, 'And this young husband, your gallant prince, do you love him still, my lady?'

Her answer was a little too quick. 'Of course!'

'And as for me? Do you still love me also?'

She blushed at this and then said again, 'Of course. But differently. You are my friend.'

He gave a short laugh. 'That man has given you nothing but hard living and tragedy. He has destroyed your easy life, and taken many other women, and yet you still love him.'

She raised her head defiantly. 'He is my husband, and he has given me my son.'

Dewi looked suitably penitent. 'I'm sorry, my lady.'

Gwenllian leaned over and took his hand. 'My dear Dewi, you have given me everything it is possible to give, ever since I can remember, and I have given you nothing in return.'

Dewi's eyes burned. 'That is not true my lady, you have given me my most precious possession.'

'And what can that be?' she questioned.

'You have given me the vision of a truly noble woman.'

Two days later they arrived at Aberffraw, to be met with rejoicing from the inhabitants, who streamed out from the gates of the settlement to meet them as they approached.

Gwenllian had never complained about living in the open, as she had done for most of the time since she left Aberffraw, but she had dreamed. She had dreamed of warm baths, and warm food, and warm wash cloths and warm footcloths and warm stones in her bed and the warmth of her mother's embrace, and now, at last, it was all there. The child was soothed and sighed over, and even her father welcomed her when he came to dinner in the great hall, and called for Meilyr to sing a song of welcome for her and the child. This the bard did, and very sweetly, but there was a pathos in his voice which was not there before, and at dinner there was no talk at all of the recent events at Aberystwyth and Cantref Mawr. At last Owain, as handsome and full of wit as ever, could stand it no longer, and said loudly: 'And when, my dear sister, may we expect your husband here? We have heard much of his exploits and have spent many a merry hour discussing his battles and his campaign, we should like to hear more from his own lips…'

Gwenllian glanced quickly at her father, who had paused in the act of raising his drinking vessel. He said nothing however, and Gwenllian answered, 'Unfortunately brother, there is a price on his head and he moves from place to place, so I have no knowledge of his whereabouts.'

'And if you had, you would not tell us, would you?' The King had joined the conversation. 'I understand my dear child. Owain is right, we have watched his campaign and have been thrilled by his success, at one time I almost thought he could do it.' His voice softened. 'You should never imagine Gwenllian, that we were not with him in spirit. But I could not join or support him, and I was right in that. We have prospered here at Aberffraw, because at last King Henry leaves us alone to live out our lives as we must. Of course, he exacts heavy tribute, but it is not so much that we cannot survive and prosper, as long as the harvests are good.'

'But you are still his lackeys are you not?' Gwenllian could not help saying.

The king smiled. 'I'm sure you will see us as that, and there is some truth in it. But as long as we keep the peace we are left alone, and at least Aberffraw stands and prospers. It is a good bargain for Henry and for Gwynedd. Both have peace and some income from the arrangement.'

'Very sensible sire.' Gwenllian's remark was sarcastic in tone, and yet if she was honest she had to admit her father had a point. She was troubled that her father seemed to have lost that fighting spirit for which he was renowned, and speculated that his policy was that of advancing age, when a quiet life seemed more important than the defence of principle.

The King was not finished. 'Your husband is now in a perilous position,' he said, 'And if he would agree to calm matters I might be able to intercede with Henry on his behalf...'

'What do you mean sire?' Owain asked.

'I mean,' said the King, 'That if he would perhaps write to Henry, stating that it is all over, and that he gives up his claim to Deheubarth...'

'That he will never do!' Gwenllian burst in hotly.

'As I was saying....' The King continued with a sharp look in his daughter's direction, 'Should Prince Gruff promise to never again raise a sword against King Henry, in exchange for his life and a pardon, the King may possibly agree. I have said he prefers a quiet life, and if that was the outcome I could welcome your husband here openly, and you could both live here with your children, and he could provide his family with a good life.' He drank deeply from his cup, and then continued, 'With matters as they are, he can provide you all with nothing but early death.'

The room was quiet. Queen Angharad had a look of pure anguish on her face, and Owain remained silent, looking grave. Even the serving women paused in their activity, aware that something of import was happening. Gwenllian stared fixedly at her plate, but did not know how to respond. Eventually Owain said, 'You have asserted your right as King to determine this matter for Gwynedd father, and you cannot therefore deny Prince Gruff the right to determine his own position for Deheubarth.'

'Of course,' the King replied, 'But I fear he has no sense, and will choose the wrong path.'

'And is the path of honour and principle the wrong path then, father?' Owain rejoined. 'If Gwynedd had been overrun and its lands dispersed to Henry's friends, would you give up the struggle?'

The King's voice was sharp. 'It would depend on the price to be paid. How many lives to be lost, with little hope of success?' His made a conscious effort to moderate his tone. 'Of course I should not want to give up, but sometimes one has to know when the battle is lost.'

'The battle will never be lost as long as my husband and I live!' Gwenllian's strong voice rose clearly across the table. 'You may be right father, we may not be able to win, but we shall never stop trying. To give up the fight for Deheubarth is to give up life itself!'

'Exactly what I was saying, daughter.' And with this retort, the King rose and departed for his gaming table.

It was only two days after this conversation that word was received from Prince Gruffudd to say that he was safe but still in hiding. Even the messenger who brought his letter had no idea of the Prince's whereabouts. The Prince warned that Gwenllian should not expect to see him for some considerable time. *I need time to rebuild the army of Deheubarth and to recover from our grievous losses,* he wrote. *I charge you to care for my son, and to protect him and teach him about his father and the Deheubarth lands. When I shall see you dear wife, I know not.*

Gwenllian read and re-read the message. She felt useless and frustrated, as she had done at the time of her pregnancy. It seemed a long time now since she had ridden out at the head of a column from Cantref Mawr to wreak havoc on a Norman patrol or stronghold. She realised she was in danger of sinking into a despondent lethargy which was alien to her nature, and so she sought out Dewi.

'I have done little since the birth of my child,' she told

him. 'I am becoming plump and will become useless in battle if I do not practise regularly. Will you help me?'

'To become well and fit? Of course.' Dewi responded, smiling. 'Although I think the extra flesh suits you very well.'

'We shall see if I can still send an arrow to the target,' Gwenllian said. 'And swordsmanship too, and the spear and axe also....'

Dewi frowned. 'As you know my lady, I have never felt entirely happy about...'

'You were not born to be happy Dewi,' she said pertly. 'Just to obey.'

And because she smiled with her eyes when she said it, and because she was his Lady, he obeyed.

It took a matter of three months only until Gwenllian was restored to her former prowess. Her brothers were amazed at the degree of skill which she now possessed. It had always been so, but now there was added a strength which had been built from the privations of life in the mountains, and which seemed to give their sister a hard edge of power which, combined with the agility which had always been hers, made her into a formidable opponent.

'I should think twice before taking her on in single combat,' said Cadwallon, after one of their practice sessions. He rubbed his arm, where Gwenllian had landed a clout.

'I don't know whether I am pleased or not,' said Owain, watching Gwenllian as she wandered away to talk to Dewi. 'She can give a good account of herself, certainly, but because she is so good she is more likely to be in the fight, and in the thick of it.'

'You cannot protect her brother,' said Cadwallon. 'For she is headstrong and will always follow her own

173

desires. She seems to have no fear of anything.'

'That is true,' said Owain, smiling. 'I only thank our dear Lord that our other sisters are married and lack the disposition to be warriors.'

As Gwenllian approached Dewi she was feeling restless. Even after the practice session with her brothers she had a feeling of unease, as if she was waiting for something to happen but was not quite sure what. Perhaps it was the beautiful spring day, she surmised. It was early March and the lambs were jumping around the pens and in the mud which covered the compound.

'Dewi?' She said, watching as he removed his mailcoat. 'Will you come walking with me?'

'Walking?' he said, as if she was mad.

'Riding then. To Abergwyngregyn, where we used to play. I have a longing to see the waterfall again, and to gather some February fair maids. I have a fancy to put some in my hair tonight, and they will be gone soon.'

He made a pained face. 'Are you not tired my lady?'

'Not at all. Oh, please Dewi! You know I'm not allowed to go alone. We can stay overnight and come back tomorrow. Do you not recall how we used to gather fair maids when we were children?'

Dewi sighed. 'Indeed my lady, how could I forget? You made me carry them home and all my friends made mock of me for it.'

'I promise you shall not carry a single one today. Let me fetch a basket.' She ran off, leaving him to remove the rest of his outer leather clothing and some of the mud from his shoes.

When she came back they set off together and enjoyed the ride and the ferry crossing over the Menai estuary. The countryside was emerging from its winter sleep, responding to the warm spring sunshine, and everywhere the signs of hope and rebirth lifted their spirits. When they arrived at Abergwyngregyn, they left the horses at the palace and walked up along their old route, until they finally reached the waterfall, which leapt down through the trees in full spate. They drank their fill of the pure sweet water, and then Gwenllian spent a happy hour gathering the white nodding flowers, which grew as thickly as a carpet, and came every year in February to herald the arrival of Spring. Dewi leaned against a tree and watched her, she seemed so unlike the young warrior in battle armour who only a few hours ago had almost unseated Cadwallon from his horse, and who could fight like any trained warrior with her practice sword swirling about her as if it were light as a feather.

She approached him now, holding the basket out with delight. 'See Dewi, are they not beautiful?'

'Not so beautiful as she who holds them.'

She blushed at this, and then said softly. 'Oh Dewi, my dearest friend.'

He turned away, and she saw him raise his clenched fists and ram the flesh into the tree bark, over and over, his eyes closed, his mouth set.

She stood awhile, and then set down the basket, unsure what to do. After a moment she went to him and gently turned him to face her. He would not meet her eyes, and so she put her hands on his cheeks and raised his head. As he met her look, she saw in his eyes the intensity of smouldering love which had endured so much, suffered so much, and received so little in return. She caressed his dear face, and traced the line of his lips with her finger.

'Kiss me, my dearest,' she said.

He hesitated a moment only, as the look of love became desire, and he murmured 'You are my heart's special love, and always will be.' And then he kissed her with a gentle longing, and their lips moved together to enclose and pursue, and the long awaited expression of their desire filled them until they knew what had to be.

In their lovemaking Dewi found there were things he could do which an hour ago he did not even realise that he knew. They seemed to come to him from somewhere deep within, and he took infinite care in the execution of them, in the slow and passionate caresses he bestowed on this woman who seemed so fragile and delicate, but whom he knew to be made of truth, duty and strength. And Gwenllian, who had always only been taken as a possession by her husband, who had borne him a child without knowing real passion, was awakened by her new lover to a world which was full of sensual pleasure and longing, until she thought she would die for the joy of it, and afterwards they lay together and laughed at the canopy of trees above them, and then at the world and then at themselves.

During the next week, love was all around them and inside them and everywhere they looked, or travelled, or even thought. Dewi felt his life had begun at last, the years flew from his shoulders and he was a young man again. For her part, Gwenllian was almost living within a reverie, a dream of calm and peaceful contentment enclosed by a wall of safety, and although they were careful to keep their secret from prying eyes, she and Dewi took every opportunity they could to be alone together. At any other place and with any other man this would have been impossible, but everyone at Aberffraw knew of their long friendship, and that Dewi ap Ifan was the Princess Gwenllian's lifetime guard. Their lovemaking continued to amaze and delight them both, and each found sublime refreshment in the other.

Sometimes Gwenllian thought of her husband, living in the privation of the mountains and the wild wood with his few followers. At these times she felt no guilt, for how could she feel guilty about the revelation of love which she was enjoying, and which made her feel that life was worth living after all? Rather, she felt a piquant mixture of sadness and pity that her dear husband, the Prince who had tried for all and lost so much, should be so cast down. She had heard from him by the good offices of a priest, who was travelling from his own church to attend further instruction at Bangor. The priest brought the news that the Prince and his men were alive but exhausted after the harsh winter, and would try to attend at Aberffraw for a short recuperation if they were sure of a welcome. Gwenllian was somewhat humbled and grateful when her father replied that the Prince of Deheubarth was always welcome in the house of Gwynedd, as long as the visit was made in secret. Gwenllian also sent word with the priest to urge her husband to seek shelter with them, and to assure him that Anarawd was thriving.

Two weeks later the lovers were enjoying the Spring sunshine on the mountainside at Abergwyngregyn where they had so often climbed as children. Satisfied and self indulgent, they lay on their backs and watched a curlew ride the wind above them, listening to its plaintive cry.

'I can recall,' said Gwenllian, 'When my father talked to me of the curlew when I was a child. He showed me how to know it by its long curving bill, and said that its cry was a cry of mourning, a cry of heartbreak.'

'I think I remember that day,' Dewi said. 'It was when we were celebrating something, I don't recall what.' He laughed. 'We should remember it. There were not many such days.'

'Of celebration? No, I suppose not.'

'I meant more that there were not many days when your father even spoke to us when we were children.'

'He did what he could,' Gwenllian said defensively. 'When he was here.'

'Exactly,' said Dewi. 'I suppose I resented it because whenever the King was away he took my father with him.'

'And so we were both deprived of our father's attention.' She laughed, and then became serious. 'I am glad that he will welcome my husband, as long as he comes here secretly.' She turned on to her side and traced her finger gently down Dewi's face. 'Is that a problem for you?' she said softly. 'What shall you do if my husband comes to claim me?'

'What can I do? He is your husband.' Dewi's face became set, that look of stoic obstinacy Gwenllian knew so well. He glanced at her and then said: 'whoever you love, all of you and yours, I must perforce also love. I would never do your husband any harm or wish him any ill.'

'Do you not think you have done him harm already? By becoming my lover?'

'Not so much as he has harmed you. He has so many women...'

'But it is not the same for me,' said Gwenllian. 'The rules are different. He is allowed as many concubines or slaves as he wishes, but for his wife there is no forgiveness, unless of course he is killed and I should be taken as a war prize.'

'That you will never be while I live,' said Dewi. 'And as for forgiveness, does not our Lord speak of forgiveness for the woman taken in adultery?'

'Indeed, but what is said in the pulpit stays there, within the Church. The teachings do not often seem to change men's behaviour.'

'No they do not,' said Dewi, pulling her close. 'And that is why they do not change mine, at least where you are concerned.' And as a tired blade, when tempered over and over, will regain its lustre, so Dewi ap Ifan regained

178

the demanding fire which had nothing to do with his Welsh blood, but only with the closeness of this woman, his inspiration and his life.

When they returned next day to the settlement at Aberffraw, Rhiannell ran to meet Gwenllian at the gate. 'Come, my lady,' she said. 'There is good news! Our dear Prince is here and awaits you!'

As she watched the colour drain from her mistress's face, and saw the look that passed between her and Dewi ap Ifan, Rhiannell wondered if it was really good news after all.

Late that evening, Gwenllian lay awake in the big bed which she now shared with her husband. She turned softly so as not to wake him, so she might more closely examine him now he was asleep. She had been shocked at the first sight of him, although he had already bathed when she entered the bedchamber. He had become thin and haggard, with dark lines etched under his eyes and a look of bone weariness which seemed to bow him down, diminish his spirit as well as his body. Now tears sprang to her eyes as she saw how the last months had used him. He had explained that although his supporters had been kind and welcoming, the winter had been hard and they had barely enough to feed themselves, never mind a hungry guest and his men.

'If it had not been for the little money Nest managed to send me, we might have starved,' he told Gwenllian. 'But it was difficult. I had to keep on the move, a few days in one cottage and I felt I had to go, so as not to be a burden on them.'

'You are safe now,' she soothed, 'We shall build up your strength, and Spring is here and the warmth will help.'

'Your father is more than kind,' Prince Gruff said. 'I

cannot tell you how wonderful it is to be here and have hot water and to sleep in a clean bed and decent food. I would have slept in the stable if your father wanted it.'

'My father has always wished you well,' Gwenllian said.

'Except when he wanted to kill me.' Gruff answered pointedly.

'That is all over now, it was a bad time when he had to put Aberffraw and his people first,' Gwenllian said. 'King Henry has not bothered him these many months; we pay heavy tribute and keep the peace, so he lets us alone.'

'He does not let me alone,' said Prince Gruff bitterly, 'There have been patrols looking for us all winter. He has taken Hywel, you would think that would be enough for him!'

'Perhaps it would,' said Gwenllian softly. 'If you would give up your claim to the Deheubarth lands and agree to live here peacefully with us.'

'Never!' His answer was immediate and vehement. 'You must never even think it! Do you not understand? It would be a betrayal of my father's memory and I shall never do that. As long as I live I must fight for Deheubarth.'

'Of course I understand,' Gwenllian assured him, 'And I shall always stand with you, and fight for Deheubarth to my last breath. I am only telling you what my father believes. He thinks he might persuade Henry to pardon you in those circumstances.'

'Pardon me? I accept no pardon from that usurper!' In spite of his tiredness the Prince responded in quick temper, and when Gwenllian saw the spark in his eyes ignite, she knew the argument was hopeless. Now, as she watched him sleep, she felt only sorrow and understanding of his plight. To give up the struggle for his lands would be a betrayal of all he had ever known.

He would live to fight another day and she would be there beside him. Her life was bound to his by duty and birth, and she would not let him down. She thought briefly of Dewi ap Ifan, and his hard set expression at dinner, when they had all listened to Prince Gruff tell of his experiences after the escape from Cantref Mawr. He had not been able to meet her eyes, and she knew his feelings.

Her husband had taken her as soon as she had entered the bedchamber, in his usual quick and demanding manner, and then had said, 'I am sorry wife, I had need of you, and there are few women to give me pleasure these days.'

'You have suffered then,' Gwenllian said.

'I said I am sorry, I had no time for your enjoyment, and I can do nothing about it now, for in this bed I am sure sleep will carry me to the grave, and last until morning.'

It was true, he was sleeping as if dead. Gwenllian turned and tried to sleep herself. No matter what, she would do her duty, and she knew that Dewi ap Ifan would do his. And in a few weeks, it would be time for her small family to return to the mountains again, and Dewi would be left behind at Aberffraw, to carry out his duties as captain of the guard.

ELEVEN
'HIDE AND SEEK'

Prince Gruffudd ap Rhys returned from hunting to the small camp which had been home for the last week. He had a hare and two birds and several rabbits, which he slung down at the feet of Rhiannell ,who was teaching the children some silliness with acorns. He had been hunting on foot so as to spare his horse, which had developed some kind of abscess on its front foreleg. He glanced briefly at Rhiannell, and wondered, not for the first time, if they could ever survive without her. He walked back towards her.

'Are my sons behaving themselves well for you, Rhiannell?'

She blushed profusely. 'Oh yes, my lord. They are good boys.' She smiled proudly at four year old Anarawd, and the chubby Morgan, who was now almost three years old. Both the boys had become tongue tied in the presence of their father, and Morgan hid behind Rhiannell's broad frame, while Anarawd stared with wide eyes which threatened tears any moment.

'Yes, of course they are good boys,' Prince Gruff said, smiling. He put out his hand and ruffled Anarawd's hair, and the child began to relax. Prince Gruff stayed a moment longer, and said, 'Rhiannell, I want you to know that I understand how much you do for us. The boys love you and you work so hard for us, we are in your debt. The princess could not manage without you.'

Rhiannell could not reply for a moment, she was so astonished at these words. Then she said, 'It is my delight and my duty sire.'

'Yes,' said the prince. 'But when...when we come to our lands and our inheritance in Deheubarth, you shall not be forgotten, Rhiannell. We shall remember those who have been with us in this time.' His voice was so quiet that she could hardly hear his words, and his look was downcast. But he raised his head and smiled, and then said lightly, 'Where is the youngest one, my little Maelgwn? With his mother I expect?'

Rhiannell laughed. 'Yes sire. A young woman came from the settlement below with some fresh milk for the little one. The mistress is giving it to him now, and I believe there will be some for these two also, when it is their bedtime.'

'That was kind.' The prince looked down the mountainside towards the miserable settlement from whence bounty had been bestowed upon himself and his family. 'They are good people, and I think we are fairly safe here.' He made an effort to rid his mind of the depressing truth and said, 'Did you have a chance to look at my horse?'

'Yes sire, I have put a poultice of herbs upon his leg. It is a good mixture which works well for men when wounds need cleaning after battle. I do not see why it should not work on horses also.'

'Thank you,' said the prince, taking the children by the hand. 'Now come along, my two brave young kinsmen, and see your mother. We must leave Rhiannell to prepare the dinner.'

Inside their hut Gwenllian was feeding the babe on her lap, and he was sucking greedily at the milky rag which transferred the goodness to his mouth. The two small boys ran to their mother, and Prince Gruffudd kneeled down to watch.

'You did not tell me your milk had failed,' he said eventually. 'We could have found a wet nurse.'

'It has been gone a week or more,' she answered. 'And there is no wet nurse to be had up here.'

'I will do something! I will not see my sons die from lack of nourishment!' The prince's frustration showed in his tone, this was more than he could countenance. He was a man of action, but hunger was not an enemy he could cut down with a sword or spear. He had never, in his life, been reduced to such circumstances. He paced the small hut.

'I have not complained, my husband,' said Gwenllian calmly.

'I know you have not!' Prince Gruff retorted. 'You would seem happy to let them die!'

In a second he was contrite, seeing the look of disbelief on her face. 'I am sorry dearest wife, that was not true and I should not have said it.'

'No, you should not.' Her tone was quiet, but her face remained stony.

'Perhaps...perhaps the answer might be to send my sons to Nest. She will take care of them and they are, after all, the sons of Deheubarth...'

'It is because of their birth, that they will not be allowed to live if we send them there!' Gwenllian raised her voice now, she was becoming angry. 'Do you think Henry will allow them to live if he knows they are at Pembroke? If we must send them away, they must go to Aberffraw...'

'Again? It is but four months since we were there for your birth time.'

'Yes, and we are always welcome there, and always will be.'

Prince Gruffudd bit his lip. 'I know...I know. Your family have been more than generous, and to be honest I know we have only survived these last winters because we were able to take rest there, and to build up our strength.' He stooped down, and ran his finger gently over little Maelgwn's head, as he continued to suck noisily at the rag. 'My sons are my pride Gwenllian, and you and our dear ones have given me much joy. You are a wife without equal, and I give you my thanks.'

Her face softened a little at this, and he continued: 'Aberffraw is our refuge when life becomes unsustainable for the boys here. When they are at Aberffraw they enjoy the company of their grandparents and your brothers and Dewi, but it is not their true home. Deheubarth is their home, and their inheritance, and if they do not spend time there how will they come to know it?'

'If they do come to know it, my lord, it will be the last thing they know.' Gwenllian ran the last of the milk down a corn stalk and into the babe's mouth drop by drop. She held the child up so that Anarawd and Morgan could see him, and they came close, and little Morgan must have the babe clasp his finger, bringing a smile to his parents faces.

Gwenllian smiled at her husband. 'Let them be sire, let them be for this time when they are so small. They will be true warriors for Deheubarth, and so shall I, but not yet. You have to be patient, and enjoy watching them grow.'

'I fear for them,' Prince Gruff said. 'This is not the life my sons should have...'

He was interrupted by the arrival of a messenger. For a moment the Prince thought it was a warning, for on many occasions a follower who had sworn undying loyalty to their cause, would be lured by the promise of the substantial bounty which Henry had placed on the royal heads, and they would have to move fast. This time however, it was merely news. Apparently in Powys, Maredudd ap Bleddyn, the uncle of the late Owen ap Cadwgan, had joined up with Owen's three brothers, and intended open revolt against King Henry. They had let it be known that Prince Gruffudd ap Rhys would be welcome if he wished to join them. Late into the night

Prince Gruff sat with the messenger, who had gleaned the information from several churches in the area, where local people could at least gather each Sunday and talk without persecution. Prince Gruffudd was able to discuss in detail exactly what was proposed, and who had joined the revolt, and Gwenllian smiled gently as she watched him, realising that any activity for her husband, even if it was only a discussion of strategy, brought him welcome relief from the drudgery of these days in the mountains, as indeed it did for her too.

When he eventually joined her in their bracken bed, Gwenllian said immediately, 'What is it to be my lord? Shall you join Maredudd and Powys against Henry?'

'I shall not, my lady.'

'I thank God for it.' Gwenllian felt she could breathe again. 'I did not wish to speak about it, but I hoped that you would not join him.'

'I can hardly imagine anyone thought I would,' said Prince Gruff. 'The revolt is surely to avenge that fool his nephew Owen, and Maredudd seems to have conveniently forgotten that Owen tried to kill me and almost succeeded. Not only that, but he torched our settlement and killed over half my men. Do they really think I would join with them after that?'

'It is strange,' said Gwenllian, 'That it was your sister's husband who finally killed Owen. They were supposed to be on the same side.'

'I heard he was pierced by arrows in the confusion of that day,' said Prince Gruff. 'The Norman soldiers obviously mistook him for us.'

'Yes,' Gwenllian agreed dryly, 'And I suppose the fact that he had kidnapped Nest for several years had nothing to do with Sir Gerald's revenge?'

Prince Gruff smiled. 'I do not blame him for what he did,' he said. 'I would do the same if any man ever took you.'

'Would you?' Gwenllian said quietly. 'Would you really do that to any suitor of mine?'

Gruff laughed. 'He would be a brave man who would attempt it,' he said. 'You would probably slit his throat!' He turned to face her. 'Anyway, if it happened he would not be a suitor would he? You would never allow that, and so he would be taking you by force, and would deserve all he got. Unless of course,' he mused, 'I was already dead, and the victor therefore had some rights in the matter. Even so, I trust he would behave with honour as befits your birth, and would marry you when he could.'

'Such things are not to be thought of,' murmured Gwenllian, moving to safer ground. 'I am sure my father will not help Maredudd either. If he would not help you, he certainly will not help them.'

'Your father is too astute to help anyone other than himself and Aberffraw,' said Prince Gruff, and rolled over onto his side, indicating his intention to sleep.

The planned revolt by Maredudd and his nephews went ahead without the support of either Prince Gruffudd, who remained in hiding, or the King of Gwynedd, who kept his council quietly at Aberffraw. There were some early small victories by the rebels, not decisive, but enough of an affront to King Henry that very soon he appeared in Powys at the head of a mighty force. Expecting this, and knowing their numbers could never match the Norman army, Maredudd had planned carefully to seize the initiative by one great stroke, nothing less than the assassination of the Norman king. To this end he positioned a large group of his best bowmen within the trees adjacent to the route, and then admonished them to 'unleash Hell's missiles upon his person' as Henry approached.

It was a fine morning, and as King Henry's column came into sight, the hidden bowmen could easily see their target, as he rode behind his banner, surrounded by a large guard. The hail of arrows was so heavy and so accurate that the rebels almost succeeded. Several of the guard were killed or injured, and Henry was only saved by his breastplate, which was actually punctured over his heart, but not completely pierced.

Shocked by the closeness of this attack, Henry immediately retreated to a safer place, and as soon as he reached his campaign tent he sent for Sir Gerald de Windsor, whom he had insisted accompany him on this, his second foray into Wales.

'What think you now of your beloved Welshmen?' King Henry shouted as soon as Sir Gerald entered. He spread his arms as his breastplate was removed. 'Look at this!' He indicated the dent in the breastplate. 'Any one of them will kill me if they can! They have no loyalty whatsoever!'

'Oh sire!' Sir Gerald looked shaken. 'We must give thanks to the Lord for your safe deliverance...'

'Thanks be damned!' King Henry flung himself into a chair. He took a swig from a goblet which was handed to him by his body slave. It seemed to calm him somewhat.

'Yes,' he said testily. 'We must give thanks.' He motioned to the body slave. 'Send Father James to me,' he said. He took another swallow at the goblet, and picked up the breastplate. 'We must give thanks to the Lord, Sir Gerald, and to my good London silversmith, what think you?'

'Yes sire, the armour is a good piece of work.'

The king fondled the breastplate again, the events of the morning had unsettled him considerably. Then he drew in a deep breath and said, 'What now then Sir

Gerald, can we take these rebels?'

'Indeed we can sire, their numbers are not enough to worry us, although they can inflict some damage. I just wonder…'

'What?'

'I'm thinking of the ultimate outcome sire. If we fight them we shall win, but what shall we win? There will be many dead, some of ours but mostly theirs, and a province of muddy marshes and miserable mountains which will yield nothing for years. Whereas…'

'What?' said King Henry again.

'If we offer them a way out? They know they cannot win the battle. Offer them tribute or death. No-one wants to die sire. They will accept, and then they will be in debt to your pleasure…'

King Henry let out a loud guffaw. 'God's Blood Gerald! You are right! I will set the tribute at much more than they can hope to pay, something really fanciful… five thousand cattle perhaps…no, ten thousand…!'

'But sire, they cannot…'

'Of course! Exactly! When they say they cannot pay I shall say 'Pay tribute or die…' His tone changed and became gentle, persuasive. 'And then I shall show mercy and allow time to pay…so much a year for the next ten years…they will be in debt to me for ever…and I shall have the tribute and their indebtedness, which will keep them quiet and the land productive.'

Sir Gerald winced, but he only said, 'Of course sire,' as the King sent for his Captain of the guard and arranged for a message to be taken to the rebels. Then he poured more wine for himself and a glass for Sir Gerald. He handed him the goblet. 'Sir Gerald, it is good to have you here. You have the measure of these Welshmen.'

Sir Gerald took a sip. 'It is interesting sire, that neither King Gruffudd of Gwynedd or the Prince of Deheubarth allied themselves to this latest uprising.'

'Yes. I knew King Gruffudd would not assist them, he is too wise and knows he cannot best me. But I did think that perhaps that young Prince from Deheubarth might join Maredudd...'

'Apparently not sire, it is said he has no liking for that family. Also, he is no threat now, he has no army and his brother was killed at Aberystwyth.' Sir Gerald took a deep breath, but then pressed on gently, 'It might clear up matters if we withdrew the bounty on his head, he is hardly worth the bother now, or the expense...'

'Of course!' The King's eyes glittered cynically. 'I recall there is a blood relationship...your wife Nest... ah!' The King smiled in reminiscence. 'The lovely Nest! She is his sister is she not?'

'Indeed sire, you know that she is...'

'And you are so enamoured of her you will plead for that young reprobate...?'

'No sire!' Sir Gerald remonstrated and then began to smile. 'I agree that it would help my marriage if I could assure the Princess Nest that her brother was safe, you are right about that. But I was thinking of wider concerns...'

'Are there any?'

'Perhaps not very important ones. But do you recall that young Prince Gruff is married to one of the daughters of King Gruffudd, the princess Gwenllian? I know your actions have led the king to swear fealty and to raise much in tribute. The peace works well in that area now. The King of Gwynedd is bound to be worried about his daughter, apparently they live hand to mouth in these infernal mountains, it must be a terrible life...'

'So?'

'If you were to remove the price on their heads, in return for them agreeing to keep the peace, the King of

Gwynedd will be even more grateful to you. He could even become supportive, and I know you value the tribute from that region.' Sir Gerald raised his glass. 'Long may it continue.'

King Henry stared at him coldly. Then he said, 'They would have to live openly where we could find them easily if we wished.'

'Of course sire, that wouldn't be a problem.'

'They would live in an area we control.'

Sir Gerald nodded. 'Of course.'

King Henry glared. 'The prince would have to swear not to make any further acts of violence towards the Crown.'

'He is broken, I'm think he will do that sire.'

King Henry continued to ponder as Sir Gerald held his breath. Suddenly Father James entered the tent. 'You need me for prayers sire?'

King Henry nodded. He turned to Sir Gerald. 'Nest may have her brother safe under those conditions,' he said. Then his face broke into a smile. 'On your knees now Sir Gerald. You must pray with me, for I have had a blessed deliverance this day.'

And Sir Gerald sank to his knees, and thanked the Lord for his own deliverance also.

A week later Sir Gerald de Windsor left his horse with his captain of escort, deciding to trudge the last mile on foot, up towards the border of trees which fringed the hillside. Although he wore body armour, he had discarded his helmet and any signs which might distinguish him as a Norman soldier. The directions received from Nest's uncle Rhydderch had brought him to a God forsaken place, he reflected. He stopped and surveyed the forest ahead, how could a royal Prince and his family live a proper life in there? What kind of people must they be?

He had never met the Prince of Deheubarth or his Lady Gwenllian, as when they had been at Pembroke he had made sure he did not know about it.

I must be mad, he thought to himself. *The Prince will no doubt want to kill me on sight, and here am I walking towards him, with only my dear wife's name to shield me. I hope to the Lord that he loves his sister as much as she seems to care for him!*

He began to walk again, and became aware that he was being watched. The hair prickled on his neck but he strode on openly, until the feeling became reality and he saw two small and sturdy men, both long haired and in filthy rags, emerge from the edge of the trees to confront him. They held axes, and raised them in readiness.

He stopped and smiled. 'It is a fine day,' he said.

Their lowering brows gave their answer. They raised their axes further. Sir Gerald said, 'I am come to see Prince Gruffudd, I have a message from his sister, the princess Nest.'

The axes lowered slightly. He was not sure if they had understood him. Then suddenly one of the men gave out a great cry. It was like the howl of a wolf, and rang eerily through the air and into the forest like a warning battle cry. Sir Gerald froze. The men did not move, but continued to stare at him, axes at the ready.

Sir Gerald sat down upon the grass, trying to show that he had no bad intent, and within a few minutes the men were joined by another. This one was a little taller and cleaner than the wild creatures, but still he approached with suspicion. Sir Gerald repeated his credentials, but the man said quickly, 'How do I know who you are? Obviously you are a gentleman, but that does not signify in these times.'

'I will give my sword into your hands,' said Sir Gerald, taking it gently from its sheath and offering it to the man hilt first.

The man did not take the sword. 'It is not fitting for me to take this sword,' he said. 'I am Idris, the Prince's manservant. I will trust you and take you to him, for I see you are alone.'

Within ten minutes the manservant had led Sir Gerald into a clearing, with the two mountain men following behind. Not knowing what to expect, Sir Gerald was horrified to see a man almost as ragged and unkempt as the others, emerge from a roughly built hut and announce that he was the IPrince of Deheubarth.

Sir Gerald stared, *surely this could not be his brother-in law?* He said, 'I have come to see the Prince of Deheubarth, and I will have no conversation with any other. Take me to him now, if you please.'

The man stared back, and Sir Gerald thought he saw a faint flush develop beneath the dirt of his features. After a moment he said: 'I am Deheubarth, and I know you sire, you are Sir Gerald de Windsor, and married to my sister Nest. I had never thought to meet you in person, except perhaps on the end of a sword tip.'

A hint of venom had crept into his voice, and Sir Gerald said quickly. 'I am sorry I did not know you my lord, but you will see I am here alone, and bring a message from your sister.'

'Is she well?' Sir Gerald did not miss the hint of anxiety in the question.

'She is well, and sends you and your family her best love and affection.' Seeing the Prince relax, Sir Gerald added, 'How did you know me my lord? I took care to ensure we never met.'

Prince Gruff smiled slightly. 'At Pembroke. I was at the bedroom window and saw you leave with a troop of horse.' He smiled again. 'I admit it, I spied on you. I wanted to see what my sister had married.'

Sir Gerald hardly knew how to answer, so he said, 'And did her choice meet with your approval?'

Prince Gruffudd's face darkened. 'I do not think choice had much to do with it.'

Sir Gerald bridled. 'For me neither, we both did as we were told.' He met the prince's eyes and then said. 'I admit I had the better bargain. As for Nest, I have done the best I can.'

Prince Gruffudd lowered his head. 'She speaks highly of you,' he said. 'I am grateful to you for that.' He gestured to the hut. 'Come inside,' he said. 'We cannot offer you the same hospitality you have shown to us at Pembroke, but you are welcome nevertheless.'

Once inside, Sir Gerald was anxious to be out again as quickly as possible, as the small space was filled with fetid air and smell of cooking and scrambling children, so that he felt he could hardly breathe. The Lady Gwenllian was better attired than her husband, and seemed at least to have had her hair dressed, but she sat with a child in her arms and another clinging to her skirts, and could barely raise a slight smile in greeting. The hut seemed to house about eight people, and in the dim light he could see a swarthy and very ugly woman bent over a large cooking pot on the central hearth, from which smoke rose to add to the choking atmosphere. The manservant Idris was sitting on the floor in the corner, skinning a couple of small animals, and Sir Gerald felt nauseous as he speculated as to their origin and purpose. Having forced himself to utter a few pleasantries, he was so horrified by his surroundings that he could not stop himself from saying so.

'How can you live like this?' he gasped, as he and Prince Gruffudd emerged once more into the fresh air.

'And what choice would you have Sir Gerald, if you were hunted like a dog and feared betrayal at every turn?

194

In any case, I can overcome these circumstances; I do not need ostentation and a court to know I am of royal blood.'

'Perhaps not.' Sir Gerald thrust his face forward to squarely look the Prince in the eyes. 'But what about your lady wife and family? They also have to suffer for your pride.'

Prince Gruffudd turned away. 'You are right,' he said, 'But what choice do I have? Henry will have us all killed if he can.'

'That is why I am here.'

Sir Gerald watched as the Prince turned, and saw the look of mistrust re-assert itself on his exhausted face. Sir Gerald said, 'I don't know if you have heard, but the uprising by Maredudd ap Bleddyn is over, and Powys is at peace again.'

'I heard it was settled without much warfare, because King Henry got too near an arrow for his comfort!'

'There is some truth in that,' said Sir Gerald, 'But Powys is to pay tribute, a very heavy tribute and for years to come.' He smiled. 'Your father-in-law at Aberffraw got a much better bargain by simply keeping the peace.'

'Paying tribute from one's own lands to a foreign invader can hardly be described as a good bargain,' said the Prince sarcastically.

'Nevertheless, perhaps it was the best thing available,' said Sir Gerald evenly, refusing to argue. 'You may do well to emulate the King of Gwynedd.'

'How?'

'I am here to make you an offer. King Henry will withdraw his hostile intentions from yourself and your family, and will grant you the right to return to a normal life. In return, you will agree to live at a location under our control, and swear to refrain from future violence against Henry's crown.'

Prince Gruff did not comment immediately, he seemed taken aback by the offer. Then he said: 'I will not swear fealty to Henry.'

'He does not ask it,' Gerald assured him. 'The king understands your position; he knows you could not in honour do such a thing.'

The Prince did not reply, and Gerald continued: 'Think of your family sire. You cannot continue to live like animals up here in the mountains. Your sons need to be properly sheltered and fed, and educated to understand and live up to their noble birth. The Princess Gwenllian also, should receive her proper place.' He hesitated. 'My wife, your own dear sister, will do all she can to help.'

The Prince was still cautious. 'What abode have you in mind?' he asked, suspiciously.

'Well sire, after your victory at Carmarthen there was little left of the town,' said Sir Gerald, smiling. 'But the settlement is being re-built, and there are homes for Henry's lesser nobles to be had there. I am sure the King would agree to your family having one of those.'

The Prince still did not comment, and Sir Gerald said with some impatience, 'You must accept this offer sire, it was wrung from the King with difficulty, and if you refuse I fear the chance will be lost.'

The Prince met Sir Gerald's eyes. 'And you sire, what is all this to you?'

'I have no interest either way, except that it will please my dear wife to know her brother and his family are safe at last. She worries about you all, and I will calm her fears if I can.'

The Prince nodded absently. 'Yes. Yes, I can see that.' After a moment he turned to Sir Gerald again. 'I do believe you have a true regard for my sister, and I thank you for coming here. To accept goes against all I have been trying to achieve, but you are right, I doubt we can survive much longer in these conditions, and my family deserves better.' He swallowed. 'I will accept the offer for the sake of my wife and sons, and agree to keep the peace.'

Sir Gerald's face broke into a broad smile, and he could not resist clapping the Prince heartily on the shoulder. 'Well done, sire!' he exclaimed. 'I am sure you shall not regret it. Gather your household as soon as you will, and come down into the valley, where I have a troop waiting. We shall escort you to Carmarthen and your new home, and you shall have the protection of my banner.' His voice dropped, and he said quietly. 'You and yours shall be properly housed and fed, brother in law, I promise.'

And as Prince Gruff saw Sir Gerald's enthusiasm and his big smile, he reluctantly managed a small grin himself.

TWELVE
'A SAFE PRISON'

When Prince Gruff and his family had been in Carmarthen for two years, Anarawd and Morgan came home from a boyish trip into the woodland badly beaten and bruised. It was not uncommon for them to be harangued and spat at by their neighbours, who resented the imposition of a family of what they called 'the Welsh rabble' amongst them, but this attack was different. Both boys had serious wounds, and told how they had been set upon by a pack of young bloods, and nearly beaten to death.

'They dared not kill us, mother,' cried Anarawd, as Rhiannell tended his injured body. 'For I heard one of them say, "Take care, for they are under the King's protection," and then they stopped beating at us, and went away.'

Gwenllian, who was attending to Morgan, muttered under her breath, 'They are cowardly scum.'

'Indeed they are,' agreed Rhiannell, looking across at Prince Gruff, who was surveying the scene with a look which was akin to madness.

'It is nothing, my lord,' she said. 'We must keep the boys close and not allow them to go into the woods again...'

Prince Gruff gave her a look of contempt and went out.

The new buildings at Carmarthen were arranged in something like a rough square, and Prince Gruff strode straight into the middle of it. He drew his sword and began to shout, 'Come out, you cowards, come out and try to best me if you can! Or do you only pick on children for your sport?'

A number of people came out of their houses and gathered round, and one of them, a soldier who had just come from duty, said 'What is the noise about? Can I not have a bit of peace to take my dinner without this shrieking?' He came across to Prince Gruff. 'Is it not enough we have to put up with you and your rabble of a family thrust upon us without this? You are supposed to be of royal blood. Can you not at least live quietly?'

Prince Gruff yelled, 'We do live quietly! And how dare you say we are thrust upon you? My ancestors have been here for thousands of years! It is you, -you ...' He gesticulated wildly around the growing crowd - 'who are the invaders here, not me and mine!' He strode towards his dwelling, and was joined by Gwenllian, who also now held her sword. Prince Gruff gestured to the soldier to follow them. 'Come and see what your neighbours have done to my children! What kind of people are you that you take out your hatred on boys who are yet unable to fight?' He stopped and called out, 'Rhiannell! Bring the boys out here!'

Rhiannell appeared at the entrance with Anarawd and Morgan clinging to her skirts. More people had arrived now, and fell silent at the sight of the young boys, blood streaming down their faces. They broke free and went across to their parents.

'See here!' yelled the Prince, 'See what your brave young men can do to children! Come and see what you can do to me! I will take on any of you, or any three of you at a time, but I expect you cannot fight in fair combat.'

Gwenllian leapt forward. She was like a wild cat, and hissed, 'Anyone who injures my children will do well to care for their own!'

The soldier hesitated. 'This should not have happened,' he said. 'We do not make war on children...'

'What?' The Prince was beside himself. 'Of course you do! I have seen the women and children you have killed, I have seen the results of your handiwork throughout this Kingdom!' He turned to the assembled crowd. 'I warn you all,' he announced, making his point with his sword, which he brandished fiercely, 'Do not dare to touch any member of my family again unless you wish to meet your Maker.' His eyes raked the sullen but interested neighbours. 'Look upon my wife, the princess Gwenllian, and upon these my sons, who are princes of this country you now inhabit by force. Know, and know for ever, that they and I are more nobly born than anyone here, and that even your King Henry will not have us mistreated. If anyone doubts that let him now come and try me, and I will release him from this world!'

There was a little jeering and a few comments about the sanity or otherwise of the Prince, but no-one came forward, and gradually the people went back inside their own houses, muttering about the incident, which would provide gossip for some days. Rhiannell collected the boys, and took them inside to bed, and Prince Gruff and Gwenllian, both still frustrated and angry, prowled the area for a while before they re-entered the house.

And as the two boys nestled down together to sleep that night, Rhiannell would not leave them, but sat herself beside the bed, and sang gently in the old tongue,

Quick thaw, long frost,
Quick joy, long pain,
Once found, soon lost,
You will take your gift again.

The house which had been allocated to Prince Gruffudd ap Rhys by Henry's constable at Carmarthen was only a very simple design, but it had been made into a reasonable home by presents of basic equipment, furniture and linen provided by the princess Nest, which were sent up on carts from Pembroke. Gwenllian had also asked for permission for items of clothing and other small luxuries to be sent to her from her home in Aberffraw, and she was allowed to write to her mother Queen Angharad requesting these. When they arrived, Gwenllian was subjected to the indignity of having them first approved by the local constable, before she was allowed to accept them. Scornfully she informed the constable she would do without in future, as anything was preferable to having her precious items pawed over and scrutinised by envious Norman eyes. Nevertheless, she and Prince Gruff now had a home for their family, and the boys Anarawd and Morgan seemed to be thriving, except for the continuous harassment from their neighbours whenever they left the safety of their home. Since the incident when Prince Gruff challenged the community however, their tormentors took care not to be too aggressive when either he or the Princess Gwenllian was nearby, for all knew that any action against the young princes would be paid for dearly. As for young Maelgwyn, now almost seven years old, he showed no antipathy or resentment to anyone, but grew strong and straight, accepting the terms of his life with happiness and enjoyment. He had a nature which endeared him to everyone, carefree and happy, and even their Norman neighbours sometimes were forced to remind themselves he was 'one of those rebels.' Gwenllian had taken on the education of her boys herself when they had been in the mountains, but now she had the assistance of a young clergyman who came each day to instruct the boys, his annual emolument having been paid to him by the Princess Nest. Their instruction in the martial arts was undertaken by their father and also by Gwenllian herself, who continued to practice her swordsmanship and archery in full sight of her neighbours, who muttered in disgust but made no open comment.

Prince Gruff was astounded by his neighbours dislike and even hatred. 'They act as if it were I who is the interloper here!' he would repeat savagely. He was clearly the member of the family who suffered most from the semi-confinement. They were not allowed to stray from the settlement except to church on Sunday mornings, and so on this one day each week the family were able to walk together, take prayers and return, having taken the opportunity to glean from other worshippers any news of specifically Welsh interest, and indeed of the wider world. The Welsh news was conveyed throughout the country by a widespread system of information passed on by the Welsh clergy, who were obliged to pay lip service to their Norman masters, but who largely remained fervent patriots. News of Prince Gruffudd and his lovely wife, the princess Gwenllian, was sought by many, and so messages between acquaintances and friends were disseminated after church services every week, with fresh news being brought regularly by the young priests who travelled between the provinces on Church business. In this way Prince Gruff was able to keep at least some contacts alive, although secretly.

Gwenllian was becoming increasingly concerned about her husband, as he chafed against the restrictions imposed upon him by their pact with King Henry, and indeed she felt the same frustration herself. After a while Prince Gruff was allowed to accompany hunting parties, in order to help provide for his family, but he was never allowed to hunt alone. As the other members of the party treated him with disdain and dislike these outings were not pleasant, and he usually arrived home in a filthy temper. On one such evening, when Gwenllian was attempting to calm his spirits after such a day, they were surprised by an unexpected visitor. It was none other than Meilyr, who was on his way north to Aberffraw. He had taken it upon himself to call into Carmarthen, and ask if he might be permitted to visit, and much to his own surprise had been directed to their house.

Gwenllian was quickly in tears at the sight of him, and even Prince Gruff's spirits lifted, as the bard regaled them not only with news from Aberffraw, (which was of no interest since it was three months old), but also of his recent travels to sacred places in the south west of Britain, and of the people he had met and the sights he had seen. After supper, he sang to them, and the young princes sat entranced, just as Gwenllian had done years before, at her father's knee in Aberffraw. Late into the night they sat, listening to the old stories and songs, and Gwenllian felt a strange lethargy enfold her, as she reflected with sadness upon all that had happened since those years of her youth. She thought of the hardships of life in the early years of her marriage, and of the birth of her young sons, but mostly she thought of Dewi ap Ifan, of his strong arms and his steadfast spirit, and the sheer comfort of him, which she doubted she would ever know again.

As for Prince Gruff, the music touched him deeply also, but for him it engendered memories of long lost friends of his youth in Ireland, and most of all the men who had fallen in the Deheubarth cause. He thought of young Geraint, and of those at Aberystwyth, and then, with a sadness almost impossible to bear, his brother Hywel.

As the music ended, Gruff ordered that the boys be taken to bed; they were already dozing and did not complain. After they had gone only Prince Gruff, Gwenllian and Meilyr remained, and Gruff poured more wine.

Meilyr said: 'I see you are both thinking of times long ago, and people and places you have loved. I have a song for those who are parted from their homeland.' He took the harp again and began:

This song is for the ones who know
When duty calls and far they go
To leave their homes and those they love,
Yes, this I call the longing.

No time will ever heal the heart
Of those life's torn or split apart,
A power that draws us to our source
Yes, this I call the longing.

On winds across great foreign lands
Our thoughts are blown like grains of sand
And borne back home to those we love.
Yes, this I call the longing.

Who calls us in the dead of night?
Familiar sounds that soon take flight
To where the lonely curlew cries,
Yes, this I call the longing.

No grass so green or air so sweet,
Prostrate we lie at Nature's feet
And plead for sight of native soil.
Yes, this I call the longing.

We've travelled far, we've travelled long
And bones are weak but will is strong,
At last we rest on native land,
Gone has all our longing.

As the sweet sound of the harp died, Prince Gruff sighed.

'Those are the feelings I had when I was in Ireland,' he said. 'I doubted I would ever see Wales again.'

'And I admit, I have those feelings for Aberffraw,' said Gwenllian. 'It seems so long since I was there.'

'We have indulged ourselves too much,' said Gruff, indicated his empty glass. 'We are becoming maudlin.' He rose and gave an arm to Meilyr. 'Come along dear friend, Rhiannell has a bed prepared for you.'

'There is one thing I can suggest,' said Meilyr, stroking his beard thoughtfully. 'Have you considered asking permission for a visit to Aberffraw?'

'I very much doubt it would be allowed,' said Prince Gruff. 'We cannot go anywhere, except to church.'

'But your time here has changed things,' said Meilyr, 'I see the Normans are not as nervous as they were. Things have been quiet for a good while. For example, I called here a year ago but was not allowed to see you, tonight I was allowed in with no trouble.'

He turned to Prince Gruff. 'Try it, my lord,' he said. 'Put in a plea for you and your family to make a visit to Aberffraw. If granted, it would do your dear wife and sons much good to see their grandparents, and such an excursion would give all your spirits a lift.'

Prince Gruff still looked doubtful, but said, 'I suppose it would do no harm to ask. They will probably refuse,' he smiled at Gwenllian, who was already bubbling with delight at the prospect, 'so do not expect too much my dear, and no word to the boys in case we are disappointed.'

'But you will make the request?' Meilyr was delighted. 'I will tell your father and the queen. They will be so pleased to see their grandchildren if it is possible. I wonder....?'

'What?' said Prince Gruff.

'It is just a notion,' said Meilyr. 'It might be better for the Lady Gwenllian to make the request, rather than yourself sire. Might look less threatening, if you see what I mean.'

'Yes, I do see.' Gruff considered a moment. 'Yes, it will be better. Ask for all of us to go my lady, as a family, but it may be that I shall not be allowed to accompany you.'

Gwenllian's face fell. 'But my lord, we cannot go without you!'

Prince Gruff smiled. 'It is doubtful if any of us will be allowed to go. But if we get the chance we must take it. It would be good for the boys. Let us see what transpires.'

'And would you agree? If they say we can go, but without you?'

'Of course,' said her husband, with a gentle smile. 'Half a loaf is better than no bread.'

Prince Gruff was proved to be right in his assumptions of the Norman mind, for although Gwenllian's request to visit Aberffraw was accepted with no adverse comments, the answer was delayed whilst permission was sought from higher echelons. 'They still think we are a problem,' said Prince Gruff, with a degree of satisfaction in his voice. It took a month to receive their answer, which was that Gwenllian and her two younger sons were allowed to make the trip, but that Prince Gruff and his heir, Anarawd, must remain at Carmarthen under Norman surveillance.

'You must go within the next few weeks,' said the constable to Gwenllian. He had paid her the compliment of coming in person to give her the decision. 'Also we cannot provide an escort; we cannot afford to send soldiers on such a trip. Nevertheless, you will not be allowed to travel without one, as I am responsible for your safety.'

'Then we cannot go!' said Gwenllian, her face showing all the anguish she felt. 'You make conditions which are impossible to keep!'

'It is not intentional,' said the constable. 'I have a suggestion. If you send word to your father, he may be able to send a troop for you, and they can escort you safely back to Aberffraw. Horses too, he should provide, for we cannot supply them. We would have no objection to that. Also, you must stay no longer than for a month or so, we expect you back within six weeks.'

It was not what they wanted, but it was something. Gwenllian nodded.

'I will send word to my father right away,' she said.

Only a week later the eight man escort from Aberffraw arrived, with Dewi ap Ifan at the head of it together with an extra three horses for the journey to Aberffraw. Gwenllian felt her heart leap with gladness at the sight of him. Together with Morgan and Maelgwn, she was already prepared, and next day they began their trip, leaving behind Prince Gruff and Anarawd, who was disappointed not to be going, but very conscious of his status as heir. He stood beside his father, watching the little group depart, and felt a certain pride when Prince Gruff explained that the reason he had to stay behind was that the Normans considered him too important to go.

Despite the close proximity of Dewi ap Ifan, Gwenllian had no opportunity to converse closely with him on the journey. The distance between them had to be preserved, both for the sake of their own reputations and the boys trust. So it was that they both burned, and suffered, permitting only a swift look between them, or a slightly overlong contact as Dewi took her hand as he assisted her from her horse when they stopped to rest. Nevertheless, Gwenllian felt a sweet release and a sense of freedom as she journeyed through the countryside denied her for so long, and when she came into her beloved Gwynedd, Dewi and his men noted the gentle tears which ran unregarded down her cheeks. As Aberffraw came in sight Dewi left the front of the troop and moved back to ride beside her.

'You are glad to be home,' he said, smiling.

She smiled in return, but said carefully, 'My home is with my husband now, and therefore must always be Deheubarth.' Seeing the look on Dewi's face, she added quickly, 'Of course I am always happy to come to Aberffraw.'

Dewi's face was still clouded. 'You say Prince Gruff is your home, but what has he ever done for you?' he asked quietly. 'He has destroyed your sweet life for one of hardship...'

'He has given me three sons!' Gwenllian retorted, 'And I have been proud to support his struggle...'

'To what end? Your husband's struggle has only tightened the noose which King Henry has around you both!'

'This is not the time Dewi!' The old hint of arrogance returned to her voice, and she watched in sadness as he pulled his horse away, and led the small group over the bridge and to Aberffraw.

The first week was a long round of happiness, with her parents and brothers all overjoyed to see her and her sons, and Gwenllian began to understand what Dewi had meant when he referred to the 'sweet life' being denied her. It was indeed a good life at Aberffraw in these times, and Gwenllian watched as her young sons responded eagerly to all the new delights which awaited them. They went hunting with her brothers, and flew falcons with the King, who doted on them. Gwenllian was surprised to see how recent years had aged her father. It was not just the silver hair and beard, and the slight stoop which afflicted him, but he seemed to have become less irascible and quick tempered, and more inclined to listen rather than to rant. During the evenings he seemed to enjoy nothing so much as to have her near him to tell of all the events which had occurred, and of their life at Carmarthen. This depressed him, but he said fondly, 'I know these times are hard for you my daughter, but your husband has behaved as a man of honour, and no man can do more. I did not agree with him, but only because I felt it was not the time. No, sadly my child, this is not the time...' he drifted away, and Gwenllian was emboldened to say, 'But when is the time father? When will it be the time for my husband to take his kingdom?'

'Ah!' said the King. 'That is the question is it not? I have been waiting a long time, but at least I have made the waiting bearable for me and mine.... When is the time? Perhaps Meilyr can tell us!'

He gestured to the bard, who was still at Aberffraw, and whispered into his ear, 'Have you any predictions for us Meilyr?'

The bard hesitated. 'I have only a vision of the scourge which afflicts you my lord,' he said.

'What?' said the King, astounded. 'Am I to be ill?'

'No my lord, not for many moons yet. It is not that kind of scourge, in my vision it was a great King, with much power...'

'Henry!' said King Gruffudd with delight.

'I am not sure sire, but in my vision he is suddenly no more. I am not sure it is Henry, for the vision is not in this land....'

'Where then?' the King demanded.

'That I could not tell...except....except there were fishes....'

'Fishes?'

'Yes sire, fishes.'

'What does it mean?' asked Gwenllian.

'I will think more about it,' Meilyr promised. 'Sometimes a vision returns to me and I see a little more.'

The King waved him away and said, 'The old fool knows nothing, a scourge which is a King, but is probably not Henry, who is not in this land but disappears, and there are fishes? What kind of prediction is that?'

'I have no idea,' said Gwenllian, smiling. Then she said, 'Perhaps it *is* Henry father, and he goes to France and is shipwrecked and drowned, and the fishes eat him!'

They both roared with laughter, and the King said, 'Even Meilyr could not think up a prediction as wonderful as that!' And Queen Angharad came up and sat next to them, but she had little to say. She only sat, and looked at her husband and her beloved daughter together, and was as happy as she had ever been in her life.

It was over a week before Gwenllian managed to arrange time alone with Dewi. He seemed to be avoiding her, and she realised that because of their slight altercation he had decided not to put her under any pressure, but to leave any future contact to her. She understood what he was doing, and loved him for it, for the freedom of choice he allowed her, so lacking in any other man she knew. Eventually, in the hearing of several people, she asked him to ride with her to Abergwyngregyn, so that she could walk on the hillside where they had walked as children, and he had agreed, saying, 'If you must walk my lady, I expect I must obey, as usual.'

Their conversation was desultory as they rode to Abergwyngregyn, and when they had left their horses at the hall and were eventually walking up the hillside, there seemed suddenly nothing to say. It was enough that they were here, together.

At the top they stood and looked at the view of the sea in the distance, the bracken already greening in the warm spring sunshine, and felt the soft breeze on their faces, and listened to the cry of the curlew. Gwenllian said, 'This does not change, thanks be to God.'

As she leaned towards him, the light through her hair turned it to burnished gold, and Dewi caught his breath. Despite the effect she had on him, he was determined to be angry, and said harshly, 'You said your home is with Prince Gruff, and I know that it is true. You did not have to say that to me.'

'No. I did not,' she said gently. 'I am sorry.'

In a slightly softer tone he said; 'Will you never tell me the truth?'

'What truth?' Her voice was quiet.

'You know very well. You said your husband had given you three sons.'

She did not answer, but walked away and sat down on a large rock, which had been their touching stone for games of tag when they were children. He came and sat beside her. 'I am right am I not, my lady? Morgan, he is mine, I know he is mine. I have always wondered since he was born, but now... now... when I look at him I see myself, not so much in features...'

'No, not so much in features,' she said softly. 'There is a little likeness in the hair, Anarawd and Maelgwyn have their father's dark hair, it is fortunate that my own hair is so light...' She stopped, and then continued with a happy smile, 'It is his stance, the way he walks, have you noticed it? When I come upon him sometimes from behind it is just the image of yourself when you were a young lad...'

Dewi smiled. 'I had not noticed that so much,' he laughed, suddenly, joyously. 'I am not used to seeing myself from afar so had not noticed that.'

Gwenllian laughed too. 'It is something about the gait, the bearing. That is why the men call you 'The Stag.' It is an apt nickname.'

Dewi took her hand, and there were tears in his eyes. 'He is such a fine boy,' he said. 'You have no idea how much this means...'

Gwenllian's face clouded. 'Dearest heart, this secret of his birth is now acknowledged between us, but he is still Morgan, second son of prince Gruffudd ap Rhys, and must always remain so. This knowledge we have makes no difference at all.'

'You are wrong, dearest,' said Dewi. 'To have it acknowledged, just between us, makes all the difference in the world.'

And then he allowed the wonderful grace and warmth of her to take him over, body and soul as it always did, and took her into his arms at last.

Their opportunities to meet over the next few weeks were scarce, but they took every chance they could. Gwenllian insisted that she be allowed to re-train in the fighting arts with her brothers and her sons, and Dewi was instrumental in this. She had not lost her skills, and her archery was still impressive, but she had to regain strength in the use of the sword and pike, as at Carmarthen they had not been allowed to use real weapons for practice, but only the wooden replicas which Prince Gruff had ordered, so that at least his sons could be taught moves and strategy. Morgan and Maelgwyn were astonished at their mother's expertise, and also at the weight of the weapons at Aberffraw, and ended the first days complaining of aching shoulders and arms, but they quickly adapted, and joined their mother and their uncles in the daily exercises. Sometimes Dewi would devise games, with points being awarded for particular skills, and for the first time the boys were treated with respect and encouragement, as they entered into everything with great confidence and much hilarity.

Gwenllian noticed to her delight, that Dewi and Morgan seemed to have a particular friendship, and her heart warmed as she watched day by day as Dewi explained to the boy how to bind arrows, sharpen his sword or fly the falcon, knowing how much this meant to him.

The leave-taking when it came, too soon, was inevitably painful. The same escort was assembled, and as Gwenllian said goodbye to her family, at least she had the knowledge that Dewi would be with them for a few days more as the troop travelled back to Carmarthen. As before, there was little opportunity for private discourse, and Gwenllian felt a deep depression bear down upon her spirits a few days later as they approached the settlement.

When they arrived however, Prince Gruff met them at the door himself, and it was clear that he was very disturbed.

'Dewi ap Ifan, I thank God you are here,' he said immediately, almost ignoring his family. 'There is great trouble. Please, all come inside, I have need of advice.'

Apparently, while Gwenllian and her two sons were at Aberffraw, the living had become even more tense and difficult at Carmarthen. It had started with some of their neighbours taking the opportunity to surround and bully Anarawd when he went out to visit their livestock, kept behind the house. Anarawd and Morgan had usually worked together, and now they found Anarawd alone, the local young men found it easy to surround and attack him. He put up a spirited defence, but was no match for six, who called him 'The Welsh peasant,' and delighted in mocking his royal status. When he managed to stagger home, bleeding and bruised once more, his father tried to complain directly to the constable himself. He was turned away by an overseer, and told that his complaint would not be heard. He was then warned 'not to make trouble.'

'Since then,' said Prince Gruff, 'life has become impossible. Rocks are thrown at us as soon as we leave the house, and two nights ago Idris was just in time to put out a burning faggot which had been thrown into the byre.'

'Perhaps it will calm down,' said Gwenllian, 'We have had these troubles before.'

'No,' said Prince Gruff. 'This time it will not go away. I am pleased to have you back dearest, but if I had possessed the means to stop you from returning I would have done so, for all our sakes.'

Rhiannell entered the room with ale and tankards, which she placed on the table.

When she had left Dewi said, 'There is something more, isn't there?'

'Yes, and this is why I am so glad to see you here.' The prince's face was gaunt with worry; he looked grey and haggard, as if he had not slept. 'On Sunday, when I took Anarawd to church as usual, after the service the young priest sought me out.'

'Father Thomas?' Gwenllian queried.

'No, it was the young monk who came from Bangor, he has been here for some weeks now, I don't think you know him. His name is Brother Francis, and he quietly said he had a message from Father Thomas, who could not speak to me himself as he was being watched. It was not easy. I walked a few yards away and then asked Brother Francis to bless me. He came over and I knelt down. He made the sign of the cross as if he was giving the blessing, but in fact he muttered to me that our overseers are writing to King Henry to say that we are conspiring to rise up again against his rule, and are planning actions against the community here.'

'But that is not true!' Gwenllian burst out.

'No, it is not true, but that will not make any difference,' said Prince Gruff bitterly. 'The plan is that we shall be sent to London to stand trial for treason, it has happened to others. False condemnation is an easy way for our neighbours to remove someone they don't like. Apparently the message was sent yesterday. We are sure to be arrested any day now, and this time dearest, I do not think even my brother in law Sir Gerald can save us.'

'You must go,' said Dewi, brief and to the point. 'Tonight.'

Prince Gruff nodded. 'You are right, but it is so difficult,' he said. 'I am fairly sure we could slip away from the back of the house, but what then? We are allowed no horses of our own, only those we are allocated if we particularly request it, and sometimes that is turned down.' Prince Gruff handed a tankard of ale to Dewi. 'Do you think Gwenllian and the boys could go back to Aberffraw?' he said, 'If I knew they were safe I could take my chances.'

'Much as I like that idea I do not think it would work,' said Gwenllian. 'It would put my father in a difficult position...'

'If what you say is true my lord,' Dewi interrupted. 'I doubt there is time for your family to get there. Perhaps when things have died down they could go to Aberffraw,

215

but if a price is put on your heads again that will be the first place they will look.' He paced a moment and then said, 'I have a better plan I think. I and the troop will leave as planned within a few hours. The horses are being fed and watered now and will be rested enough. You will all be seen waving us away.' He leaned over to Prince Gruff, his fair head almost meeting the dark one, and continued in a slow and careful tone: 'Outside the settlement, and over the river, there is a stand of willows about half a mile down the track...'

'I know it,' said the Prince.

'I will leave three horses there, those which Gwenllian and the boys rode here, together with another two, all we can spare. We shall have to take turns to double up on the way back to Aberffraw, and so will you, when you make your escape. One horse each for you and your manservant. Gwenllian will have to double with Morgan on another, and Anarawd and Maelgwyn together. That leaves one more for Rhiannell and Olwen...yes, that will work I think...'

'I can't thank you enough,' said Prince Gruff.

'Don't thank me, thank King Gruffudd,' said Dewi, 'They are his horses. I am desperate to join you in the escape, but I feel that might cause a problem. If the constable decides to send out a search he may well catch up our troop. It will be best if I appear to know nothing, and we return to Aberffraw as expected.'

Gruff nodded. 'You are right, let us pray it works.'

It worked without a hitch. After Dewi and the troop had left, the family gathered together those very few items they could take with them, and Anarawd, Morgan and then Maelgwyn, took it in turn to leave the house one by one to join Idris, Rhiannell and Olwen already hiding in the byre. They waited until it was dark, and then at the normal bedtime their rush lights were put out and Gwenllian and Prince Gruff quietly collected the family and they made their way across the fields to the river. Prince Gruffudd was aware the bridge might well be guarded, so he led them down river to the shallow crossing used by local farmers and their cattle, and one by one they slid quietly down into the freezing water and made the crossing without a sound. Once assembled on the far side, soaking wet and with their teeth chattering, they made their way across the fields again as fast as possible, and found the horses at the stand of willow as Dewi had promised. In moments they were all mounted, with the few possessions they had brought with them, and before midnight they were well on their way up into the cold but welcome safety of the mountains once again.

THIRTEEN
'HUNTED'

The news spread through the Welsh valleys and mountains like wildfire. The escape of the Royal family of Deheubarth was seized upon as a source of gossip, comment and dire prediction.

During the years of their house arrest, news of the family had become a signal for patriots to give a sad shake of the head and a resigned sigh, as if to acknowledge that all the efforts of the gallant Prince and his equally brave wife had, after all, been entirely in vain. 'After all, what had changed?' asked the parishioners as they gathered together to discuss latest events after attending church on Sunday mornings. Then would come the sad shake of the head and the sigh, usually accompanied by a reply and ensuing discussion along the lines of: 'Nothing. After all the bloodshed of our men, including young Prince Hywel, nothing has changed. The Normans are still with us, to bleed us dry and make merry at our disgrace and defeat. The damned English, those who are left, lie down wearily under the yoke, and make no protest since the death of the renowned Hereward from the Fen country, he who they called 'The Wake'.'

Now the conversations were changing. The escape from Carmarthen had provided new impetus, some gossip at last, a thread of hope from which to draw strength. At first the reports were disjointed and with little detail other than that the family had disappeared. This talk was quickly replaced by a rumour that they had been killed by their Norman neighbours at Carmarthen, (who were known to have no love for them), and lurid accounts of the dismemberment of their bodies became the appalling talk of the countryside, growing ever wilder in its fanciful imaginings, until the morning when Father Thomas and Father Francis together, held a prayer meeting after the usual service on Sunday, for those known to be loyal to the Prince. Visibly moved, Father Thomas revealed that he had received a message from the Prince, stating that he and his family were safe in the mountains. The meeting became a true prayer meeting then, as the congregation sank to its knees to give thanks that their Prince had once again escaped from his enemies, and lived to fight another day.

Then the news was carried throughout the countryside, from peasant to priest and from neighbour to neighbour, and with the coming of summer in that year, the hopes of the loyal Welsh were revived somewhat, and the depression lifted, even if only for a while. In this spirit of new found energy, the clergy closed their eyes to the many signs of thanksgiving which appeared at local ancient sites, the offerings of food, wine and flowers, which appeared as if by magic, to placate the spirits of long revered goddesses of the old religion. Officially non existent now, the old ways and superstitions still lingered in the deep consciousness of the Welsh, and at times such as these it was easy to revert to the ancient truths told them by their parents and grandparents.

For Prince Gruff, Gwenllian and their sons and servants, life had quickly adapted to the hard but bearable conditions which they already knew so well. They had travelled at first to their old mountain fastness at Cantref Mawr, and stayed for a while on the charred site of their old camp, where they were able for the first time to see the full effects of the late Owen ap Cadwgan's handiwork, although the site was already becoming overgrown.

Gwenllian said, 'I'm glad Sir Gerald had him killed. He was such a traitor, and deserved it.'

'From what I gather,' said Prince Gruff dryly, 'Sir Gerald took pains to do the job himself.'

'I don't blame him.' She gazed into the leafy canopy of trees above, and said, 'In spite of all our hardships here, I would not be back in our house in Carmarthen.'

Prince Gruff sighed. 'I too, would not care to return there. I am glad you are content, because now we need to make a choice. We can write to King Henry, and explain our situation, tell him that we only fled from Carmarthen for our own safety, and that the stories he received about us from our neighbours were false; or we can remain here, in the mountains, in which case we shall certainly be hunted down.'

Gwenllian was silent for a moment, then: 'If we try to explain to Henry,' she said, 'Will he believe us?'

'We cannot know his mind dearest, it is a risk, certainly. Perhaps if Sir Gerald put our case to him...'

'I think not,' said Gwenllian. 'That poor man has done enough for us already, and is probably in trouble now for our escape.'

'That is true,' said Prince Gruff. 'I have already sent word to Nest to tell her of the true situation.' He paused, considering. 'It is strange, is it not, that this man who should be our enemy, has probably kept us alive this long?'

'That is only because of your sister, whom I love with all my heart.' Gwenllian rose to her feet and gently kissed the Prince on the cheek. 'That is your greatest attribute my lord, that you have such a beautiful and influential sister, who melts all hearts, including Sir Gerald's.'

Prince Gruff smiled. 'She surely does that, but I think...it is strange, but apart from our ties by marriage, I found I was drawn to Sir Gerald. I think he is a good

220

man, I doubt he would harm us if he could help it.'

Gwenllian laughed aloud. 'I never thought to hear it, and from your own lips! *A good man*, and a Norman too! Is it possible?'

'Well,' Prince Gruff began to smile himself, 'He was not born in France you know...'

'Neither was King Henry,' Gwenllian quipped. 'In the shire of York, so I believe. In any case,' she continued, 'I think we must not trouble Sir Gerald further, it may put him in disfavour with the King, or bring trouble to Nest herself, which we must never do.'

Prince Gruff nodded slowly. 'Yes, you are right. In future I shall contact Nest only in strictest secrecy, Sir Gerald should know nothing of it. And just in case there is an immediate manhunt for us, we must not stay here. Sir Gerald found this place once, and could find it again.'

'I thought you said he would not harm us if he could help it?'

'Perhaps he would not,' said Prince Gruff grimly. 'But he may be under strict orders, and others might be sent to look for us. It would be foolhardy to stay here. We must move on my love, hard though it is. We must find a new site for our camp, even more remote, and cut ourselves off in order to survive. I do not mind for myself,' he smiled, and spread his arms wide. 'I enjoy the fresh air and the sense of freedom.' He laughed, and for a moment Gwenllian saw the boyish look of years ago, as he said, 'I am like a cock bird which had its wings clipped to keep it close to the farm!' He spread his arms again and almost shouted: 'Now I can fly again in my own land!'

And Gwenllian could not help but agree, for his enthusiasm was infectious, and she leapt up to join him, and together they danced a few moments around the clearing, prancing and singing like wild things, until

Rhiannell and the boys arrived back from their plant hunting, and joined in too. Amid their noisy jubilation, the Prince stopped suddenly, and as the family followed his example, they saw that he was staring, to where a group of about twenty men, heavily armed, stood watching them. For a few moments there was silence, and then one of them, an older man with a huge smile on his face, came forward and dropped to his knees in front of the Prince.

Prince Gruff leaned forward and lifted the man to his knees. 'My dear old friend,' he said, 'I knew not if you were dead or alive!'

'I have been lying quiet,' responded the old man, 'Since Aberystwyth.' He lifted his head and laughed. 'Here we are my lord,' he said, 'there are thirty four of us. We come to join your great army, and find you sporting with the women and children!' And then the whole group approached them from the forest, and there was a great deal of laughter and celebration, and Rhiannell ran quickly to fetch ale.

There was of course no great army, and none arrived. A few more men at arms straggled in, and were made welcome, but there was no great enthusiasm for another campaign against King Henry, for the lesson of Aberystwyth had been a salutary one, and had not been forgotten. Prince Gruff and his group of followers, now swollen to around fifty in number, moved further into the fastness of Cantref Mawr, and within weeks another new settlement had been constructed, and the whole group undertook rigorous training in the fighting arts. Before long Prince Gruff was leading war parties to attack the Norman patrols which came to seek them out. Gwenllian meanwhile would undertake the instruction of her elder sons, who were now old enough to draw a bow and throw a spear, and the blacksmith forged small swords for the boys, realistic weapons which had always been denied them, except at Aberffraw. Sometimes, wearying of the camp and its restrictions, Gwenllian would replace her husband at the head of a patrol, and would lead the warring raids herself. This time there was no demur from the men, as they were by now all well aware of the fighting prowess of their own warrior princess. In this way, the company of patriots managed to keep themselves alive and their persecutors confused, and as the months dissolved into years Anarawd and Morgan grew strong and straight, and in turn taught their young brother Maelgwn all that they had themselves learned. It was not an easy life, but it was a life of freedom.

It was in the spring of the year 1132 that a messenger arrived from Aberffraw with some dreadful news for Gwenllian. Her brother Cadwallon, he of the generous nature and hearty appetite, had been killed by the Normans after being captured during a raid on their positions in Nanheudwy.

'What was he doing there?' Gwenllian cried out in horror. 'My father has forbidden my brothers to take up arms against the Normans!'

'I believe he was attacking a Powys position,' said Prince Gruff. 'That family of turncoats still do not know which side they are supporting. They pay homage to Henry, but still carry out incursions wherever they can into Gwynedd lands, they are a law unto themselves, but often have Henry's might behind them.' He took his wife in his arms. 'I am sorry for the loss of your dear brother,' he said. 'He was a good man and a great fighter, which he has proved with his death as a patriot. I do not think he was deliberately disobeying your father. It must be difficult for your brothers to obey now, as I hear that your father the King is now somewhat infirm in his old age.'

Gwenllian stared at her husband, it had been over two years since her last visit to Aberffraw. 'I must go home,' she said. 'Home to Aberffraw. My mother will need me.'

Prince Gruff agreed. 'This is a time for you to be with your parents,' he said, 'and to show solidarity with the family. I shall accompany you, and the boys too. It will do us all good to live comfortably for a few weeks, and we shall mourn Prince Cadwallon together.' Gwenllian nodded, but turned away quietly, not wanting her husband to know or even suspect the thought which had surfaced unbidden at the news. *If only it had been Cadwaladr who had been slain, he is always so unkind to everyone, and has such a vicious streak. But it had to be our darling Cadwallon, who was brave and true, and such a dear brother to me.* She pushed such unworthy thoughts away; even Cadwaladr did not deserve this. Her brain disobeyed her and the thoughts returned with even more vehemence. *Thank God it was not Owain. In all our troubles and tribulation Owain is the rock upon which we depend. If it had been Owain, how could I have continued to live, let alone continue the fight?* A dreadful fear suddenly gripped her and she turned again to the messenger. 'Were others killed also?'

'Yes my lady, seven soldiers of the King's guard who were with Prince Cadwallon.'

Her throat was constricted. 'Not...not Dewi ap Ifan?'

'No my lady, he was not with the Prince, he was at Aberffraw with the King. He does not leave the King's side much these days.'

Gwenllian nodded calmly as her heart lurched. She turned to her husband. 'I will make ready for the trip my lord,' she said, and walked quietly from the room, her heart still beating like a great hammer.

Dewi ap Ifan was at the palisade to greet them when

224

the family and their escort arrived at Aberffraw a few days later. It had been a difficult journey, as they had travelled secretly in order to avoid any chance Norman patrols, and the eyes of would-be traitors. As Dewi handed her down from her horse Gwenllian met his eyes, and saw there the depth of love which met her sorrow and held it, close and true, with deep understanding. There was hardly time for a greeting however, before she was shown to the Queen's room, where her mother wept with happiness to see her and the boys. Gwenllian was shocked to see how her lovely mother had aged, she was still tall and straight, but her face had lost its youthful lustre, and her eyes had become dull and lifeless. Nevertheless, she had ordered everything made ready for them, and the family were soon again enjoying the warm and comfortable living conditions so long denied them in the mountains.

It was not until supper that they talked of Cadwallon. The King had joined them, and Gwenllian saw that her husband had been right, his sight was almost gone. He came into the room on Dewi's arm, and as soon as he was seated Gwenllian and her husband paid their respects, and were gratified at the pleasure the King obviously derived from their visit.

'I wish it was not such an unhappy time for us,' the King said. 'But we are very glad to have you with us, and it is right you should be here.' He put his face close to his trencher as Dewi helped him to meat, and then said, almost belligerently, 'I cannot bury my son you know, cannot even bury him in our traditional way.' His head bent even lower. 'Where is Gwenllian?' Gwenllian rushed to his side and he said to her, almost piteously, 'They will not allow us to bury my dear son whole. Instead, they must cast his body parts in many places. Is it not enough to kill him, without denying him paradise? Is there no honour left in this wicked world?'

Owain said gently, 'Do not distress yourself father. I do not believe Cadwallon is denied paradise because he has no grave. It is a superstitious tale for the peasants, not a teaching of the Church.'

'It was always widely known that a body must be buried intact!' the King responded, with a touch of his old vigour. 'It has always been the Welsh way, even in the most bitter struggles we would not deny our opponents the right to bury their dead whole and in the proper way.'

'I know father, I know,' said Owain. 'You are right, it has always been our way. That is why the Normans make sure we do not bury our dear ones whole. Their practices are inhuman, but they do it only to make us afraid of opposing them. They wish us to receive the message that if we rise against them we will not only lose our lives, but our immortal souls. That is why I do not believe it. They do not have dominion over a man's soul, only Our Lord has that power.'

There were murmurs of 'Amen, amen' around the table, and the King seemed a little appeased. He nodded and said, 'You may be right Owain. I pray that you are.'

It was a sad supper with everyone very aware of the young Prince who was absent from the table. When all had eaten their fill the Queen said, 'There is much food left. That is because Cadwallon is not here.' And the family looked at each other and smiled, even Cadwaladr, and thought of Cadwallon, who would never brighten their supper table again.

A few nights later, Prince Gruff came to the big bed in the room Gwenllian occupied. She was surprised when he reached for her. She had thought that when he was at Aberffraw, and could choose a concubine or a slave girl to be his nightly companion he would do so, having been denied feminine company for so long in the mountains.

226

'What is this my lord?' she asked. 'No other woman to be found?'

'Plenty,' was his reply. 'But my needs are not as strong as they were, and I find that increasingly they cannot be satisfied by a mere girl.' He smiled at her and said, 'You know you have always had my true heart, and when I can have the best wine, why should I make do with sour ale?'

Then he laughed out loud, and Gwenllian joined in, and they pretended they were young again, and found comfort together.

Outside in the byre Dewi ap Ifan sat with the young Prince Morgan, showing him how to whittle wood, and as they sat together, Dewi told him stories which had been passed down by his father and his grandfather.

The time passed too quickly, but as autumn turned to winter Prince Gruffudd knew that he must move his small family soon and return to their mountain stronghold. He held out as long as he could, hoping that they could see out the winter at Aberffraw, but as soon as the first signs of Spring appeared they made ready to move. They left before their whereabouts could become common knowledge, before spring had attained any real warmth, and before Dewi and Gwenllian had found an opportunity to speak privately together. It was also before Anarawd and Morgan had learned all they wished from Dewi ap Ifan and his men. But not before Gwenllian had realised that once again she was pregnant.

At Cydweli castle the Norman lord Maurice de Londres started peevishly as the door opened when he was making his ablutions. He did not take kindly to interruptions, and was about to let forth a tirade of abuse at his manservant, when he realised he had an audience.

'What is this?' he enquired suspiciously, lifting himself from the chair where his body slave had been trimming his beard. His manservant was accompanied by a group of at least ten others, and as one of them pushed himself forward Maurice de Londres recognised him and relaxed. 'Oh,' he said shortly, 'It's you again.' He sat down in his chair again and motioned for his slave to continue.

'I apologise for disturbing you my lord,' said the man, who was clearly Welsh but fairly well presented. 'You said to let you know the moment I had news of the Prince Gruffudd ap Rhys and his followers.'

Maurice de Londres looked across at him with disdain. The man was a local leader named Gruffudd ap Llewelyn, whom Maurice had used as an informant on several occasions. The man was a fawning traitor to his own people, but a combination of threat and bribery had made him a reasonably reliable source of news.

'You have given me news of this rebel Gruffudd ap Rhys in the past,' he said. 'It has never been enough for us to snare him.'

'He is clever my lord,' said the Welshman defensively. 'He moves from place to place and has many people loyal to him.'

'He is *not* clever!' Maurice de Londres said sharply. He got up again and waved away his slave, wiping his face with a cloth. He leaned towards Gruffudd ap Llewelyn and his face twisted into a threatening mask. 'Never tell me that rebel is clever! He is like a wasp that buzzes here and there, here and there, stinging where and when he can. He is not a danger to me, and never could be.' His voice rose, *'He annoys me, that is all, but he who annoys me shall pay the price for it!'*

He walked away towards the window of his chamber in Cydweli castle, where he had been overlord for the last two years. He did not know it, but the room had once been used by the princess Gwenllian. He stood looking out, and then said in a normal tone, 'Tell me your news. Surprise me with your information. Convince me that the large amounts of gold I have spent on that veritable chain of spies under your control is actually going to produce some result at last.'

Gruffudd ap Llewelyn licked his lips. He was terrified of this man, who had been known to put out the eyes of his friends, never mind his enemies, and who was celebrated for the particularly vicious methods of torture he devised. 'He has been at Aberffraw, my lord,' he said, 'and all his family with him. His wife, the Princess Gwenllian...'

'Ah! There is another!' Maurice de Londres became incensed again. 'Her head is needed on a pike for a warning sign. She too leads patrols against us! It is said that her followers shout her name over and over when they attack!'

'That is true my lord, they say she fights as well as any man...'

'That is *disgusting*. So... what news of the she-wolf?'

'Her brother was executed at Nanheudry, so they travelled to Aberffraw to stay with her family. We had no news of it until they left, but their escort was spotted by one of our spies. They are on their way back to their stronghold in the mountains, and our man sent a message to us, and is now following them to ascertain where their camp might be...'

Maurice de Londres nodded. 'That is at least promising. If we catch them this time you shall be rewarded.' He nodded dismissively. 'Go now, and send me my Captain of the Guard. He will need to start out immediately. We will catch this wasp, and I shall flay him alive, and put down the whole nest. King Henry will be pleased when they cease to buzz.'

It was three days later when Gruffudd ap Llewelyn presented himself again at Cydweli castle, accompanied by the Captain of the Guard. They had discussed strategy, but both were terrified as they approached the great hall, where Maurice de Londres was waiting.

'What news?' he said, as soon as they entered.

'The rebel has got away, taken to his heels like the scum he is,' said the Captain.

'What do you mean?' de Londres demanded. 'What of our man? Did you find him?'

'Yes indeed my lord, we found him quite quickly, but his throat was cut.'

'And there was no message? He had said nothing? No witnesses?'

'Nothing my lord.' Gruffudd ap Llewelyn spoke for the first time. 'When Prince Gruffudd ap Rhys silences someone, they are silent for ever. They are back in the mountains again, and we are no nearer to finding them.'

Maurice de Londres smote his huge fist down on the table. 'We shall follow him there,' he roared. 'Surely we can find him...'

The Captain was brave. 'The problem with that strategy my lord, is that he always finds us first, before we even get near to his camp. That is how we lost so many patrols.'

Maurice de Londres knew the truth when he heard it. He breathed deeply and swallowed his anger.

'Nevertheless,' he murmured. 'The time will come. Be assured, the time will come.'

FOURTEEN
'MAES GWENLLIAN'

Gwenllian sat on a skin rug and cuddled her two year old son to her. She stroked his brow and ran his long blond locks through her fingers. She had not ceased to delight in her wonderful child since his birth, and still found herself laughing with joy when she looked at him. They had named him Rhys, after his grandfather Rhys ap Tedwr, and his birth had been difficult and painful in spite of Rhiannell's best efforts. However, Gwenllian had quickly recovered, and the child had grown strong, with a pair of lungs which his father likened to 'the biggest bellows in the smithy.' Now Gwenllian and Gruff had four sons, and although she had secretly hoped her last child would be a daughter, when she first beheld the tiny boy she had cried tears of happiness. She cuddled him closer, but he wriggled and squirmed and wanted to be let go, since he had begun to walk he could not keep still for two minutes together.

'Wait a moment,' she admonished him now. 'Let me put on your warm cloak, for it is so cold today, and you will be chilled.'

She fastened the deerskin cloak around him, which Rhiannell had made with love in every stitch, for she too, doted on the child. She let him go and away he went, through the door of their hut and straight over to the far side of the clearing, where his brothers Morgan and Maelgwyn were practising swordplay. He stopped next to Anarawd, who was barking out instructions and encouragement. Gwenllian, watching from the door of the hut, saw Anarawd pat the child's head as he stood there, clinging to his brother's leather thigh boot, and jumping with glee.

What joy have I here, she thought, *with Anarawd almost twenty now, and Morgan and Maelgwyn eighteen and sixteen, and all healthy and strong. I am fortunate to have reared each child to maturity, and how they all love the little one!*

Her reverie was broken by a shout from the camp perimeter, where a palisade of sorts had been erected to ward off any attack from the west. It was a guard, who ran in to say the patrol was on its way home, they had been sighted a mile away. Gwenllian was surprised, the Prince was not expected back for another two days at least.

'Are they followed?' she asked the guard.

'No my lady,' he answered. 'It appears all is well, but they come apace, perhaps there is news.'

'Rhiannell, we need food and ale,' Gwenllian cried. 'The Prince and his patrol are with us!'

Rhiannell ran to organise the women, who set out the tables, which they put together when the Prince was home and wished all to eat together, despite the fact that it was December and bitter weather. By the time this was done and the fires loaded for a good blaze, the patrol was cantering into camp.

Apprehensive, Gwenllian ran to meet the Prince. 'Welcome my lord,' she said, 'But why so soon? Is there trouble?'

His smile was answer enough. 'No trouble,' he said, laughing. 'I can hardly wait to tell you, my dearest wife.' He was down from his horse in a second and embraced her heartily. He grasped her arms and looked long into her face. 'It is Henry,' he said. 'King Henry, our scourge and tormentor, is dead!'

'What?' Gwenllian's mouth dropped open. 'But how? Are you sure? I thought he was in France…'

'Yes, he was. And I am sure. I had it from Uncle

232

Rhydderch himself, who had a message from Nest. The King was at a place called St Denis le Fermont, at a hunting lodge where he was staying overnight after the days sport. Apparently he ate a large amount of lampreys, of which he was very fond. He had been told that it was not the season and he was advised not to eat them, but he would have his way and made a pig of himself! He died with a great stomach ache!'

The Prince by now was embracing his sons, who had gathered around, listening, along with everyone else in the settlement. He picked up little Rhys, and turned again to Gwenllian, 'What think you my lady? Armies have tried hard enough to kill Henry, but in the end he is beaten by a platter of fishes!'

Gwenllian was bemused. 'There is something... I know not what...but something...Yes!' She turned to her family. 'Meilyr! Meilyr knew it! When we were at Aberffraw some time since, he told the King that he had a vision. A vision of a great scourge, which was suddenly gone, and that there were fishes ... it must have been Henry after all!'

Prince Gruff scowled. 'Visions, predictions, that old man always has one to suit every time and event,' he said. 'It appears Henry died on the second of December, so the tyrant had been gone a week before we even knew it! Come wife, it is time to celebrate and to talk over what this means for us all.'

What the momentous event of King Henry's death meant for them was not immediately obvious. Over the succeeding weeks it seemed to Gwenllian and Gruff that the whole world was silent, awaiting events, and then it became clear that the Norman dynasty, so powerful for so long, was at last showing the strain of change. Henry had always intended that upon his death the titles of both

King of England and Duke of Normandy should pass to his daughter Matilda, and Prince Gruff was already making plans on this assumption. Only days after the news of Henry's death however, a message from Rhydderch affirmed that Henry's nephew Stephen had already assumed the title of Duke of Normandy, and had rushed to London to seize the English crown for himself. He was assisted in this enterprise by several French nobles and English lords who could all envisage something to gain.

'To think Stephen would usurp the throne in such a way,' said Prince Gruff, as they sat discussing events around the fire. 'One cannot imagine such a traitorous thing, especially since nine years ago he swore to Henry that he would accept the succession of Matilda when the time came. It is clear his word means nothing.'

'If Henry had thought for a moment that he would not accept Matilda, I doubt Stephen would have lived until now,' said Gwenllian. 'We must wait and see what happens, we cannot change events, but I can only think that this scramble for power will do us no harm. The Normans are divided at last.'

'We must hope so,' said Gruff. 'And I hear that the Marcher lords on the borders are to come out for Matilda. Robert, the Earl of Glamorgan, has already done so. They may well join together and take up arms against Stephen. If they do, the Normans will have more trouble than they can imagine, and become more divided than ever. Perhaps our time is coming at last dearest.'

It seemed that others felt the momentum of the times also, for during the next two months, men-at-arms began to gather once again in Cantref Mawr, and the strength of Prince Gruff's force gradually grew to over five hundred.

Even the weather seemed to be predicting momentous events. Shortly after Henry's death a huge storm devastated middle Wales, and the superstition was voiced by many that this was an omen which heralded a time of great change. Lakes had burst their banks, and in one uncanny incident, it was reported that a pool had emptied itself, including fish, into the adjacent valley. Wild rumours flew through the valleys, fed by the lingering superstitions of the ancient religion, and the cry arose that the great Arthur himself would surely return to rid the land of all invaders. Many of the Flemish smallholders, who had followed the Norman army into Wales to scavenge what they might and resettle the land, were equally fearful, and began to pack up their belongings and join the caravan of terrified souls leaving the country to escape they knew not what.

Prince Gruff's newly gathered army were becoming impatient, but still there seemed no clear information to inform the prince as to the best course of action. He was discussing the possibilities with Gwenllian and his newly appointed captains on a cold morning just after the Christmas celebration, when a messenger was announced. The man was jubilant, and could hardly wait to spill out the news.

'There has been a huge uprising in the far south, my lord,' he cried, still gasping for breath. 'Near Swansea!'

'Ah!' the prince responded eagerly, 'That does not surprise me. I have had word for many years of the harsh rule of the Norman lords there. Every kind of cruelty has been practised on that region.'

'Indeed my lord, and it seems the people had reached the end of patience. The uprising just began like a great bubble, and became larger and larger, and there was much confusion. Have you heard of a local leader there my lord, the one they call Hywel ap Maredudd?'

'I have indeed,' said the prince eagerly, 'He has been a thorn in Henry's side for several years. I admire the man.

He has kept the flame of our freedom alive at times when it was almost extinguished in that poor ravaged countryside.'

'It was he my lord, who raised the army. They were heavily outnumbered of course, but they wreaked havoc on the Norman and Flemish forces at Penlle'r-gaer, and secured a resounding victory, with over five hundred Norman troops left dead on the battlefield!'

There was an immediate outbreak of celebration inside the prince's hut. As everyone crowded around the messenger eager for more information, Prince Gruff turned to his wife.

'This is the sign we have been awaiting,' he said, 'It is time to strike at last.'

'You are right my lord,' she responded seriously. 'The Normans may still be secure within their local settlements, but the whole Welsh nation are surely ready now, and the Normans can no longer muster a large army if we confront them with a serious and well armed threat.'

'I agree,' said the prince, 'But nevertheless, I have not forgotten Aberystwyth, and I am not about to be impetuous.' He paced the hut, which had now become quiet again, with his captains hanging on his every word.

It was to Gwenllian that he turned however. 'I am sure that the time is now,' he told her, 'but we need even more men. I believe that with Henry dead and confusion in the Norman ranks, your father may at last agree to help us. Either that, or he will perhaps leave the decision to Owain. I think I should go to Aberffraw to ask for his cooperation.'

'Yes,' said Gwenllian, 'now is the time. And I will write to my father.'

She wasted no time, but sat down right away to compose the message. She decided to send it to Owain, as her father's sight was now so poor, and she knew that

Owain would read her request truthfully to the King. She wrote:

Dearest father and mighty king, to demonstrate the sincerity of our request, my husband makes personal attendance upon your court, and I beseech you to consider carefully his intentions.

It was with some apprehension that the family divided the next morning. Prince Gruff had decided to take Anarawd with him, so that he might learn from the negotiations, and also little Rhys, so that his grandparents may see him for a few days. He was attended by a large troop of men, but left the bulk of the army behind with Gwenllian and the princes Morgan and Maelgwyn, to defend the settlement. There had been many reports of lawless robbers and bandits roaming freely in the countryside, now that the Normans had withdrawn many of their regular patrols to consolidate the defence of their castles and strongholds. As the Prince's party prepared to depart there was a palpable silence overlying their affectionate leave taking, as each member of the family feared for the others. Gwenllian kissed little Rhys, and lifted him up to Rhiannell, who was to travel with him as his nursemaid, and he was quite happy, as he loved the big ugly woman who had cared for him since birth. Then she bid the party God speed, and they set off for Aberffraw.

At Cydweli castle Maurice de Londres sent for Gruffudd ap Llewelyn. For weeks rumours of uprisings and wanton acts of violence against Norman strongholds and settlements had reached the castle, and he realised that the situation was becoming serious. When the Welshman entered, he came straight to the point.

'Well sire, in these days of rumour and confusion, where lies your allegiance?'

The Welshman felt his knees turn to water, but he smiled broadly and said confidently, 'Where it always has, my lord. With yourself and the English crown.'

'Ah! The English crown…' Maurice de Londres voice was low. 'It seems that we have Stephen to look to after all. He had himself crowned quickly enough to daunt those who would have opposed him.' He turned to face his companion. 'Whatever happens to the English crown I shall remain here at Cydweli, and that will not change. There is much disruption and no doubt more to come, but there is no doubt of the eventual outcome. I hope you realise that.'

'Of course I do, my lord.'

'Then tell me what you think of this latest information, that the wretched wasp of Deheubarth has drawn a new army to his side up in the mountains. Will he attack?'

Gruffudd ap Llewelyn relaxed a little, he was on firm ground now. 'I have fresh news for you my lord,' he said. 'The Prince has left the mountains and is on his way to Aberffraw. It is thought he means to ask Gwynedd to join him.'

Maurice de Londres paled visibly, but he said 'King Gruffudd has not taken up arms against us for years. He swore fealty to King Henry…'

'Yes. To King Henry,' said the Welshman pointedly. 'The King of Gwynedd is old and feeble now, and may well leave the matter to his heir, Owain, who is known to favour war against the English crown. It is possible they will join together to form a new great army. Gwynedd and Deheubarth are joined by marriage…'

'Yes, and where is that she-wolf, Gwenllian?'

'She has remained behind in the mountains with most of the new army and two of her sons.'

'We can never root them out, in those accursed mountains,' mused de Londres. He seemed to come to a decision. 'I have a plan,' he said briskly, 'which is already begun. But we must act quickly, and draw out the she-wolf before the army is strengthened from Gwynedd. Last week I obtained a concession from the Crown, and already a large detachment of well armed and battle hardened men are on their way from London to reinforce us. We will put a stop to this uprising before it starts. That,' he said pointedly, 'is where your spies will be helpful.'

'Anything my lord, just tell me what is to be done.'

'Arrange for Gwenllian to get the news that the reinforcements are to come by sea, and will land on the west Glamorgan coast next week, to strengthen my hand. She will know she must act quickly to attack us before they arrive, and will be drawn out with her army. She will not allow us to gather strength and form a combined force when she knows the Prince and his followers plan to meet us soon.'

'How will that help? If she attacks before we have the reinforcements we may lose...'

'She will not. She cannot.' Maurice de Londres smiled. 'She will believe our false information and think she can defeat us before the reinforcements arrive. But they are on their way now and will already be here, all in place, and waiting for her.'

Gwenllian paced the mud floor of the hut, her brain in turmoil. She looked anxiously at Morgan and Maelgwn who stood beside her, their faces serious. She turned once again to the messenger.

'Are you sure?' she asked again. 'Quite sure?'

'Yes my lady. The man who told it was straight from Cydweli, and was in his cups to be truthful. But all there know that Maurice de Londres is determined to attack us.

His words were that he will 'finish the rebels once and for all.' He knows that Prince Gruffudd has gone to Aberffraw and intends to build up another great army to move against him, so he intends to attack first, before the Prince returns.'

'And the reinforcements from England? How do you know they will really come?'

'Their message was intercepted, my lady. It said that they promised one thousand men-at-arms, battle hardened in France. They will come by sea, to arrive on the west Glamorgan coast next week.'

'What shall you do mother?' It was Anarawd who spoke. 'Shall we send a message after father to ask him to return?'

'I fear that will be too late,' Gwenllian responded. 'They are probably at Aberffraw already. We shall send a messenger certainly, to inform them, but it would be foolhardy just to wait and allow Maurice de Londres to consolidate such a great force.' Gwenllian drew in her breath and then said, 'I must speak to all our captains of troop, and make sure they are all with me.'

The leaders of the Deheubarth army were quickly gathered, and Gwenllian explained the situation to them. Some of them asked their own questions of the messenger, and then Gwenllian addressed them.

'If we allow these Norman reinforcements to reach Cydweli we shall be allowing the tyrant de Londres to build up a great fighting force to move against us,' she said. 'I believe we should take the attack to them whilst we have the vital element of surprise. The reinforcements will not arrive for a few days, and if we move quickly, under cover of darkness, we can travel quietly and surprise them before they get to Cydweli.'

There were some murmurs of assent, and Gwenllian continued. 'Before we discuss any plans, I need to know

240

that you are all with me, and will accept me as your leader, as my dear husband your Prince is not here.'

'My lady,' said a young captain, bending down to one knee before her, 'I am your man, and swear my allegiance and my life, lead where you will.'

It was in the time honoured chivalric tradition, and all the other leaders followed suit, kneeling one by one and swearing allegiance. When all had done so, the Princes Morgan and Maelgwyn did the same, and Gwenllian was hard pressed to suppress tears at this evidence of loyalty.

'Thank you, gentlemen,' she said, 'And we must find out if all our followers are also willing to accept me as your campaign leader.'

They went outside and the whole army was gathered together within minutes and the question put. The answer was a roar of approval as they chanted, '*Gwenllian! Gwenllian! Gwenllian!*' for now her reputation as a warrior and freedom fighter was well known.

When it was clear that all were ready to follow her, Gwenllian held a meeting to plan the strategy. The decision was that they should split their forces into two halves. The first, led by Gwenllian, would travel to a secluded spot at the foot of the wooded hill known as Mynydd y Garreg, which was near the river and within a mile or so of Cydweli castle, and to wait there. The other half, under the direction of their most trusted captain, would make their way to intercept the Norman reinforcements before they could reach Cydweli. Although they would be outnumbered, the Welsh forces would have the element of surprise with them, and if the Norman reinforcements were not completely wiped out, they would at least be severely reduced in number. When the reinforcements had been stopped, the Deheubarth men would join Gwenllian for the attack on the castle. When the plan had been agreed, and all were quite sure of their orders, they withdrew to prepare themselves and their men, for they were to leave that evening as soon as darkness fell.

Gwenllian realised the full enormity of what she was about to do, and told Olwen to bring her full military dress. She wore a mail hauberk, split at both the front and rear, which ended just above the knee, and tucked her long blonde plait underneath it. She put on her good leather riding boots, and on her head she wore a chainmail hood for added protection. Over these she wore a crimson calf length surcoat. Lastly she swung her kite shaped shield over her back, and put on her scabbarded battle sword. She suddenly wished that Rhiannell was there, to say some word of encouragement and kind common sense, but Rhiannell was at Aberffraw with young Rhys. So she smiled at Olwen, and went out to her waiting horse.

She rode at the head of the great column of men, with Morgan and Maelgwyn at either side of her, followed by the ranks of cavalry, foot soldiers and the company of archers, following a predetermined route intended to cloak their approach to Cydweli. Down the great valley of Dyffryn Twyi they travelled, passing through Dinefwr, the traditional seat of the Kings of south Wales, and in particular the revered King Hywel Dda. As they passed under the hill fort ruins which towered above them, Gwenllian told her sons that one day, it was her dream that Castell Dinefwr would be rebuilt.

'One day,' she told them. 'When your father and I have regained Deheubarth, we shall see it rise again, to appease the spirits of our ancestors. Remember this place, my dear sons, as a reminder of our heritage, and the justification for our fight.'

They rode on, skirting the settlements of Llandeilo and Caerfyrddin with as wide a margin as possible, as they knew there would be enemy informants in the area. At Llandyfaelog they split into their two respective halves, and Gwenllian and her group, by a combination of stealth and an intricate knowledge of the countryside, arrived a few hours before dawn at the foot of Mynydd y Garreg, where they were to be joined later by their friends to attack the castle at dawn.

As she waited, Gwenllian took the opportunity to talk to Morgan and Maelgwyn, for this was the first real combat for both of them. Then she walked among the ranks of soldiers, making sure all knew what was expected of them when the attack on the castle took place. Her spirits rose, as she found that confidence abounded, and morale was high. She was just beginning to wonder why her other troops had not yet rejoined them, when a sudden hail of arrows descended upon them in a veritable deluge. As men fell around her, she looked up in horror, only to see hundreds of men storming down upon them from the heavy bracken covered slopes of Mynydd y Garreg above. Suddenly, the unsuspecting camp was attacked by a seeming avalanche of swords, shields, spears and battle axes, supported still by the hail of deadly arrows from the hillside above. It was the army of Norman reinforcements that had already arrived, and which had been hidden on the slopes of Mynydd y Garreg, awaiting them. The plot hatched by Maurice de Londres and his ally Gruffudd ap Llewelyn had been well planned.

In the initial moments, the shock of the attack sent men and horses scattering in all directions, but Gwenllian quickly re-grouped her forces to form a shield wall just as the first wave slammed into them. These were seasoned troops, but Gwenllian's soldiers, once they had realised what was happening, fought with ferocity and courage. Amid the carnage and clashing of swords and axes and the screams of the horses, for some time it appeared that not much progress was being made by either side. As the furious battle continued, Gruffudd ap Llewelyn, on the edge of the action, moved freely amongst the French troops. 'The rebel princess is in the crimson surcoat!' he shouted, pointing to the centre of the fray. 'He who kills or captures her alive shall have ten gold coins!'

Immediately a spearhead of Norman shields thrust towards Gwenllian, and burst through the Welsh interlocked shield-wall, which allowed half a dozen of them to close in on the princess and her sons. Both Morgan and Maelgwyn fought frantically to protect their mother, but under the storm of axes Maelgwyn's once dependable shield disintegrated, and a Norman sword pieced him through twice. Gwenllian shrieked, and bent to aid him, but her young son was already dead. Fired with anguish, she leapt once again to battle, and skilfully applied her sword to deliver death with consummate ease. The unique blend of ferocity and efficiency which had been the envy of her brothers was now evident in its deadly wrath, and although heavily outnumbered, she and Morgan stood their ground in a savage exchange of hand to hand fighting. Suddenly, Gwenllian was struck in the upper arm by the edge of a French sword which knocked her off her feet, and as her attacker thrust forward to deliver the *coup de grace*, Morgan threw himself forward and the sword pierced his shoulder instead. Somehow, Gwenllian's dwindling supporters managed to reform and place a shield around her, and, with the princess at their centre, they prepared to fight to the last and die with honour, as had their many companions now strewn about them.

Suddenly, Maurice de Londres himself, having ridden out from the castle, appeared in heavy armour at the head of at least fifty horsemen armed with lances. Brashly they rode straight at the Welsh defence wall, killing at least a dozen as they did so. At this the few remaining survivors realised all was lost, and dropped their arms in surrender. Gwenllian was seated on the grass with Morgan in her arms, trying to staunch his dreadful wound. Two Norman knights approached her on foot, and the eyes she raised to them were bloodshot and tearful. Realising then her situation, she got to her feet, smoothed down her surcoat, and turned to face her enemies, pulling off her chain hood. As she did so, the soft dawn sunlight now appearing over Mynydd y Garreg caught her blonde hair in a sudden glow of gold, and the noisy throng around her abated.

Her audience was made up of a few exhausted and demoralised countrymen, and the Norman soldiers who only moments ago had been jeering wildly, elated by victory. Now all were silent as they awaited the judgement on her fate. It was not long in coming. Maurice de Londres spoke in a low tone to Gruffudd ap Llewelyn, who came to the clearing around Gwenllian. Her hands were tethered behind her, and she was dragged to face the Welsh traitor.

He began in a loud voice, 'For your crimes...' Gwenllian spat in his face, and he stopped. He wiped his face on his sleeve and began again. 'For your crimes against the English crown, you, Gwenllian, wife of the rebel Gruffudd ap Rhys, shall receive swift justice at the hands of our finest swordsman.'

There was a slight movement in the crowd, as her few remaining supporters tried to rush to her side. Their disbelief was evident on their faces, but they were stopped, and turned their attention to assisting Morgan, who could barely stand.

Gwenllian acknowledged her sentence with a nod, and then turned to her distraught son and followers.

'Morgan, my son, my heart, you and your brave knights must swear to live on, to tell our people what happened here this day.'

A Norman soldier clad in chainmail stepped forward with his broadsword unsheathed.

Gwenllian spoke again, and her voice was clear and firm. 'In my final moments my dear son, I send my undying love to you, your father and your brothers.'

Her brain reeled into panic. *I must do this well, dear Lord, help me!*

Morgan could only nod, as the tears ran down his bloodstained face.

Now two more soldiers stepped forward. One gathered her thick plait and held it taut on top of her head. *And is this how it ends? My poor Maelgwyn never to know a full life, and Morgan...can he survive such a wound?* The soldier stood facing her, the long rope of hair still in his hands to keep it out of the way of the sword blade. The other soldier stood behind her and held her arms fast. *Thank God Anarawd was not here, I know he will care for my darling Rhys...* With a tug on her hair at the front, she was forced to bend from the hips, exposing the smooth skin of her neck. *Dear Lord, receive me...*The Norman executioner now stood at her side and looked to Maurice de Londres for the sign. With a mere tilt of his head he gave the consent. Slowly, the visibly nervous swordsman raised the heavy sword above his head, and with one hand on the hilt and another on the pommel, he drew in a deep breath. A split second before the razor edge reached its target, a final cry escaped Gwenllian's lips.

'*Remember me!*' she cried, and the sound struck against the still air, and reverberated along the valleys, to merge with the cry of the curlew.

AFTERMATH

At Dinefwr castle the three brothers and their old friend Dewi ap Ifan, gazed into the fire, now burned low. Each had his own sombre thoughts. For Anarawd, the remembrance of that dreadful evening when the news had reached Aberffraw that his mother had been executed and that Maelgwyn had been killed in battle, was a memory which had never left him.

'We were all so busy,' he told young Rhys. 'We were making preparations to invade the Norman held territories. When the messenger arrived it was so unexpected...such a shock.' His eyes misted. 'I recall our father and Queen Angharad just clinging together, and then sinking to their knees. They tried to give each other comfort,' he explained to Rhys, who was listening intently with wide eyes.

'Yes, but there was no comfort to be had,' said Dewi. 'I remember I was trying to find out if you were still alive Morgan, for you had been so badly wounded. Then at last I was told you had been taken prisoner, and so at least there was some hope for you.'

'Where was grandfather, King Gruffudd?' Rhys asked. He had never heard the full story before, and wanted to know all.

'He was in his bedchamber,' said Anarawd. 'The news was taken to him there. He asked to be left alone, he wanted to reflect on his daughter's turbulent life. It was a severe blow to him, and he was already frail, and as you know he died within the year.'

The brothers fell silent, each with his own thoughts. Anarawd reflected on the bravery of his mother, and inwardly decided that as his father's heir, he would try to live up to his great inheritance. Morgan gave silent thanks that he had at last been able to return to Wales, and to find his family and Dewi again. He determined that one day he would make the pilgrimage to Rome, and give thanks at the great church of St. Peter. Both of them remembered Maelgwyn, and his stoic and pleasant nature.

Dewi ap Ifan had different feelings. When they had talked together through the old story, he had kept back certain aspects of Gwenllian's life, those events which were hers and his alone, and now his own precious and closely held secret. It was only now, after the passage of five years, that he was able to bear thinking of his dear Lady. He glanced at Morgan, who for all his suffering still seemed to be the open and honest young man he remembered, and suddenly he was glad, glad to have lived the life he had, even with all its tribulations.

'I wish to say something.' Rhys was on his feet. The others regarded him with affection.

'I am the youngest, I know,' said Rhys. 'I have heard the story of our father and mother and it has made me very proud. I want you all to know that as soon as I am old enough, you will all be proud of me too.'

'Of course we shall,' rejoined Anarawd, smiling.

'I have not finished,' said Rhys. 'What I intend to do is build up the lands of Deheubarth again and I shall accomplish what our parents could not. One of my most important tasks will be to rebuild this castle of Dinefwr, as our mother wished. I shall build it in stone, as the Normans do, to last as a monument to her and father. Do not doubt me,' he added, as his companions gazed at him indulgently, 'For I assure you, it will be done.'

EPILOGUE

The resting place of Gwenllian's body is not known. The Normans carried out their procedure for disposal of remains by ensuring that her body was not preserved intact, as they had done with Cadwallon.

King Gruffudd died in his bed, aged eighty two, and was buried with all honour in Bangor cathedral.

His son Owain joined with Prince Gruff and together they continued the struggle against the Normans, with great success, their first victory being the re-taking of Aberystwyth, where Gruff had learned such a hard lesson, and had lost his much loved brother. As they rode into battle together, the massed troops always gave a resounding battle cry - *'Gwenllian! Gwenllian!'*

After receiving a serious wound in battle at Crug Mawr, Prince Gruff failed to recover, and died just over a year after his wife. Local supporters were convinced he died of a broken heart. Owain continued to rule Gwynedd with great wisdom for many years, and became known as 'Owain Gwynedd.'

Dewi ap Ifan continued to support and teach Gwenllian's children until his death.

On the death a few years later of Sir Gerald de Windsor, the Princess Nest married another Norman lord, Stephen, the castellan of Cardigan, and had more children.

Prince Anarawd succeeded to the title of Deheubarth,

and an unprecedented collaboration between Gwynedd and Deheubarth lasted until the hot headed and unpredictable Cadwaladr had Anarawd murdered over a territorial dispute. A great outcry followed and Cadwaladr was forced to flee Wales. Morgan succeeded his brother in 1143 and continued to rebuild the Deheubarth army with Rhys at his side. In 1155, with his health failing, he handed the title to his young brother and embarked on a pilgrimage to Rome. He died on the road within sight of the great city.

Rhys ap Gruffudd ruled Deheubarth until his death in 1197. He made treaties which brought peace at last to the troubled land, and earned the title of 'The Lord Rhys.' Before he died, he commissioned the rebuilding of the castle of Dinefwr, in accordance with his mother's wishes.

A century and a half later, this powerful bloodline produced another descendant who could boast a direct hereditary link to Gwenllian. His name was Owain Glyndwr.

The curlew still flies above Abergwyngregyn.

Lightning Source UK Ltd.
Milton Keynes UK
25 November 2009

146685UK00001B/5/P